DEATH
THE
RED
FLOWER

DEATH
THE 🌿
🌿 RED
FLOWER

Oswald Wynd

HARCOURT, BRACE & WORLD, INC. · NEW YORK

B.10.65

Library of Congress Catalog Card Number: 65-21042
Printed in the United States of America

To my only collaborator, J. G. W.

'Death is the red flower
Of war,
The unfolding petals slow
In the stillness
At the heart of fear's din.'

Anonymous, twelfth century

PROLOGUE

Red sand from the Gobi desert stung into the cabin of the old jet the moment the door was opened. Deputy Chairman and Foreign Minister Liu Fa Tsu felt the bombardment against his skin even where he stood in the aisle, still between seats. He thought once again what he had often thought before . . . as a Southerner . . . that Peking had a climate fit only for pigs, wolves, and Manchus. Healthy, the Northerners called it. It all depended on what you meant by health. In winter you could get frost-bite in the hard sunshine during a ceremonial march past, and in summer you were periodically frizzled when sixty-mile winds brought heat from the great Mongolian blast-furnace.

It was a sixty-mile wind now, shaking the plane. Somewhere down below, in whirling sand, was the reception committee. It was important to see at once who they were. Liu went to a window and rubbed it with his hand.

Seven men were bent double out there. It was an auspicious number, if one believed any longer in these things, which one didn't of course. Still, there was a certain satisfaction in that seven. Liu recognized the plump shape of Han Shi, the Minister of Agriculture, whose weight became a political embarrassment during a famine year. Han had been ordered to go on a diet until his tunic flapped, and he certainly appeared thinner. Part of his summer uniform was now streaming away from his body like a flag, though it was still a gross pole holding it.

I

Sha Li Tsao, the party organizer, was down there too, and this was auspicious indeed, the narrow-eyed Sha contriving to avoid any laudatory receptions for his colleagues unless personally ordered to attend by the Leader. And was that Sha carrying flowers? Liu smiled.

The Deputy Chairman went down the steps from the plane to a round of congratulatory hand clapping scarcely heard above the wind's howl. The Minister of Agriculture gave a thin yelp that might be taken for a cheer, and then they all closed about Liu, as though to protect a prize lily from the bite of the desert.

Liu did not smile at his fellow labourers in government. He disliked the grit of sand against his small, perfectly white teeth. He began to march off towards the airport buildings, the others in convoy behind, now silent, battling the wind, but in all likelihood straggling out into a line of precedence derived exactly from their platform stations at the last party congress. They were all fools except Sha, who was a killer black wild-cat from north of Mukden, as lean as the perpetual hunger of a northern province.

Glass doors opened. In the main reception hall it was hotter than outside, the air suspended in a dry, brittle stillness that had no life in it. The Leader's portrait, vast and in high colours, stared down towards all the arrival bays.

Sha Li Tsao had been carrying the small sweet roses of Shantung, in red and white, buds marked by tiny bruises. He thrust these out. One side of his mouth drooped.

'From our great Leader, Comrade. Congratulations. Successful and delicate mission accomplished.'

Sha hated the Russians and a faint irony was there, something none of the others would have dared. From Sha's machine had come the mixed blast of new proletarian and traditional Chinese invective which had sometimes rather winded even Moscow. That propaganda would now have to be shut down. It was a hurt to this Manchu animal, who enjoyed the use of the tearing fang.

'A truly united Marxist-Leninist front,' said fat Han, on whose round face were little spots of perspiration.

Liu lifted his hand in a gesture which indicated that he had

2

no intention of making a speech. He then walked, holding the roses, towards more glass doors and through them to the big black car which showed its age even through new paint. He got in out of the wind noticing that there was sand all over the carpet.

It was not an official reception, there were no crowds. It was hardly a day for crowds anyway, though Liu enjoyed them when they had been properly arranged in the new Peking, where the vast, wide streets had been designed for rallies. The car moved slowly against flying sand and the back compartment, glazed away from guard and driver, held an oven temperature and little dusty cyclones of its own from draughts in the ill-fitting doors. Liu took out a Russian handkerchief and sneezed into it. This didn't make him feel any better.

He wished he could go straight home. At fifty-five he recognized in himself the old man's yearning for the known cosily about him. It was a feeling that only flicked at him on occasion, but he knew it for the threat it was. A man could not have two lives, one behind a wall, the other in the world. In a way he had done this. There were some who knew he had done it. And there was talk.

Not that talk frightened him. Up where he was talk was no more than a noise of tom-cats. He lifted the roses and caught just the faintest of fragrance which had survived the heat. He remembered garlands in India, the smell of flowers continuing through all the faintly ingratiating talk of the weak who know their position. He had enjoyed India, moving through it as a smiling threat, copying their graceful greeting and speaking of friendship in a thin Chinese voice where intonations can be made to announce a careful remoteness. They had offered him too much food and he had seen a thousand dancing girls. Well, they would need to do more than dance down there, and they would be taught to do some new steps.

In Africa the black hands clapped. Everywhere he went were the black clapping hands of the comrades and the smell of their bodies under white suits. The leaders had flesh on their bellies and fat wives with gold in their ears. Everyone was too big physically, with the suggestion of the human frame over-nourished in its planting and turned to showy growth that left

3

a soft pappiness of stem. On his return he had spoken to the Leader of flashy savages. The Leader had quoted Lenin on Marx on Colonialism.

After they had gone through the *Hatamen* gate the other cars in the convoy turned away, clinging to the broad new avenues while Liu was taken through an untouched old quarter, quite slowly, towards another wide road not yet completed which was to run along the inside of the huge city walls.

For some reason the walls of Peking always depressed the Deputy Chairman. Their sheer massive strength had so often proved an illusion in fact, and so many conquerors had taken the city without a fight. As a young man Liu himself had seen the Japanese goose stepping through the main gate behind an eastern barbarian frog-general on a horse. The Mayor of the Imperial City had bowed low in obeisance, very low.

But the Leader was fond of his walls. The great drum towers had been repaired and one of them was now hollowed out and rebuilt for a new purpose, the curved tile roofs relaid over steel sheeting, while beneath this twenty thousand tons of concrete gave a contemporary heart to old stone. It was to this corner tower that the Leader had withdrawn, most often rumoured away from the city on his farm, but in fact always here, in a mausoleum designed for the living.

You never saw him. All you heard was a voice, the pundit's voice coming from the corpse of the man of action, with still the same little squeaks of ardour, and the awful dull lapses into pedantic preaching which went on and on, the gospel of the Leader on Marx and Lenin, the true light here only.

'He would rather kill me,' Liu thought, 'than have me as his successor.'

The truth was that the Leader, like Stalin, wouldn't consider a successor. When he was dead there was no life in the world. He made no plans for such a time, the unthinkable.

.   .   .   .

A door closed behind him. Liu looked with distaste at the teak table and chair in the centre of the floor. On it was a bottle of wine, a glass, a pad, pen and a lamp, nothing else. You sat in

4

the chair and waited, sometimes quite a long wait. You were a man expecting no one because no one would come. You were exposed, your face and movements seen, but all that was available from your side was a voice coming out of a hidden speaker. Camera eyes peered at you during the silence before the voice began.

Liu sat down. He took out his cigarettes and was irritated to notice just a faint trembling of his fingers as he lit one. Once again he looked about him, trying to spot the exact concealment of the camera eyes, but this was impossible for there was a frieze right around the square box of a room, this broken only by the door. The frieze was about five feet off the floor and covered in some kind of opaque plastic which glowed faintly, giving a vaguely decorative effect.

Delay was one of the Leader's tricks, to let your mind wander in a vacuum, to let expression seep into your face. Liu had always tried to keep his mind empty at this stage, his body frozen into a controlled composure, but today the discipline wouldn't work. He was suddenly thinking of the Leader's disease, and of whispers heard in Moscow. That particular cancer didn't always kill quickly. It ate the body on the surface but left the organs whole underneath, for a long time.

A dying man was watching him now, but a man dying slowly, almost in his own time and with plans pressing against his mortality.

'Liu!'

The voice was strong, though perhaps amplified.

'Yes, Party Chairman?'

Liu was straighter in his chair. He had tried not to make that movement, but always did.

'You're quite comfortable? Smoking, eh? I don't smoke, Liu. Not any more. I'm conserving my health.'

'Yes, Leader.'

'You're thinner, I think. The heat in Moscow is worse than Peking?'

The Leader enjoyed a mocking farce of bourgeois civilities. Liu could recall sitting opposite a drunk man who expected to become the most powerful in the world, hearing this jeering of small courtesies, a lolling head and a loose tongue sending them

5

out in a kind of parody of human intercourse. It had become even more of a parody in this room, an old joke revived between the living and the sealed away in a tomb.

'So you've fooled the Russians have you, Liu? You made a good job of that? You spoke of my deep concern now to be on friendly terms with our brothers? You convinced them?'

'I told them that the time had come for a united front of all workers' parties throughout the world.'

Liu heard a chuckle and then that travelled over into a cough which became a dry crackling on the speaker. It was cut off, a switch turned.

'How ill is he?' Liu thought. 'How ill?'

'I'm very well,' the Leader answered. 'Except for a cold. I went up on the roof for a view over Peking. At night. The wind was strong. This gave me a cold. Did you know that I can go up on the roof and look out over Peking, Liu?'

'No, Leader.'

'Oh, yes. A curving staircase. The climb is steep but the exercise is good for me. Up to my eagle's nest. I can walk up there and look down on you all. I see you all, Liu. You think I'm shut away here. But I see you.'

The Deputy felt a prickle of sweat on his spine and the palms of his hands were moist. The Leader still kept his lines to the world, an octopus who might at any moment allow one tentacle to wither and fatten another. He could even now be using Sha more than any of the others on the Central Committee. Sha might have come to the airport straight from a session here.

'Is something troubling you, Liu? Aren't you as confident of your success in Moscow as your despatches suggested?'

'I'm confident. Solvonoff was convinced. I'm sure of that. What I asked for was a very big thing, big enough to hide completely what is behind it.'

'I hope you're right. What d'you think of their new Chairman?'

'Solvonoff is a party man, no more.'

'You're quite sure no more? He got the position. How did he get it?'

'A neutral choice, as you suspected, Leader. A civil servant.

6

He holds office because three men stronger than he want him to.'

'Dogs fighting on a dunghill! It would have sickened Stalin. Was Stalin a party man, Liu?'

'No.'

'Neither am I. Remember that. The party is there to be told. The people are there to be told.'

'Yes, Leader.'

'You're a civil servant too, at heart, Comrade Liu. You could've been a professor. Have you ever killed a man with a gun?'

'No.'

'I was sure not. How quickly the new grows, replacing the old. But not in China, Liu. Not so quickly. Not yet.'

As certainly as if he had been told Liu knew that the Leader's line to the world was now Sha. It was a shock and frightening. But he had been frightened before. When a situation is plain you can fight it, and the dreaded facts can even prove a stimulus to confidence. It was to be Sha or Liu Fa Tsu. The Leader thought he had decided but it was a decision that could be reversed. In struggles of this kind the more intelligent man tended to survive. When Liu spoke again his voice held a note of acidity.

'Comrade Solvonoff and I have established a high degree of mutual trust and friendship. As one civil servant with another.'

For a moment there was silence. Then a cackle.

'You have your uses, Liu. Who else would I have sent to Moscow?'

'Perhaps Comrade Sha? After *that* conference the Russians would have dropped a megaton bomb on Peking.'

There was silence, no sound, not a hint of breathing. It was hot in the room with the glowing frieze. Liu was sweating. He wished there wasn't this stickiness on his body. It was like trying to keep your composure in southern India when you were sure the perspiration was wetting through to your chair.

Liu had used this approach to the Leader before, but not often. Usually he had the manner of a principal private secretary, keeping the flat hardness as a reserve. Once after he

7

had produced it the Leader had reached across a table to hit him in the face. And then laughed. A voice could not hit you and there was no laughter. The Leader was ill now. Stalin had gone mad in the end. Liu waited, his lips still holding the smile he had used with his words.

'What guarantees have you brought back?'

The voice was perfectly calm.

'None,' Liu said. 'The Russians make the first move and until this we do nothing. They announce a new blockade on Berlin through the East German government. Three days afterwards we attack Quemoy with paratroops. Solvonoff will go through with this. He must establish his authority, for there's still trouble in the Central Committee. Solvonoff needs a display of the old bear in a temper to harden his position. The Americans have even suggested that he's a weak man. They'll find that the time of vodka parties in embassies is over.'

'Dare the Russians risk war?'

'They must risk moving nearer to it, Leader. Solvonoff wants a top level meeting with the American President and he'll get it this way. Quickly. It happens that we both want to put pressures on the West at the same time. Of course Solvonoff talked to me of the justice of our cause in Quemoy.'

'That island!' The Leader's voice was loud. 'So the man's fool enough to think I want to waste time killing fleas?'

Liu said nothing. He lit a new cigarette. His fingers were no longer trembling. He was listening now for every nuance of tone in the Leader's voice. Something was not right, though he couldn't be sure what it was, an undertone of petulance, perhaps, which was quite new. The whisper startled him, as though spoken with a mouth hard against a mike, and splintered by shivers of static.

'And our strike against the paper tigers, Liu? You're still ready for it after Moscow? And all it means?'

The Deputy took a deep breath. The thing they had started to make still frightened him sometimes. This was one of the times.

'I'm ready for it.' His mouth was dry. 'The new alliance East-West will cause all the alarm we need in Washington and London. The Berlin trouble will bring a general alert. There

8

will be war talk in Europe and America. In the Democracies you can count on fools making the kind of noise which will bring things near to panic. We'll use their panic.'

The thing became whole again when you talked about it, stripped of its dangers, an uncomplicated perfection of planning too simple to be discovered either by the West or the Russians, who had got out of the habit of simplicities. The Chinese were the original chess players, after all, some thousands of years before any of these barbarians developed the minimal intelligence necessary for the game. The Russians, of course, had been practising hard for some time now but the Chinese had no need to practise.

'I don't want Peking destroyed,' the Leader said.

It was a child's voice, with a whine of lament in it. Liu did not stiffen in his chair, but every nerve in his body felt tugged from some central control. The Leader was dying, slowly. Dying in the mind, too, the responses there coming and going, the periods of clear lucidity difficult to maintain for long. Someone was there with him, someone who could turn off a switch at the right moment. The switch was off now.

A face came into Liu's mind, the face of a man who had somehow found his way into the heart of a stone monument. It was the face of Sha, the hungry Manchu.

. . . .

Liu dismissed his car and walked past the last sentry. He hadn't the nervousness about moving around alone without a guard shown by some of the other members of the Central Committee, indeed rather saw himself as the Deputy who dared to meet the comrades in the street, a man wearing as his right the clothes that were so much better than theirs. He would even go into one of the little bourgeois shops and talk to the owners who still survived under the grace and favour patronage of the State, conscious of voices building up out in the road, whispers identifying him. And then he would turn with his quick smile of brother to brother and a session of clasped hands in the street, un-Chinese physical contact which startled, slightly repelled, but was remembered.

9

Today Liu walked for another reason, moving between the Leader's voice and another life as slowly as possible, wanting to put down time as a barrier. His feet spaced out the distance and allowed perspective to return. He was almost soothed by the illusion of freedom and walked, though unaware of it, with the deliberate, restricted steps of a skirted Mandarin in another age, out carrying a bird-cage to give his favourite budgerigar an airing in the sun.

The wind had dropped suddenly and light was now a copper sheen over the city. The heat was close and adhesive, with almost no stirring of air down in the pattern of lanes Liu had chosen. About him walls offered a stuccoed blankness to the world, with plain gates under demurely tiled overhangs. It was still the city of ten thousand officials who, when they had achieved an opulence to hide, tucked it away carefully like a hand up a padded sleeve. The inner walls of the Forbidden City still permitted a small, parasitic adhesion of what had once been rich men's houses and might even still be.

A noise made Liu turn his head. The lane had been empty for Liu, but now there was one other in it, a beggar. The man must have been crouching unseen in some shadow and yet there wasn't much shadow. He was following, too, shuffling, but fast enough, a bent-over hump wearing a waterfall of coloured rags to which strange light gave a kind of iridescence.

Beggars were not allowed in Peking by law, though they remained in a furtive underworld sheltered by the shabby mass of the city. They appeared sometimes like a blight, emerging from holes when the capital was disciplined and orderly for an occasion like the Leader's birthday, marring it with a jolt comment on continuing misery, as indestructable as rats.

Liu turned. The beggar stopped. Part of the sewn-together tatters were lifted up over his head and the face stayed hidden. Liu didn't want to see that face. He looked at the hand thrust out to him, a whole hand, with all the fingers, but the man still might be a leper, there were plenty about. The thought of the disease always gave Liu a feeling of sickness, recalling a small terror, neatly put away, but which had been with him since a boy. Once a beggar had caught his hand as he passed and rubbed a raw red stump against healthy flesh. Then laughed.

The dream that had come to Liu after that still came back. He heard now the expected whine.

'The Lord is rich. The Lord is good. The Lord will give to the poor.'

'There are no Lords now, man!'

'I see what my eyes see. The Lords are still here, Master. A bowl of rice for my belly. In three days I haven't eaten.'

'Then you don't work.'

'There's no work for me. I'm a farmer with no land, Lord. They took my land away. My wife is dead. My children are dead. A bowl of rice for the emptiness in my belly.'

'I give you nothing!'

Liu found himself waiting for the beggar to take another step nearer, waiting with a compressed hysteria in a corner of his brain that could suddenly spill out over the rest of it. He began to feel that there was something below the surface of the accidental in this meeting, as though he was being accosted by a spectre from his own past and the past of his country. Everyone had uniforms in China these days, even the beggars crept around in very old ones. These rags were weird, suggesting a stage property for the fool, a designed foil for the glittering brilliance of embroidered costumes still allowed in the theatre, but nowhere out of it.

The man was big, too, crumpled down to hide this, but stretched he would be as tall as any Manchu, looming in this lane, a giant under the copper sky. This was one of Sha's men!

In the moment that he knew this Liu remembered the pistol. It had been given to him in Moscow, amongst many presents. Like a toy it looked, but it was loaded. They had made a joke of the loading at a Kremlin reception, where vodka flowed. He hadn't wanted the gun, but then he had seen how pretty it was, with handle inlaid in Caucasian mother-of-pearl, and had worn it home like a small talisman to touch against his ribs.

Today the Leader had asked him if he had ever killed a man with a gun!

The beggar was moving. He was taller. His foot came out for a step forward. Liu saw the man's eyes, glittering, no humility there. He fumbled inside his tunic, as though searching for a wallet, and as he did he saw the beggar stretching and tensing for a spring forward. Terror flooded from that compartment in which it had been held.

Liu fired first with the gun still up at his chest, then pushed it out at the end of his arm and put two more bullets, low, into rags, each small crack stinging at his hand and his brain.

The beggar's movement forward continued for seconds. Then he seemed to go on his knees in a kind of dreadful, deliberate supplication. The patchwork fell away from his head, showing it shaven, without sores. There was a bubbling from wide lips, then suddenly a heap on uneven cobbles, and a moaning. The knife was there, shining on dull stones.

No gate in the long walls opened, and the lane stayed empty, as though this had been arranged. Even the rumble of the city was shut away and distant.

Sha could have got to the Leader first from the airport, for the car which had taken Liu had gone slowly. That had been arranged, too. Yesterday he had been the Foreign Minister and Deputy Leader of China. Today he was under sentence, eliminated if not yet dead. There had been a slight miscarriage of planning due to the unforeseen. None of his aides had been able as yet to report on that Russian gun carried by a man who did not like guns.

The mission to Moscow had been a success and this was all that was needed . . . from Liu. The Leader didn't want him for the next phase, he had Sha for that, Sha and his secret horde of Manchu wolves. It was a time for the true killers again, when you pushed professors aside.

Liu began to walk again. He wanted to get home. Behind the security of his walls he could use established calm, a big gate closed and locked, safety a recess. Ching Ling would be waiting. He was suddenly an old man desperately needing the thing she had given him that two other wives had never done . . . the offering of her youth, like a sacrifice, all of it.

He had been fifty-three when he married her, and Ching Ling nineteen, the gap between them a chasm, even in China where the old had long taken the young. And she had come to him not from any phalanx of young women Marxists, but like a girl under the Manchus moving from one shelter to another,

her whole life between walls, and with a total acceptance of this. Liu remembered his first wife with bitterness, a student's choice, the emancipated new Chinese woman ready always with the clenched fist raised, and still ready with it on party platforms. His second had been a doctor, a bad one, now banished to Fukien after medical deviationism, but really because she had bored him stiff, bringing to their bed a lingering pungency of surgical spirit and a kind of intellectual detachment in sex. Ching Ling was like the dream of a young man given reality late. He went through his gate to her and was in another world where the raucous noises of his political activity seemed at once cut off in a hermitage that didn't demand celibacy. Beyond his gate was the China that had once been, hidden and faintly furtive, but his real living.

It was still there. He had only to get to it.

Liu turned into his own lane, which was empty, too, except for one man pulling a hand-cart. The cart was laden with what looked like household goods and the man strained against a woven shoulder strap like an overworked horse, bending forward, his head down. The cart creaked. It was the only sound.

A wind stirred, a last flurry from the sand-storm, lifting the dust in the road and producing a sudden banging Liu couldn't identify. It was a heavy noise, of weighted wood hitting the immovable.

His own gate! This was set in the middle of an old stone wall that was a false front to concrete ramparts behind, an old Peking gate of weathered wood with iron studs in it and a steel backing that was a recent addition. A tile roof, more ornate than its neighbours, leaned out into the lane and was ornamented with two griffins in Imperial yellow, ceramic porcelain. The gate was in two halves, one almost never opened. But it was open now.

Liu moved through a moment of frozen time, of the unreal which must be penetrated. He put out a hand to the loose gates and the used half swung back in a total, oiled silence, showing the forecourt empty.

He stepped over the foot-high sill, into his sanctuary. Nothing moved. The house was hidden beyond the ten-foot-high carved white marble dragon screen which had once

belonged to the puppet Emperor Pu Yi, the last of the
Manchus, and still alive, serving new masters. It was a big
house, but one story only, sprawling, its roofs tucked back into
a discreet obscurity.

Liu secured the great gates, sealing himself into whatever
was here. He moved over to the little guard-room. Empty. The
receiver of a wall phone dangled on its cord. A stool was over-
turned. That was all.

He went around the dragon screen. He saw the rocks of the
formal outer court, tumbled rocks like something from an
eruption. He saw the roofs of his world undamaged and the
windows shut, but nothing moving, not even full fat peonies
in a cobalt-blue garden pot.

'Fu Tan!'

The servant always ran to him, but there was now no sound
of feet. And then Liu saw the house door, wide back. He went
through it, noticing that the hall wasn't right, it held a new
emptiness as on a moving day. The treasures had been taken
first, two ebony stands left, but the twin Tang horses carried
away. He shouted again and there was a roar reaching into the
recesses of the house, down corridors, past courts, to the inner
rooms. No voice answered.

Then he did hear a sound, distant and pulsing. He went
quickly down the corridor towards the rooms his wife kept to,
not checking strangeness in passing, not noting things gone,
but dimly aware of this. The sound grew into singing.

Ching Ling's television! She had it on through all the controlled hours of transmission, switching off when he came, but
keeping her vigil for him in an almost passionate attention to
the screen, as though in some way her life grew from that box
and had meaning through it. He had joked with her about this,
but gently. He was always gentle with his old man's prize, it
came easily after the other two, both of whom he had often
wanted to beat with a stick and had done on three occasions,
twice with the party leader, and once with the doctor.

The sound was a programme of military marches, with the
choruses sung by girls' voices. He recognized the tune as he
opened the last door.

His wife's room smelled of flowers from a window open onto

14

a courtyard where there were rigid masses of bloom packed into stone boxes. The television blared sound but the picture had been lost, the shimmering square shot across by dagger tremors of interference.

She was not in her chair. He didn't run when he saw the shape on the floor behind the set. He walked, with these seconds pounding and real, as if with a voice in his mind screaming that there was no escape now, no way of pulling down a sound screen on a ticking clock. He saw her feet that should have been bound when she was a baby, but hadn't been, small feet still, but not the wrapped lily buds of the south. He saw her legs in pale blue Shantung silk, and the tunic embroidered at cuffs and hem. He saw her head folded into an arm, the black low bun of hair still neat, though a jade comb lay near one clenched small hand.

'Ching Ling?' he said, as to a child asleep.

His hands found the truth, groping hands, feeling and lifting, turning that head. In Ching Ling's forehead was a small round bullet hole. Her blood was darker than the dark floor.

Liu Fa Tsu made no sound then. His hands came away from his wife's body and his legs pushed him up, with one hand out to the booming set. He groped along to a knob and brought silence into the room. Then he looked down.

He remembered a girl brought to his bed, weeping in the pain of a virginity torn from her with a violence that had shamed him afterwards. He began to cry, not even aware of it, slow tears forced from ducts that would soon be withering, the last tears of a man who now has nothing to shelter or protect. He heard a distant banging without terror, as though fear couldn't reach him, but the noise made him turn from what he had once been to the present.

It sounded like a ram against the gates, a boom, then silence for the swing-back before another thud. His hands came up searching for the Russian pistol, groping in the inside pocket of his tunic but finding it in an outside one. He looked at the little gun. There were three bullets left in it, three Russian bullets with which to take the whole of China, and after it the world.

.   .   .   .

15

Liu had never fired a machine-gun. For a little time in the guard-room he had felt panic. What if he couldn't find how to feed in the cartridge belt? He was certain this was an old model, and, as an issue to protect members of the Central Committee in their houses, it might well be one of the Leader's little jokes. But the thing was well oiled.

A click and the belt was holding. He picked up the gun and lugged it across the outer courtyard. A crash at the gates snapped one of the bolts, and half a door bulged six inches at the base. Liu pulled himself up onto the narrow ramp topping the concrete of the inner guard-wall. A skin of stone three feet high protected him from the lane, but he had to bend down not to be seen, pulling the gun behind him as he crawled. He got his breath and looked over the wall.

Ten men were down there, not police or soldiers, Sha's wolves. The lane was empty, terror keeping the curious at bay. The wise man stayed small and inconspicuous on an evening like this, allowing someone else to tell him later of what the night had brought, and that in whispers. Sha's men had got hold of a log from somewhere, a slow way to break in, but they had been expecting the gates to be open.

Liu lifted the gun and pushed the snout over the wall, aiming it down. The men below were chanting now, in a final effort at the shattering gates, their leader whining out something that might be one of those songs born out of an agony of living up in their frozen wastes. The killers were singing. Liu lowered the gun a little further.

When he pulled the trigger he found himself holding spitting, shaking metal which fought control. He half sprawled over the gun, sweating, but keeping the nose down while the ribbon of cartridges chattered through, coughing bullets, the cobbles below sparking fire. The screaming didn't begin for a little time, not until Liu managed to move the muzzle of the gun back and forth, then back and forth again. He heard the boom of the log falling. Men started to crawl away. He eased the firing, using individual bullets on his targets. The crawling stopped. He noticed that he had smashed one of the porcelain griffins.

The lane was empty at both ends. Liu came down from the

ramp and eased himself through the shattered gates. He had his pistol out, looking at the sprawled figures. Some of them were moving, but none tried to stop him. He walked down the lane into the dusk, through a held terror of new silence where no door opened and no face peered. In the shopping street there was also the quiet, with people back under cover. Bicycles lay scattered along the drainage ditch. Liu picked what looked the newest, got on it, and rode north into an area beyond the freeze, where news had not yet run ahead of him. Here he turned west, pedalling hard.

.   .   .   .

The sentry at the outer gate to the drum-tower courtyard was the first test. Liu walked towards the man, waiting for recognition and the gargled scream of respect, or recognition and no scream. The gun might come down if news had travelled ahead of a bicycle.

He got the salute and went past with lifted hand, crossing an area of smooth concrete towards a small steel door and the second sentry. To this man he said:

'Get your Captain!'

The officer on duty was the one who had earlier met Liu. He seemed surprised but not astounded. It meant no news to this level . . . yet.

'Comrade Deputy . . . ?'

'I've come to talk to the Leader. It's urgent. Take me down the passage.'

They went between faintly sweating concrete walls, under hard, naked bulbs. The Captain was just slightly uneasy about this unannounced visit but he was also young, frightened of authority. He didn't look any veteran of the Korea or the Tibet fighting, which was careless of the Leader. The guards, even in the approach areas to this fortress, should have been hand picked. Or had Sha been at work here too, replacing regulars with raw recruits?

At the steel doors to the lift the Captain reached out for an internal phone.

'No!' Liu called out. 'I don't need to be announced.'

17

'But, Comrade Deputy, I must . . .'

'You challenge *my* order?'

The Captain only hesitated for a second. Then the lift doors opened. They went into the box and were sealed away there. The movement started. Liu knew that the Captain was thinking about regulations broken. He might also be thinking about his professional prospects. In a job like this, which brought you in touch with the high ones, it could be literally fatal to give serious offense.

'I don't want you to come with me into the inspection room,' Liu said. 'Stay in here.'

This was another breach of the rules.

'Do you understand?'

'Yes, Comrade Deputy.'

'I don't like the way your hand is sitting on your revolver, Captain.'

The boy's arms dropped to his side. Liu smiled.

The lift doors opened, and he stepped out into a perfectly square box three times the size of the lift behind. He was facing another set of steel doors which stayed shut while the visitor was inspected on close-circuit television by another guard in the room beyond. That guard would have some kind of automatic warning of the lift's ascent, and Liu was counting on the man's surprise to make him open doors. A hiss of compressed air behind told Liu that he was alone in the inspection chamber, sealed into it. This lasted for all of a minute, then the panels in front of him rumbled back.

The nearer one got to the Leader the less the guards about his person appeared to respect other members of the Revolutionary Council. The man sitting behind the desk in there did not rise. He was almost entirely bald and any hairs left had been taken off with a razor. His neck creased down into his collar. He looked what he was, a thug, with the thug's bestiality of manner only slightly covered by his new role of receptionist. There was a big revolver in his hands and it was pointing straight at Liu.

'Why weren't you announced?' the Guard asked.

'I didn't choose to be!'

The man blinked. He knew nothing about death in a Peking

18

lane. But this was not a state of affairs likely to last long. The man glowered, caught in something well outside his norm. If you use brutes you can't expect startling cerebration. Under a bald head a brain ticked with all the massive, deliberate solemnity of a municipal clock. His indecision was obvious. Liu stepped forward.

'Wait there!' the guard shouted.

'Don't talk to me like that, you Manchurian pig!'

Liu saw anger come into small eyes, like a rush of blood. The hand holding the gun began to shake. The man looked down at a panel on his desk, then back at his hand. Anger was rattling him, and through it he felt fear, almost as though he sensed something that could be an omen of change undermining his little dog's world.

'What do you want . . . Comrade Deputy?'

'That's better! I've come to talk to the Leader. It's most urgent. Take me to the room and then tell him I'm here.'

Liu waited for that to penetrate, then added.

'Close these doors again. And put that gun away.'

The guard turned a switch on the desk and the doors rumbled. He stood, still with the gun, but caught Liu's eye and put it down. Then with an almost curious, lumbering docility he began to move towards a passage, leading the way.

It had always angered Liu to be led to the viewing room, but not now. He came quite close behind the man, who seemed to have recovered from nerves, possibly from the thought that no one could harm the Leader in the viewing room. Liu came very close and shot the guard neatly in the back of a thick neck.

It was a little like the slaughter of oxen he had once watched on a State farm, this creature's fall almost as heavy, a great thud on concrete, noise enough to warn a relief if there was one at this level.

Liu didn't really expect this. He listened for a moment, then opened doors, to the viewing room, cupboards, a kind of kitchen, and finally the dead man's kennel, a small place in which spartan furnishings were brightened by pin-ups on the walls, pictures offering the kind of erotica not encouraged in the New China. One bed. There was no one else to contend with at half-way house.

Liu stepped over a heap and walked back to the reception desk, sitting in the chair. His mouth felt a little dry. It seemed that killing made you thirsty. He poured water from a carafe and sipped. Then he lit a cigarette.

He was sure he couldn't be watched at this desk, which was the control centre in a kind of neutral zone. The danger now was that Sha might report back to the Leader direct by telephone, but this didn't seem too likely. Sha would have to report total failure in the little matter of an assassination and it wasn't the kind of news the Leader, even as a sick man, liked to hear. Almost certainly Sha would wait, with his men out scouring the city, tearing into any hides to which the Deputy Chairman might have gone. There was a little time, but not much.

He looked about him. A second set of steel doors led up to the citadel, and these would certainly be controlled from above, which meant that it was time to contact the Leader's women.

There were two of these, his wife and his sister. There were no servants up there, the sister did the cooking. The Leader had reduced his living to the bare essentials, but then he had never been a man who cared for the little luxuries. Liu looked at the switch panel built into the desk. The guard had been a simple man, drilled in easy duties, and the most important switch would be the one nearest to hand. Liu turned it.

A ceiling speaker made a sound like a ventilator clicked on, a faint hissing. Nothing happened for almost a minute, then there was a woman's voice, faintly peevish and very loud.

'Yes? What is it?'

Liu held his handkerchief over his mouth. The secret of sounding like a Manchu was to be noisily half inaudible.

'Comrade Sha. To see the Leader.'

'The Leader is resting. He can't see anyone.'

'Comrade Sha says he must.'

'Well . . . I'll find out.'

Like a maid-servant in a nice bourgeois household going away to see if the mistress is officially at home. Liu waited in a kind of conscious calm. He felt propelled at speed on the great wave of his purpose, riding it easily so far, managing the

20

balance that was needed at the foaming crest, as though he had suddenly mastered the trick. His wave might disintegrate into a roaring tumble of surf, sucking him under, or it might hold to shoot him high up onto a solid beach. It was either life or death. He had a packed schedule of plans for one, and could look at the other.

This was how you took power, by having no alternative. Everything latent in your living, ill organized in some areas, was suddenly directed to one ultimate, massive gamble in which failure was the dark but success would make you a god even against the ticking minutes of time.

The speaker in the roof crackled.

'Comrade Sha can come up. Ten minutes only.'

The condition sounded like a woman trying to assert an authority she knew she couldn't maintain. He rose quietly, stubbing out his cigarette, conscious of the continued hissing of the speaker. He went over to grey steel doors and was surprised to hear a faint whirring behind them. Somehow he had expected a stairway here, not another lift. He remembered the Leader's dislike, from his earlier life in the open, of being confined in small rooms or climbing boxes.

The steel doors opened to show a lift big enough for four people, brightly lit, with an upholstered seat the length of its back wall. Liu got in and pressed the one button. Very quickly the faint shaking of the climb began. He stood in the middle of the floor, quite still, only lifting his hand once to pat the pocket which held his gun, then take it out, holding it pointing at the doors.

The lift stopped. Rigid Liu waited for the hiss of compressed air. Instead there was a click, then a crackling. The woman's voice said:

'Comrade Liu, you are the Leader's prisoner. You will surrender!'

His head jerked up, to the voice and the eyes watching him. He stared back at that dazzle-bright cornice. The final check was in this cabin. The woman had made it.

His mouth was so dry he couldn't have brought a sound from it, but his hand came out to press the one button. It didn't move the lift.

His wave was breaking, too soon. It was anger he felt then, an uncontrollable surge of it, beyond reason, something never quite known before. It was anger that put him up onto the seat, smashing at the glowing cornice with the pearl-handled butt of the Russian gun. He could hear the woman's voice squawking at him as he tore the covering away, shattering one bulb, reducing light to half, then pounding at the lens eye, breaking round glass, poking the butt into the hole until he felt something give. It was the speaker next, a little mouth to be silenced. The voice stopped.

He had stillness again, for his sweating and a laboured breath. His body shook, but it wasn't from terror. His eyes had seen the square in the roof, an escape hatch from the box. He reached out for the release catch and the hatch cover dropped inwards to hang down into the cabin. A damp coldness came to him and a smell of oil.

Liu put the gun in his pocket. He didn't think about age as his fingers closed over an outer rim. His body was muscled still, and light, with no spare fat on it anywhere. It hurt his shoulders to pull himself up and breath shouted from his lungs. But he got through, teetering on the edge of a hole before sprawling out onto the gently curving roof. His hands slithered up a greased cable, getting an uneasy hold on it. He pulled himself upright.

The one bulb in the cabin lit the shaft in a pale, eerie greenness. It was smooth concrete without a break for thirty feet up to one set of high doors. He still had his head back, staring, when the cable trembled a warning under his hands.

The lift started again, pushing up to doors that could only be opened by compressed air when the cabin had made contact with a projecting sill. Liu slumped down for a better hold, crouching, and for seconds shut his eyes. He opened them when the cable stopped vibrating, then reached in through the hatch to smash the remaining bulb in the cabin. The shaft went black about him. There was total silence until the hiss of the doors opening.

Noise was a flat assault on ear-drums, the terrible hard banging of an automatic rifle fired into a steel box. Liu pushed back from the hatch opening as ricocheting bullets stung through it.

Then silence again, complete. Liu put his hand in his pocket and brought out the Russian pistol. A woman said:

'He must be dead. I've emptied the gun. Put on a light.'

Someone was weeping down there.

'I said . . . put on a *light*!'

The cabin was lit faintly from somewhere beyond.

'What . . . ? That hatch!'

The lift trembled as the woman stepped into it. She was almost beneath Liu, pointing an empty gun up, as though, in shocked surprise, she'd forgotten it was useless. The light from behind didn't show her face, but her eyes somehow caught it, like a cat's in half dark, a shimmering of orbed surfaces. She pushed the gun barrel up at him as he put one bullet through the easy target of her head. The crack of the little pistol was a modest noise, even in the shaft.

He heard a scream as he dropped down onto a body, using it as a step. The woman in the passage backed away from him, her hands empty, both of them coming up to her face. It was the Leader's wife. His sister had been the fighter.

'No,' she said, still backing. 'No!'

Her terror was acutely personal, a little life whimpering away from death.

Liu opened a door. It was a sitting-room, with a window to a central shaft like something from a new factory, all glass and utility light, but nothing to look at. The place was about as inviting as a party committee office. It had been furnished with a random collection of junk from an official residence, hard ebony chairs, square cabinets, gross tables as platforms for ugly tea-cups. There was an ordinary key in a mortice lock and Liu turned this.

He went over to the woman.

'I won't hurt you,' he said, not for her comfort, but from his contempt. 'Is the Leader asleep? Could he sleep through all that noise? Where's his room?'

She still couldn't speak. He felt almost embarrassed by the dimensions of her spirit. And then he wondered how Ching Ling had died today, there by her television set? Like this . . .

23

staring at a round little muzzle, all living paralysed in her eyes?

'Get into the sitting-room.'

She didn't move. He had to pull her across the hall and it was like hauling along a spiritless dog who has been given a beating. He knew her slightly, from occasional receptions, a wife in the background and not meant for the public eye, but allowed out now and then wearing good silk and jade pins in her hair. She was the Leader's fifth wife. He had run through quite a few, but then he was older, considerably older.

He put her in the sitting-room, turned the key, put it in his pocket, and went on to another door. This opened onto something fifty feet square and fitted out as a centre of operations in an orgiastic worship of technological gadgets. The room announced that it was the heart of China and somehow Liu found this just slightly silly. It would be a good place to put an embalmed body. A great map of China and adjacent countries covered the whole of one wall. In the centre of the floor was a circular table equipped with instruments that suggested the control room of a power-station. Here the Leader had sat in a padded chair and pressed the buttons which let him see the man down beneath him in the viewing room, that feeble supplicant come for audience. And here Sha had leaned over the great man's shoulder. This was the world of a dying man, his nursery.

A door from the control room was slightly open. Liu pushed it back to see a cell, and very small, the last cave of a man who had for years hidden in mountains. It had nothing in it but a hospital bed, a white enamelled cabinet and a wash-basin.

The Leader was in the bed. This sight of him turned Liu's stomach.

For some years now the Leader had worn huge dark glasses and he was still wearing them, though they were no longer an adequate concealment. One side of his face was like the surface of the moon, a dreadful frozen lava relic of past eruptions. Both his hands were outside the covers and one was bandaged. The man didn't seem to be breathing.

It was only when Liu had shut the cell door behind him and gone nearer the bed that he noticed the smell. It was the stench of an ugly dying. But the Leader wasn't dead. There was a

24

scraped sound from his throat, then a movement of his head which exposed more of the horror.

'Who . . . ?'

Liu swallowed.

'It's your Deputy, Liu Fa Tsu.'

'What? I . . . heard something. Guns. Attack . . . Who are you?'

The vitality of a hundred campaigns and winters in the open was still there. The bandaged hand propped a body up from pillows.

'Who are you?'

'Liu.'

'Liu? Here? No!'

'I'm here in Sha's place, Leader.'

'Sha? Yes, Sha. I want the women. I'm not comfortable.'

The eyes must have become active again behind huge moons of smoked lens.

'You're not Sha!'

'No. He'll soon be dead, Leader.'

The neat bed was disturbed, heavings lifting the cover. A foot poked out, then another. They were bare feet, normal, reaching the floor and fumbling with toes for slippers, a great man getting out of bed like a sick child, in weakness.

'What do you mean, dead? Sha? I need Sha. What are you doing here?'

'I came to tell you that we must kill Sha.'

'What? You came to tell . . . ?'

The laughter, the sound of it coming from a twisted mouth, was like an old insult renewed. Liu watched the man find one slipper and forget about the other. He watched the body come upright, a night-shirt falling to the floor in crumpled folds.

'Get out of here!' the Leader said, loud, in his old voice.

He took two paces forward, his body shaking.

'I'll find out who let you in!'

Liu opened the cell door. He went backwards into the big room beyond, as a kind of lure to the tottering figure, not wanting to have to touch that body. He went over to the circular table and round it, to the far side. The Leader followed, holding onto the door jamb for a moment, his breath an

25

effort, then clutching out at a filing cabinet. He was staring towards the padded seat of his control, his head lifted. Liu mightn't have been in the room. The Leader lurched across a gap of space and got his hands on the table, holding himself up, panting.

'Liu? It can't be Liu. I'll find out.'

He reached the chair and sank into it, suddenly totally immobile, as though gathering strength. It was returning strength that Liu was afraid of, and lucidity with it. For the clear moments still came. There had been a long time this afternoon when the Leader still showed his grasp on affairs, even with Sha standing by his shoulder. It had been the Leader's voice, his real voice, sustained for a long time before the whimper.

'So it's you,' the man in the chair said suddenly, as if he understood now.

'Yes.'

'And Sha?'

'He's looking for me. In the city. Very busy just now. He never thought I'd come here. Leader, you chose the wrong man to have up here with you. Sha is a fool. All his wolves couldn't get me. I'm here. I'm your Deputy. This is my place, not Sha's.'

'I thought you were a professor.'

'You were wrong. And I've changed. Since my wife was killed by Sha's men.'

There was silence. Liu was conscious of hidden eyes watching.

'I don't know what you mean. Your wife?'

'Sha killed her. He's too powerful, Leader. He does what he wants. In your name, without telling you.'

'I didn't know!' That was a shout and a lie.

Liu came a little nearer.

'You know now. We must stop Sha. We can do it from here. You have only to turn a switch to get Hin Jao at security. Order a war on the wolf-killers. Hin will be pleased to obey you, Leader. He hates Sha. The wolves were becoming a challenge.'

'I didn't know this. I didn't know it!'

Liu came around the desk. There wasn't a great deal of time.

'I'm your Deputy, Liu Fa Tsu. We'll get Hin Jao now and tell him what to do. He knows your voice well. And your voice is strong again, Leader. Your illness can't be serious, since you have such a strong voice. You will speak loudly, won't you?'

'Eh? Yes, I can speak loudly.'

'We'll call the guards first. To tell them I'm here by your orders. And after that we'll speak to Hin Jao.'

Liu knew what would come then. It was necessary. He would use the last bullet in the little Russian gun.

CHAPTER ONE

Captain John Lownie hadn't had a woman during his six days in Shanghai. It left him with a feeling of unease. He lay along the settee under the open ports of the day-cabin and stretched, lifting a leg to look at it. He was wearing shorts so he could see his leg all right.

'Beautiful,' Henderson said.

'Eh?'

'I was just confirming your thought, man. You're a magnificent animal. In my time specimens like you were a fluke of nature. Now it's all done by special feeding early.'

'I never got any special feeding early. Not in this crap town.'

'You're always wanting back to it.'

'I'm sentimental.' The captain grinned. 'I keep hoping it'll settle down. That things will start jumping.'

He sat up, then he stood. He was six feet exactly, and built to fit the height. His head was squarish, with fair bristle cut to a maximum length of three-quarters of an inch in front. He was thirty-six and could, when he smiled, look eight years younger. He had very blue eyes, so blue they startled until you noticed the lines around them and decided on no comment. Or the jaw and decided on no comment. Only Henderson commented when he liked. He was sixty-one and dead to the world until it was time for whisky.

'If this damn business puts the river pilots in mourning too, and we miss the tide . . .' John said, going over to the radio, clicking the switch.

'It won't, Captain. They're efficient. They want us down river on the next tide. We'll get the pilot.'

'I could take her down myself.'

'And have the underwriters on your neck? Sit and relax.'

The radio warmed into words. It had been speculating all day about the death of China's Leader. The banned voice of Radio Manila came in loud and clear, as though in a crisis of national mourning someone had forgotten to switch on the jamming.

'Quote,' said the voice in English. 'London comment.'

'To hell with London comment. Let's get some music.'

'Shut up,' John said. 'I'm listening.'

He sat down to listen, for a moment tapping fingernails against the front edge of the settee. He was cutting down smoking and it added to a jumpiness.

'We are bringing you, relayed from the United States, a recording made in London this morning over the British Broadcasting Corporation's networks. The talk is by Sir Malcolm Lugworth, an adviser on Chinese affairs to the British Foreign Office, and who was for some years at the Embassy in Peking. He knew the Leader personally.'

Sir Malcolm's voice, in spite of a cracked transmission, suggested that he had come to the studio from a very good lunch indeed. He was modest in that authoritative way which is so much more convincing than any straight self-advertising, and he was being rather jolly on the whole about the demise of a world leader and its international implications.

'. . . Of course, it must be understood that when I claim to have known the Leader I really mean that I met him on a number of different occasions and dined with him once. But, for contact by a Westerner with a Chinese politician these days, that's really rather a lot. Especially when that politician is the virtual ruler of six hundred million people. And he *was* that, there's no question about it. Whatever the importance of the Central Committee of the Party in China, it never at any period assumed the role of the similar Committee in

Moscow, simply because it wasn't given the chance. The Leader saw to this. He was boss as a guerilla fighter in the mountains, and he was boss as the ruler in Peking. Liu Fa Tsu, his successor and second-in-command, did his master's bidding on all occasions. One always had the impression with Liu that he had a list filed in his mind of approved questions and answers carefully vetted by the Leader. And with Liu, if you wandered outside the permissible, you got no answer at all. You got a very polished smile. The problem now, of course, is what kind of a man is going to evolve from the Leader's Deputy? This is the question which is being asked in every capital in the world today and to which there will no doubt be many answers. If I were asked to give *my* answer, I think I'd risk saying that Liu is a very different kind of person indeed, who will never, even if he tries, evolve into the kind of man his late master was.'

'Top drawer and all that,' Henderson said. 'His daddy and granddaddy were in the service before him.'

'Shut up, Chief! Have a drink. The bottle's in the cupboard.'

'Half an hour to go yet.'

John lit a cigarette. He glared at the radio.

'Liu Fa Tsu might almost be called a curious anachronism, an intellectual throwback to the old China. He was the son of a top-level official in the Department of Education, and during the Communist fight for power Liu took no active part that we know of. He was a much more available figure in the Peking of my time than any of the other political personalities. But he always seemed hemmed in by the discretion of the civil servant.' Sir Malcolm laughed for the world. 'One might almost say that he had a British professional civil servant's feel for never letting himself get labelled in a manner that could be used against him later!'

'I hope you're learning something,' Henderson said. 'I'm not.'

'What I'm getting at in all this is that while Liu is the natural successor as Leader it could be said that he has no real training for ultimate authority. This is partly because the late ruler of China never delegated any real power. The Liu we saw

30

in Europe, Liu the traveller, was his master's servant, and always just that. His aims may have totally coincided with his master's, but I find I doubt this if only—to use a word that our American cousins have become so fond of—because his "conditioning" was so totally different. Liu was the student of history, the intellectual, the man brought by reason to his political convictions. And—dare I say this?—perhaps expediency has played its part in forming the man. There is no suggestion that he took any active part in the overthrow of the old regime and the coming to power of the new. He was, in fact, an established civil servant at the time of the revolution, and can be said to have accommodated himself, most skilfully, to sharp change. What the old lions around the guerilla fighter thought of him we don't know, but it is a fact that the lions have almost without exception disappeared from the scene. Liu was the new boy and a very bright one, who by sheer intelligence and adaptibility forced himself into the front ranks of the party. I would hate to seem here to be underestimating the new Party Chairman in any way. To get where he had reached under his master, against the odds of his background, can only be called a phenomenal performance. And that he has established himself as he appears to have done, at once, without the kind of Central Committee jockeying which has, in the past, been a feature of the Russian scene, suggests only one thing . . . he is a determined man!' There was a pause which might have been Sir Malcolm having the glass of whisky which the B.B.C. provides, a little reluctantly, on these occasions. 'A determined man, yes. But also a very different man. Let's put it simply and bluntly, the late Leader was a killer and a fighter. Liu Fa Tsu is sedentary by inclination, rumoured by his enemies to be almost an aesthete. The late Leader never left the borders of China in the whole of his life. Liu Fa Tsu has travelled all over the world. One was the tough peasant schoolteacher turned soldier and taking power by sheer stubborn persistence in brute force. The other is a man from a long line of cultivated mandarins who has never experienced physical violence and would probably be incapable of dealing with the kind of extrovert situation which confronted his master every day for nearly twenty years of his life.'

31

'That's a real Tory swine for you,' Henderson said. 'Sucked in all the answers with his mother's milk. There have been Lugworths running England for three hundred years. And mucking about with Scotland, too. To say nothing of killing Irish.'

'Will you shut up?'

'To sum up then, if one dares to sum up anything at so fluid a stage, I would say that I'd back Liu to hold power, largely because it is difficult to see anyone strong enough to challenge him. He has the civil servant's splendid advantage of seniority by appointment, something that other civil servants may grumble about but rarely ever take positive action against. It must be remembered in this connection that practical rule by the civil service is an older tradition in China even than it is in England . . . by some thousands of years. As a trained administrator Liu will bring great competence to his role, I'm certain of that. Authority may also give him a strength he doesn't appear to have at the moment, though I will be considerably surprised if he ever develops that faculty, so useful in a dictatorship, of being able to lay hold of a single event and make use of it with ruthlessness for his own ends. Liu's training is all against his developing this kind of ultimate lust for power. To my mind he is likely to administer China without ever attempting to shake the world with terror at his dreaded name. Prophecy, of course, is vastly dangerous, but I'm still venturing into it. I believe that the bamboo curtain will now wave in the wind of change. I think we will see a considerable relaxation of East-West tension, though possibly at the start this may take the form of an apparent Russian-Chinese united front again, with Russian influence in the ascendant. We must remember that on the site of two almost barbaric Imperial thrones we now have two new Leaders, brought up beyond the active revolution in their countries, men with a new approach. And I firmly believe that we are on the threshold of world co-operation that would have been impossible to imagine as short a time as five years ago. Let us hope that this is the case. Let us also hope that a really new China will take her place at the council tables of the world as a force for much more than her own interests, ready to work

32

for that permanent peace based on a measure of understanding which we all seek.'

'Amen, brother,' Henderson said.

John got up and switched off the radio. He turned.

'Well, what do *you* think, Chief Engineer Henderson? From what you know of the Chinese?'

'I think Chinks are Chinks. They'd still like to cut off our ears and send 'em home in the post. They've had four thousand years of history and they've always felt that way about foreigners and they always will.'

John twiddled at the knobs again, bringing in a local station. A girl's voice was singing patriotic songs in a very high soprano and in a manner which suggested she was likely to rupture her larynx at any moment. They were probably the late Leader's favourite ditties, and, though not solemn, their importance was underlined by a full orchestrated background in which national grief may have been responsible for a certain lack of musical co-ordination.

'Out with that row!' Henderson said.

Another station produced a political commentator who was reading a script that had been chopped into dignified little pauses, like an aping of Churchill. In near soprano pitch, as opposed to a dignified baritone, the effect was a little odd.

'How much of that can you understand?' Henderson asked.

'All of it.'

'What it is to be educated. Me now, I was brought up speaking pidgin out here. "Boy bringee whisky, chop, chop, velly quick." That was the time to live.'

'I can remember it, too,' John said.

'Only as an infant. Not in its full flower. My captain on the Yangtze river ships could remember the days when you kept discipline with a whip right up as high as your Chink bos'n. And there were never better run ships anywhere.'

'Here we go,' John said. 'Tell us about pirates just beyond Bias Bay when you were in the coasters.'

'I've told you. It's time for my whisky.'

Henderson poured while John Lownie looked out of a square port, kneeling on the settee to do it. They were anchored just off the Bund, in mid river, hatches covered and the ship waiting for the tide at the bar across the entrance to the Yangtze estuary. In the holds of the *Maree Tarn* were almost a thousand tons of low quality scrap iron, birds-nests packed in moss, ginger sealed in blue jars, tinned bamboo shoot, tinned bean sprouts, bottles of soy sauce, and jars of pickles. They were practically a floating Chinese restaurant. The whole cargo was very nearly a barter deal in return for British printing machinery.

Henderson made a slurping noise over his first drink which suggested a thirsty collie. John opened a door onto the deck and went out.

It was hot even in late afternoon. The river had its old look of heavily milked tea. There was a great deal of floating garbage, little sargasso clumps of it drawn together by some almost protoplasmic urge and forming small rafts of refuse, each making dignified separate courses down current towards the sea. The river was still full of boats, small steamers, and the thousand *sampans*, but of the foreign ships which had once packed in here, waiting for inadequate docking facilities, there was no sign at all, only a Japanese tanker and the seven-thousand-ton *Maree Tarn* held by her bows upstream, a nine-year-old ship, the smallest of the Tarn Line, but still large and new looking here, her white upper paintwork and yellow funnel catching the fading sunlight, mirroring it back towards a city where paint was a difficult commodity to come by.

From here the buildings looked all right, each separately identifiable to John Lownie, as though a façade over there had still the power to spin a wheel in his mind and bring it to a stop opposite some small, complete incident in a boy's life. As early as six he had spent long hours down on the Bund staring at the ships, their presence out in the river offering a promise of escape, the ships all certain to move away on the long sea-patched ribbons of their courses to the world that wasn't China and wasn't Shanghai. John stared at the bulk of the Cathay Hotel, its tower built in a pride that hadn't long to go before a humbling. His mother had worked in there, in the flower shop, just another White Russian making a living from amongst the dirty dishes of a plush world. She was a

34

superior servant where the other servants were soft footed Chinese, shut away in her little booth with the Shantung roses, smiling, answering the phone, speaking always softly in the careful English taught her by an *émigré* father in Harbin.

A lucky girl Natasha, really, for a White Russian, marrying a Scotsman on a B.I. cargo ship instead of just living with him, being a supported wife for all of seven years until Hamish Lownie had shifted to Atlantic liners and Shanghai became as faded in his recollection as the impulse to send maintenance cheques.

'You're a Scotsman, John,' Natasha had said. 'You've got a good Scots name.'

What could you buy with a name? A country?

As a boy John had never been in the hotel where his mother worked, though once he had seen into it through revolving doors, standing flanked by two Sikh policemen while his mother was fetched out, dead pale under the curved braid of her long, tow-coloured hair, her lips moving for the words she couldn't quite shape. His mother had come out from the smell of cigar smoke and the softness of Tientsin carpeting to stare down at her slightly undersized little delinquent.

John leaned on the rail, but turned his head to detail of his portable world, checking without a frontal awareness of it the greasing on a lifeboat davit mechanism. After painting, the moving parts could be left to a slowly feeding rust. The boats hadn't been moved for a month. It was time for a surprise drill. He tucked his elbows into the sides of his chest and felt the prod of joint bones against hard flesh. He had always eaten well, Natasha had seen to that, sometimes from the hotel itself, left-overs in paper napkins, part of the terrible humanity of the Chinese for the white skins towards whom they could feel a total contempt.

'Stinking whore,' John said out loud to the city.

But it was the old city, not this one, not this place occupied by a new planning which forced weird patterns on something designed for another use. Today the very traffic in the streets was as alien as the faces, and the clattering din of joy for sale was totally silenced under a blanket of austerity so snugly fitted down you could find no corner to lift. The little boy who walked beside Captain John Lownie in these streets was a stranger, too.

In all the ugliness of flat China there was no uglier place in which to have set a city, the little side tributary river with two moods, flood and ebb, and always carrying its offal of living between mud banks, the buildings swelling from these on imported rubble and stone, pompous and crowded. There was no hint of distant hills to be seen, just an arc of dusty sky in summer and in winter an antiseptic application of snow, giving relief from stench. The ships which had brought life here had gone, the bulky French liners with swagger literary names, the Japanese cargo-passengers, built with finicky economy, but efficient; the huge, braggart white Empresses that no longer sailed the Pacific at all, and the Dollar Line, a motley of Presidents, popping in and out of Asiatic ports and always losing money, but offering the Stars and Stripes and a five-piece jazz band. You still saw the Blue Funnel sometimes, waving the British flag, but not often in the new Shanghai. One ship came up now, or two, and hung about waiting for an underworked pilot to free them from these waters.

John remembered the Sikh policemen, huge and turbaned and bearded, one on each side holding a small boy's shirt. Natasha's words had finally come as a cry:

'But . . . what's he done?'

The Sikh's English was like a little toneless song for a reed pipe, thin sounding from such a big man.

'He has stowed away, Ma'am. On the Japanese express ship to Kobe. He had sto-len food from the pan-try. He had taken mo-ney from a cabin. They had to lower the gang-plank again.'

His mother's eyes, staring.

'Johnny . . . why?'

He had no words for her then, and really no words for her after.

Henderson came out from the day cabin and also leaned on the rail. Two whiskies in quick succession had restored him to a good temper, a state which often produces in the Scot that pawky humour which is accepted in his own country but almost nowhere else.

36

'Never mind, my boy, it won't be long before we're in Singapore and you'll be back with your lass. Captain Lownie's Suzie Wong. What's her name again?'

'Mabel,' John said, staring at the former offices of the Hong Kong and Shanghai Bank.

'Aye, Mabel. Wherever did she get a name like that?'

'From her father.'

'Who was he?'

'Her mother could never remember. Only that the baby was to be Mabel if a girl. Her full name is Mabel Tlani Nakhon, and she is trying her damndest to blackmail me.'

'Eh? To do what?'

'Set her up,' John said, staring at a truck which came around a corner filled with workers wearing the clean tunics which indicated that they were on the way, under orders, to a mass spontaneous mourning rally for the great one's passing. Someone had artistically draped two pieces of black cloth, meeting in a bunch of flowers, across the front of the radiator, apparently forgetting that black for mourning was an idea imported from the Imperialist West.

'How do you mean, set her up?'

'In a house. I wouldn't have to bear all the expense. She would be mine when the ship's in Singapore.'

'And when you're at sea?'

'She wants to cut down to three other steady clients.'

'But man, you're only in Singapore for three weeks in the year. It doesn't sound like much of a business proposition to me.'

'It isn't,' John agreed. 'That's what I keep telling her. But she doesn't see it that way. She wants respectability. That's a house, with no mama to take a cut.'

'I'd take my custom somewhere else if I was you.'

'Mabel has something. A lot of these Thai crosses do.'

John watched a small open *sampan* with an outboard detach itself from the jetty. It spun a little on the current, and then set a course aft of the *Maree Tarn* which meant a boarding. It probably meant the river pilot, come three hours early for a square meal and whisky. These pilots were all the same, except that the Suez ones drank orange squash and, in a kind

37

of protest against deprivation, took in such vast quantities of carbohydrates and protein that they rolled through life weighted down by drooping flesh. This boy would be a party man, who had kept his office in the lean trade years by a sharp eye for deviationist tendencies in his colleagues. He would stand behind the helmsman of the *Maree Tarn*, wrapped in the invisible, antiseptic plastic against the outside world which so many Chinese walked around in these days. It didn't really help to talk the language at all, you still got looked at from behind the packaging of a safe conformity, as though contact, in the human sense, could only be degrading for the superior species, if not downright dangerous. Though John had heard that there were other places in China which were much better, like Canton, the relaxed Southerners not taking Peking as the source of all gospel. But the Tarn Line ships never went to Canton, everything transhipped from Hong Kong to keep the colonial business-wheels turning.

You still saw White Russians about up here. There had been some talk of shipping them back to the great motherland, or at least the Siberia end of it, and horrible stories, too, of Soviet resettlements in Kamchatka where the summer is like anyone else's winter and the winter is God's own hell of cold. But a few hung on in Shanghai, how it was difficult to see. How did the parasite live when the host body had been totally eliminated? John had seen his half-brothers by race in the street, seen their eyes, and then, blessed in the barrier of knowing no Russian, something his mother had always kept from him stubbornly, had walked on, as aimlessly as they were walking, but with something to come back to, when they had nothing. It must be all kinds of hell to be a White Russian caught up for the second time in a spread of the Marxist revolution from which you had run when you were younger, and had your strength. Did they still breed in their Shanghai holes, producing more of the flaxen-haired and blue-eyed for these streets?

'The Scots boy got out,' John thought, and spat in the river just forward of the gangway landing-platform.

His mother hadn't got out. He had last seen her in 1947 when he was nineteen and a junior apprentice deck officer. His ship had come to Shanghai and he had found his mother in the Cathay Hotel, behind the flower counter, but living in, up in a room on the eleventh floor which had a window onto a shaft. She was happy, she said.

'I'm happy, John. I have everything I want here. I'm happy.'

She was dying, he knew. He wondered sometimes what she had wanted from him as a son, what it was specifically he hadn't given her. He looked and even sounded like a Scots boy, and she was a Russian woman living in Shanghai, with her friends other Russians, few of them as fortunate as she with her hotel room and real heating all through the winter.

'I am happy, John.'

All right, she was happy! What the hell can you do? How can you give people what they won't take, and when you don't have any idea what they want? His mother had got on without him, for a long time, and to the end. And where was his bastard father anyway? What had he to do with all this, the great giver of a name, a steward making up bunks on ships, who might still be doing it if he hadn't gone down after a torpedo hit?

John took out the package of cigarettes which had been making a conspicuous lump in his trouser pocket. He lit one, flicked the match away, and watched the pilot boat.

'I went to the American School in Shanghai as a charity case and pledged allegiance to the flag every morning in assembly. One nation indivisible and all the rest, and somehow Oleg Mikaeloff, son of the Russian Consul, went there too, excused the allegiance to the U.S. President maybe, but under the same umbrella of an international ideal which failed to work at school just as it failed later. Oleg got a punch on the nose behind the gym from a smaller boy that was me. A little Red Russian streaming blood from his olfactory cavities. He came in a big black car and went home in it, with the chauffeur taking his schoolbag and putting it in the back.'

'That's our pilot,' Henderson said. 'Going to feed and drink him?'

'Yes.'

John turned and went for the hooded companionway which led down to the shelter deck.

.   .   .   .

The *Maree Tarn* sailed at 8.15 p.m. exactly, upping anchor, and then swinging around on the current, once a tricky manoeuvre amongst other ships but now easy enough in an empty river. She sailed from the lights of the Bund and loud military music discharged from street speakers, slowly, engines in reverse for a time against the swift flow, putting ten thousand lit windows astern.

The pilot stood behind the helmsman and only spoke to give his orders, in English. John Lownie stayed on the bridge, knowing that he was behaving like a young skipper on the first voyage of his first command. He watched while a stranger flipped seven thousand gross tons in and out of the narrow flows between often nearly invisible marker buoys. There were certainly much worse rivers for navigation than the muddy little Hwang Pu, but even here a slight miscalculation in rudder movement or in speed could send a suddenly inert mass of steel shuddering up onto a silt bank.

No moon at all didn't help. Beyond the first bend, the flat agricultural land offered no lights, as though the communes had sucked the people out of their old mud houses into supervised living far away from the fields. As the sky glitter behind them faded, there was nothing to be seen from the bridge windows but a clamped-down blackness, flecked ahead by infinitesimal sparks from the markers. It took them the better part of an hour to pick up the light at the mouth of the Hwang Pu, and this seemed to be on low power, a little feeble recurrence that might have been someone with a torch on the bank.

Eight bells and the first watch. That was something. The mate came up iron stairs, a boy from Sunderland, still in his twenties and sitting his master's ticket soon, confident that this would lead, after only a short wait, to a command of his own. Haslett was as punctilious about the dignities as a deck officer on a vast Atlantic liner.

'Duty, sir.'

'Yes. Well, we're not needed. Not for another hour.'

'I'll be glad to get out of the smell, sir.'

'What do you mean?'

'China.'

Something faintly defensive stirred in John, as though at a slight. It was still half his land they were moving through, and this ditch a ghost boy's river on which he had watched the ships and longed to use them.

'It was all right once,' John said, and then remembered that it hadn't been all right for him. Had it been all right for Natasha Lownie?

'They rather scare me, sir. I mean the faces you see. In the streets. The way they look at you. As if they didn't want you there and could see through the space you take up.'

It was quite a flight of imagination from Haslett. And it was also the truth. They did look through you these days. John could remember a time of almost clawing curiosity about the foreigner, who was followed about, aped sometimes, kidnapped, or treated with a delicacy of politeness so polished that any return seemed a blundering awkwardness. But that had been the ending of an eighty-year period which had to be set against an earlier forty centuries when for the Chinese anything from beyond their border was nothing. It was their attitude again today, not violent change under Marxism, just a return to norm, to a total contempt for the Russian barbarian and the American paper tiger. They had swept their house clean of all traces of invaders who had brought religion and business, neither of these strange bounties wanted any longer. The most numerous people on earth, breeding vastly more than they had ever done, were pushing now at old frontiers, testing them, ready to flow out when the time came, taking their China with them. It was a country swelling like a celled organism suddenly affected genetically, with an almost unthinkable monstrousness as the end product of growth.

John went over to stand by the pilot.

'Half way?'

Small eyes turned sideways, gleaming in the binnacle light. The man didn't nod or move his lips.

'If you deepened the channel at the estuary mouth, this

wouldn't have to be a tidal approach at all. But that might do you out of a job, eh?'

The pilot showed no interest at a use of Chinese. He cleared his throat and spat on the deck. Then he gave an order to the helmsman. John could feel the slight swinging movement through his feet, as much as anything from a momentary altering of engine vibration.

Haslett said:

'We seem to be hugging the starboard marker buoys pretty close all the time, sir. I wonder why he doesn't stay in mid stream?'

'Why don't you?' John asked the pilot.

There was a reaction.

'New channel made. Change all time now. Last year floods.'

'Why not move the buoys?'

The pilot shrugged.

'Not do.'

John turned and went out from shelter to the bridge over-hang, into the real dark there which seemed folded down in layers of black-dyed wadding. When he leaned over, he could hear above the ship's own noise the wash against a bank, a thick bubbling of silt-heavy water. Ahead were the marker lights, an undulation of them drawn in a gentle sloping 'S' line that never at any point would take them well out into mid stream. He turned and was walking back to the wheel-house when he was flung down onto deck boards, flat, hands and feet out. He heard Haslett shouting:

'My God, we've struck! We've hit something solid!'

The noise was not the sound of a big ship running onto a mud bank. There was a tearing of plates, a grinding.

'The forward bulkheads,' John roared. 'Haslett! See to the doors!'

The boy had been holding onto something. He began to run towards the bridge steps. The engines were in reverse by the time John reached the controls. The pilot was dead pale, trembling.

'Something in river! Something in river! I not know. Something in river!'

The grinding was still going on, and the ship rattled from

42

the screws turning back. John yanked the engine controls to stop, but he could feel, under him, that the *Maree Tarn* was free again, floating on the stream. He could feel something else, something not seen, just known, she was already heavier in the bows. He reached out and grabbed the pilot.

'You little bastard! Get us back up the river to Shanghai!'

CHAPTER TWO

Chequers, the official country residence of the British Prime Minister, is only used regularly by those incumbents who haven't the private means to go somewhere else for their week-ends. It is flawlessly maintained, well staffed, and has depressed successive generations of Heads of State. Possibly this is partly due to a rather grim air of English calm which has survived a multitude of crises. There is also a museum tone of things set in their places which it would be domestic heresy for the political transient to monkey with. So the house is accepted as it stands, a gift to the nation, and an awful monument to continuing English traditions which include immaculate gardening. The place is also subject to the tyranny of entrenched personnel who have a liferent on it, which is a great deal more than its occupiers do.

The Right Honourable James Dalrymple was another Scot who had contrived to achieve eminence in England, this in spite of the natural disadvantages of his place of birth, no especially remarkable breeding, and very little money. His appointment as Prime Minister had surprised the public, as these appointments so often do. It had also resulted, again the norm, in some dramatic resignations from office amongst his own party. None the less the compromise dark horse had jumped into office with a sprightly display of energy which confounded his critics and deepened the hostility felt towards him by people who claimed they had always rather liked the chap. He was, in his way, something very few British Prime Ministers appear to be, a man of his time, alert to it and not overly impressed by the British past. The elderly thought him highly unsound, which really meant that no one had heard of his grandfather; the young thought him too old, and the middle-of-the-roaders said he was moving left more and more every day. Certainly his Cabinet appointments, usually an area reserved for decorum and party seniority, had been eruptively startling. No Front Bencher was safe, and no Back Bencher who had been toeing the line for promotion, got it. Her Majesty's Loyal Opposition tended to resent the P.M.'s dynamism as much as his own party, it was an innovation that, however much needed, set unnerving precedents for British political life.

Gregory Hartshorn, the newly appointed Minister of Defence, walked in the Chequers gardens, not as a true admirer of the authentic English perennial border, but because the political game, played against this particular backdrop, had evolved specific rules for the place. Real work was sometimes done in the big house but everyone contrived to meet for tea and to pretend that nothing so 'uncountry' had been going on. It was a tradition to chatter on the terrace at 4 p.m. about Wimbledon or cricket, but very little else. The current Prime Minister was probably the first ever to come out into pale sunlight talking about relations with France.

Gregory moved alone down a hundred yards of grass walk on which no daisy had ever dared poke up into the light. The substance beneath his feet was like top quality Wilton carpeting with a heavy underlay, firm-bristled, but yielding. He was thinking, as so many were these days, about China.

He had been to China once, not as a politician, but a traveller, a university professor with a whim, who had wangled a visa after difficulties and travelled some eight thousand miles to find himself virtually a prisoner in his country's Embassy, drinking imported gin with very bored ladies who felt that life was passing them by while they were stuck in a diplomatic backwater. Certainly there had been the one interview with Liu Fa Tsu, arranged for him by his cousin, the First Secretary, and from this Gregory had carried away an impression of a man saying absolutely nothing at some length, and doing this with a kind of deliberate insolence beneath a veneer of almost traditional Chinese courtesy. Liu's comment on the Chinese population explosion had really been the only interesting one.

'There are many people in China. There will be many more. We think this is good.'

Feeding, Liu had assured him, would come from Chinese scientific achievements. There was even now a research foundation engaged on the conversion of wild grasses into edible protein. And did Mr Hartshorn know that most grasses, in their natural state, had a high vitamin content? 'Look at cows,' the Deputy Leader had said, and laughed. 'The world is full of grass. We must learn to eat it.'

Gregory Hartshorn's impressions of the new Leader didn't somehow march with those of Sir Malcolm Lugworth who was at this moment, until tea time, in an informal closed session with the P.M. Almost certainly Sir Malcolm was now engaged in reproducing from a mental sound track a non-edited version of his words to the world.

Gregory didn't pretend to himself that he liked Sir Malcolm. As an historian, he found punditry glib and prone to easy conclusions that could smell like the truth but almost never were. A man who has been trained to a bird's-eye view of history cannot really, if he is an honest researcher, achieve any dogmatic standpoint from which to make an impressive show in the world, a fact which is a grave disadvantage in a political career. There is a kind of residue in the mind, even with convictions, of neutrality, the feeling that allowances must always be made for the as yet unrevealed. Sir Malcolm *knew* what Liu was going to be like as the Leader of China. This seemed to Gregory impertinent nonsense.

He lit another cigarette and then looked for a place to throw away the match, but a terrible order rebuked him and he put the thing in his pocket.

It was a quarter to four. The sound track would have at least another fifteen minutes to run. The P.M. was rather addicted to these briefings from his experts, and he kept a vast stable of them, like a millionaire would horses. In a way his Ministers, too, were part of this stable, appointed for the express purpose of holding up the apex of a pyramid rather than to head their own departments. It seemed almost a natural law that as government became more complex the man on top found himself less able to delegate authority, with the result that you could no longer have an idiot in nominal control with the machine still functioning in a reasonable manner. A bad Prime Minister now simply meant bad government, and a few years of the wrong kind of head of state could reduce any democracy to chaos.

Gregory had always felt it must be a kind of hell to hold ultimate responsibility under a representative system of government. You could expect to please very few and your enemies all had loud voices. It was a minor hell to be Defence Minister, for all that, after only six days in the appointment, the new man was still moving around inside the carefully spun cocoon of his caution. He had been pushed into office in a minor cabinet reshuffle, or, as the Prime Minister put it so succinctly for the press: 'A realignment of top echelon personnel to improve the drive of the administrative machine.' The P.M.'s public utterances these days were considerably nourished by American idiom as a result of all those trips to Washington. Everyone seemed to be going to Washington a great deal of the time, the Treasury practically living there. Only the Home Secretary didn't appear to interest them in America and was left alone, but even the Secretary of State for Scotland, that ruler of a depressed appendage, was forever dashing over to wave bits of tartan at bored U.S. industrialists, while the Minister of Transport used planes to Los Angeles like buses in order to study traffic control in a technocratic age.

There hadn't been time in his six days of power for Gregory to join the great trek West, but a Pentagon conference might happen at any time, when he would fly over to be given the hand of close fellowship by American generals who had, privately and before they met him, written off his ideas on defence as the usual British attempt to keep their damn little islands afloat at almost any cost in the H-bomb era.

There had been quite a flurry in London about Gregory's appointment. The Leader of the Opposition had risen in the

House to say that, while he had personally a great respect for the Right Honourable Gentleman elevated to high office by the Prime Minister, his esteem for the man could not make him overlook profound doubts about his fitness for this particular role. In plain words: 'Why the hell an ex-prof?' Generals, admirals, and air marshals could all be expected to dislike him on sight and on principle. The Permanent Under-Secretaries, geared as they are to political change, and to ignoring it as much as possible, would be bound to elevate long noses at the appointment of a man who, however eminent in his own field, had none the less been obliged to wear spectacles from the age of twelve and had seen no active war service whatsoever. In the City they were saying that the P.M. had gone quite mad. It had been a slight surprise, even to a history professor, to find his appointment resulting in stock market fluctuations which cost uninformed punters half a million pounds. Even more startling was the fact that over in New York the Dow Jones index had dropped a couple of points that day, too.

At the end of the grass walk Gregory found himself facing a piece of garden statuary that was decidedly period in feel, not a gnome, but a little Pan in chipped sandstone on which the birds had left passing tribute. Why had he wanted to become Defence Minister? The truth was never easy to come on, but it was a matter of duty to look for it. One reason—he liked the thought of being important enough to hold that office. Another, he thought he could do it. It is a popular fallacy that history repeats itself, but history can offer at least partial answers to a great many contemporary situations, and it is so rarely referred to by politicians, possibly because it doesn't often flatter their function. Yet another reason—he liked James Dalrymple, who was one of those old friends who had become more valuable as such and not just a habit.

There was yet another reason. Gregory's wife, a Lady in her own right, the daughter of an earl who had bullied the Tory party in his section of England into total submission, thought her husband was biting off more than he could chew. Elaine was a woman of some beauty, great charm, and great candour. He still loved her after ten years of marriage, but found her almost as irritating as when they first met at somebody's cocktail party. He could hear her voice quite distinctly as he turned back up the long grass walk.

'Darling, I thought it was quite sweet when you wanted to become a Member of Parliament. But this! Really!'

Elaine had no need for any social eminence which might possibly come in the train of her husband's appointment. She had been born to more than she needed in the only world she acknowledged which was stuffed with top people. She accepted her husband's progressive views, even prepared to share them provided change came about in a nice way that didn't really upset any of her friends too much. One of the things he meant to do as Defence Minister was show his wife that he wasn't in any compartment as yet, capable of much more than safety as an academic digger of dry bones. The odds against him, however, were formidable, and he was still slightly unnerved by the P.M.'s apparent confidence in the appointment.

Tea was being served on the terrace. The Home Secretary was already settled in, looking depressed, as though a political house-party was his idea of hell. So was the Minister of Transport, obviously hearing traffic noises in the distance, beyond the trees. It was his nightmare that he wouldn't be able to get to the office one morning because the whole of London had seized up, a million cars blaring fury at him. He thought about viaducts and by-passes in his bath, and was reputed to have acute gastric trouble.

The Prime Minister came through french windows as Gregory reached the bottom step. He was being charming to Sir Malcolm, who wore the expression of a man who has talked himself out and can't imagine anything in this life more blissful.

'Gregory knows China, too,' the P.M. called down, with smiling malice.

Sir Malcolm raised his eyebrows.

'Really? How long ago?'

'Almost five years,' Gregory said.

'Oh. That's rather a long time, isn't it? And considerable changes since then, of course. Did you meet any of the Central Committee?'

49

'Liu Fa Tsu.'

'I see. What was your impression, Mr Hartshorn?'

'I thought him a very astute and able man who was simply waiting for his chance of power.'

Sir Malcolm smiled.

'That might be said of a good many politicians, don't you agree?'

'Quite,' the P.M. said. 'I was dancing with impatience for years.'

Some time later Gregory was provoked out of a listening silence. He put down his teacup and said directly to Sir Malcolm:

'I believe it's a mistake to think a man can never break through what he has been for most of his life and become something else, even something quite different. There have been explosive changes in personality that have affected the world's history. High office can often be the agent of that change.'

'Who have you in mind?' Sir Malcolm asked.

'If you want a modern example . . . President Truman. I think he was a very good President. And I believe that when the period comes into perspective it will be seen just how effective he was. Yet no one could have foreseen the change that was to take place in that personality.'

'I've never suggested, Mr Hartshorn, that Liu Fa Tsu is not a capable man.'

'The point is, capable of what? You think power is likely to turn him into a moderate, who will bring a new Chinese approach to world problems. What makes you feel this? It's not their tradition at all. Liu inherits a country that is growing stronger every day, with a massive population that he can use as an instrument against us if he wants to.'

'He's a man of the world,' Sir Malcolm said.

'I think he's a man of China. And that's out of the world as we know it, or even think about it.'

'Most interesting,' said the P.M. 'Have some cake, Lugworth. How is a Chinese out of the world, Gregory?'

'In arrogance.'

The Home Secretary had been about to help himself to an

éclair but thought better of it. Sir Malcolm put on a smile.

'I do believe,' he said, 'that you're trotting out the old yellow peril.'

'Yes, I am. I don't want to, but I am. It's considerably against my instincts to do it. It's putting a label on a huge block of the world's people and saying you won't get past that label. It's probably wrong to say that. But I think it would also be wrong not to consider it as a possible reality of our time. When you look at China you must look at her history.'

'No!' Sir Malcolm shook his head. 'In our time you're looking at a right-about face, to all intents and purposes that is. Massive change, under their concept of Marxism.'

'That I simply don't believe,' Gregory said.

He knew then that he had made another enemy. It is particularly disconcerting for a politician when this is patently obvious.

.   .   .   .

The P.M. used the library as his office. It was a room dedicated to books no one had the time or inclination to read.

'Well, Gregory, if you do that sort of thing to your under-secretaries, there's going to be interesting hell to pay. When are you starting?'

'Not in a hurry.'

'Oh. Pity. I like a good stir up. We have too many admirals not yet on the retired list. And old generals who think they have a strategy for peace. There's not much else left to them with war what it is these days. Did you mind all the papers pounding your appointment?'

'I was surprised to find it made me angry.'

'Good. You've been a man in a shell, you know. All your potential pushed into it. Take a deep breath now and expand.'

'I'll try, James.'

'Well, round one. Washington.'

'I've been waiting for this. But I thought you might give me a couple of weeks in office first.'

'Could you fly over Tuesday?'

'There's nothing really to stop me. Is it urgent?'

51

'I think so. It's something I want off my mind and settled. Ancient history really, in that it cropped up in the Cuba crisis and our predecessors in office didn't do anything about it. Of course they'd say that it was done with their full knowledge and approval, but I don't believe it for a moment. The Polaris base ship pulled out of the Clyde then. The Americans virtually packed up their base on our territory when there was a real threat to it. Their motives may have been partially humanitarian. But I'm interested in the morale factor. The sailing of that ship wasn't good for ours then. It wouldn't be on another occasion, either. See what I'm getting at?'

'Hm,' Gregory said.

'It's their ship and they've a right to do what they want with it. But the fact remains that that ship *is* the base, something we accepted with all the risks involved. The Americans could quite easily see war looming when we don't, and in this sense we are concerned. I don't want that base and its movements to become a kind of barometer of what America thinks of the world situation. If the Pentagon won't agree to the fullest consultations with us before pulling their base out of our waters, then it may become necessary for my government to reconsider the whole question of U.S. bases in this country.'

'You want me to say exactly that over there, James?'

'Yes.'

'Is it wise?'

'It's policy. And I'm very concerned with policy at the moment. Our rating in Washington is a bad third to the Germans and the French. This is something that needs straightening out. The noise of a real row with the British echoing down the corridors of the Pentagon will be an interesting change for the Americans. The right kind of row every now and then tends to strengthen the basic relation we have with these people. You know me, Gregory. At some risk to my career, I've never pretended that in this country we're now more than a second-class power. But we're damn good second-class, not an indifferent third. That's my point. Within our means we're the best allies they have in the world today. But I'm not having any sentimentality about our American cousins—a revolting phrase—cloud the fact that our interests

52

can, at times, diverge sharply. This is a small issue, but it's important to us, and it's going to be settled *our* way. It'll be interesting to see how they react to a stubborn professor.'

'They may react like Sir Malcolm.'

'Very well, shoot them down, like you did him.'

The P.M. laughed. Then he tried to get his pipe going again and failed.

'Gregory, do you really think the Chinese are an immediate threat . . . or could be?'

'I do.'

'Then we'll have to watch 'em, won't we? You mustn't be suspicious, you know, of the way I use the experts. I don't take them too seriously. But they're useful if you subtract from what they tell you what they are themselves. Then do a bit of division by your own intelligence. How far do you agree with Sir Malcolm . . . if at all?'

'His assessment of Liu Fa Tsu's background is sound enough. Sedentary. Like mine.'

CHAPTER THREE

John Lownie lay on his back in a Shanghai hotel. It wasn't the Cathay, that was now offices, but the old Astor House, mid-Victorian, with massive plaster cornices on all the ceilings. He stared at the one low-powered bulb which hung down, shadeless, from central brownish warts that had once been decorative flowers and probably gilded. Beside him, on the coverlet, was a cablegram. He could see the words without picking the paper up again.

MASTER MAREE TARN SHANGHAI STOP MINIMAL REPAIRS LOCALLY YOUR SHIP STOP PROCEED SINGAPORE STOP GIVE PROBABLE SAILING DATE STOP HAGERSON

Hagerson wasn't actually one of the Tarn Line divinities, but as their chief agent out here he came damn near it. What he said went, north, south and west of Singapore, and he was a man who liked to say a lot.

Minimal repairs! How the hell could you make minimal repairs on six bow plates which looked like they'd been torn back by a massive can-opener? And how could you give probable dates of departure when your ship was in a Chinese dry dock totally possessed by slit-eyed riveters?

The *Maree Tarn* had hit a sunk tug. The thing had gone down the morning of the day they sailed, a fact not reported to the river pilot, the wreck not marked in any way. That was the official explanation. The port officials had been positively

54

bland, looking at John not through him while they said their pieces. The presence of the sunk tug had represented a danger to navigation for which they were entirely responsible. The repairs to the ship would be done at government expense and the crew would be entertained on shore meantime with free tickets to Red culture.

He lit a cigarette. He was getting through two packets a day of Chinese stink. The rationing had stopped. Sometimes he looked at his stained fingers and saw that they were trembling. He ate the stew that was the hotel's cuisine with fingers that shook a little over lifting a fork. A shore-bound sailor with shaking fingers.

He rolled off the bed.

'God Almighty, I can't crack up.'

It was enough to make you, though. He went over to a marble basin and turned a tap. It said hot, but it came cold and in an ungenerous trickle, as though the municipality these days wasn't giving anything away, even water. You'd think they had enough water in China. It took all of a minute to fill the basin. He splashed his face and neck, took the thin towel and used it. Then he picked up the burning cigarette again. His watch said 1.30 a.m. Time for sleep.

Sleep was something you had forgotten about, even the sailor's clock-punching sleep, the ration of a watch to be risen for, or the skipper's ration of having to be awake quickly, and thinking. Even that kind of sleep was out.

John was looking at his face in the cracked mirror when the knock came.

'Uh?' he said, still looking at his face, not liking it.

'Captain?'

Haslett. The boy Haslett on the prowl in the middle of the night. He didn't like China. Maybe he'd had a nightmare.

'Come in.'

'Captain, I think something's happened.'

John said without turning:

'You bet.'

'It's Henderson, sir. He hasn't come back.'

The old man shared with this boy, John had forgotten that. Only the captain rated a room to himself.

55

'Have you looked in the comrades' convenience, Mr Haslett?'

'He's not there. I'm quite sure he hasn't been back to the room. I was asleep, of course.'

He was still of the age when sleep could be 'of course'.

'Any idea where he went?'

'Yes . . . sir.' Haslett was hesitant.

'Well, give!'

'He said he was going to stir up the town a bit.'

'The D.O.M. I wouldn't worry. He probably *is* stirring it up. He's had more than sixty years of life and a lot of it along this coast, so he ought to be able to look after himself.'

'Well, the thing that worries me is the way he's been drinking. And tonight especially. Before he went out. He wouldn't eat anything. He wouldn't even go to the dining-room. I've never seen him quite like that.'

'I have,' John said. 'He's been a bit better since you joined us, but it's an old story. He's building up for a really good party. Which means three bottles. Was he getting whisky?'

'Yes, sir. He had it in the room.'

'Scotch whisky?'

'I saw the label. Definitely.'

'East-West trade is looking up. I wonder if you can buy it in the hotel? I must try. It could be what I need.'

'I'm sorry to have bothered you,' Haslett said.

It was just slightly trying the way the boy seemed always to be standing to attention, as though a Sandhurst army cadet instead of merchant navy. There wasn't anything nautical about that guardsman's back, with the arch inwards leading up from a deep cavity above the buttocks. It was a stance which always made John feel that the characters who adopted it were trying hard to break wind, but couldn't.

'You'll find him on his knees in the passage outside before long,' John said. 'It isn't easy to get him to bed. Our chief engineer has a nasty tendency to kick when he's lit. As hard as a mule. You have to watch for that. It comes when you're least expecting it. I've seen him kick with his eyes shut. Or he may do it right in the middle of one of Scotland's patriotic songs. Call me if you need me. And come in even if the light's out.'

56

When the boy had gone John flicked off the switch and went to the window. This was draped with lace gone brown which smelled as though it had been hung about the time of Edward the Seventh's coronation and never laundered. He pushed it aside to look down from the third floor at Shanghai's night life. There wasn't any. It was remarkable what a good job the Reds had done in this area. Once the street below would still have been thronged at this hour and the din a bit much for sleep on a warm night. Now there was one pedestrian, two cats, and a policeman. The policeman was looking at the pedestrian and vice versa. For a moment John thought there was going to be a demand to see the lone walker's identity card but the crisis seconds passed and Shanghai's last reveller got away. Nothing could possibly happen to Henderson in this town unless he fell in the river, that could still drown him. He was probably asleep on a park bench somewhere, with his shoes and socks off. It was too hot for pneumonia.

'Shut-eye,' John said out loud. 'Good old bloody shut-eye.'

He started to undress. He had got as far as pulling off his shirt and hanging it over a chair back to let the armpit areas dry off, when there was a knock again. Nothing diffident about it this time. Feet had come right to the door, silenced by dusty old carpet, but the knock was official even if the feet weren't.

'Come in.'

It was a Chinese in uniform, quite a big man, professional bully-boy even. Something had happened to one of his ears, not exactly cauliflower, but it had a gnawed look. Perhaps local girl friends were turning carnivorous.

'You Captain Lownie?' He used English.

'I am. Why?'

'You got old engine man? He in trouble.'

'I thought this was coming.'

'Eh?'

'Pass it. What's he done?'

'He hit comrade with bottle.'

John didn't like that at all. He didn't like, either, the way munched ear was regarding him, as though this was very official indeed.

57

'I'm very sorry to hear about this. Where is my chief engineer?'

'Locked.'

'For the night?'

'It is offence for charging. Comrade is wounded. You understand?'

'Unfortunately, yes.'

Blast the old fool! As if enough hadn't happened.

'You want me to come with you now?'

'No. Not now. Morning. I come . . .' He looked at a sizeable dial strapped to his wrist. 'Ten o'clocks.'

The visitor left without any social pleasantries. John went on with his undressing. He pulled on pyjama bottoms and got under the sheet.

'I'm damn well not going to think about this.'

It surprised him that he felt sleepy.

  .   .   .   .

Chewed ear wasn't the escort in the morning. They went in a car, which showed the occasion had some importance, a driver isolated up in front, and using the horn a lot as though it was one of the small pleasures left in this life. The escort stared straight ahead all the time and sat rolled into his corner of the back seat as though he had been told that capitalism was infectious. John didn't try out any Chinese. He wasn't at the moment interested in how the local fauna got on under the new enlightenment. He had slept, but all it had done was underline the fact that he had been missing a lot of sleep lately. A cigarette burned between his fingers. He looked at his hands, which he liked to keep clean, and noticed that they weren't quite that.

The car went slowly. It wasn't the traffic, just plug trouble, the symptoms of this evident from the periodic coughing of the exhaust. It could be that the Javanese weren't selling their best car spirit to their near brothers up north. The Japanese were selling plenty of bicycles, though, a lot of the models shiny with a new paint that was in sharp contrast to surroundings. There were also Japanese motorized two-wheelers ridden

58

by men who mattered and had hats, instead of caps, to prove it.

The police station had always been just that. There was a lingering smell of disinfectant, as though authority had to be protected against plagues whatever happened out in the streets, and the place was humming with activity, uniformed power in mass movement.

John was shown into a tiny room like a cell and the door was pulled shut on him. There was a table and two chairs, nothing else. He sat and lit another cigarette and had smoked half of it before the door opened and a man came in who looked as though he stowed away his rice ration in cheek pouches to be masticated later on. The rest of him was quite small, a short body lifted off the ground by short legs. He looked at John with real curiosity which was something new.

'Captain Lownie? I'm told you speak Chinese.'

'Yes, I was born here.'

'How interesting. So you return to your native place. How do you find it?'

'Not my native place.'

There was no reaction to this. The man went to the other chair, pulled it out and sat.

'I am Inspector Chow.'

'I've come to see my chief engineer.'

'That will not be possible.'

'Why?'

'In China the prisoner on a serious charge must wait without visitors for trial.'

John sat forward.

'Serious charge? Inspector, I won't try to deny that Mr Henderson likes his drink. And he probably made a nuisance of himself last night . . .'

'You do not understand, Captain! I said serious charge. I mean it. The most serious. Your Mr Henderson hit a Chinese man in a People's Restaurant with a bottle of drink which he brought. Before that he had been most insulting. He used pidgin language that is not heard in China now. He said things about our country.'

'I'm very sorry. I'll see that he is disciplined if you turn him over to me.'

59

'Turn him over to you? Captain, the man your engineer attacked died this morning in hospital.'

A nausea which had persisted in John's stomach, even beyond the break of sleep, moved up and sat in his throat. He pushed his fists against the edge of the table. He stared at a thin mouth between those squirrel-pouched cheeks.

'The charge is murder,' the inspector said.

John took a deep breath before he spoke.

'I'll be getting in touch at once with our Embassy in Peking.'

'You can.'

'Inspector, I ask you again to let me see Henderson.'

'No.'

'Is he in this building?'

'I cannot tell you.'

'But I only have your version of what happened. Is that the reason I'm not being allowed to see my engineer?'

'This man has broken the laws of China. He will be dealt with in our way. He will see our justice.'

'You can't blame me, Inspector, if I don't feel too happy about that.'

'Your feelings mean nothing to me!'

There was nothing more John could do. The escort took him out of the building and back to the car. He was left alone only at the hotel entrance, going up in a shaking lift with Haslett who joined him in the lobby.

'Sir . . . is it true about the Chief?'

'If you mean a charge of murder, yes. How did you hear?'

'One of the men had it. From someone in the hotel. I can't believe it! That old man, hitting someone with strength enough to kill him!'

'He's not too old to be able to use a bottle with drink taken. Not nearly too old. There must be a black market in whisky in this place. That's how he got hold of it.'

'Captain . . . you believe this?'

'I don't believe anything at the moment, Haslett. Nothing at all. Do you understand? Come into my room a minute. I want you to get a cable off for me.'

Haslett closed the door. He stood looking around.

'What's the matter?'

60

'This place could be bugged, sir. Had you thought of that?'

'Yes. If it is they won't have much of a record of my snoring in here. And they're perfectly free to listen in to anything I have to say to you.'

'I can't help thinking about the old boy.'

'Sit down and relax. Henderson has lived through a lot worse than this in his time. He's pickled in Scotch malt and as tough as nails. And probably a Chinese jail will do his liver a lot of good.'

John knew that Haslett was suddenly disliking him. The boy still lived in a black and white world of the goodies and the baddies. He saw life tidily, everything in it as neatly arranged as his own cabin drawers. Henderson, for all his alcoholism and his Scots ribbing, was something of a father figure, and his antiquity itself commanded respect. John wondered if there had ever been any time when he had seen living along these lines, and decided that the gutters of Shanghai were not conducive to an early innocence. It was something he had missed. It probably meant permanent and early scarring on the tissues of his soul. The thought of this didn't trouble him at all.

He found he was angry, not so much at the Chinese for being themselves as at Henderson for being himself. He was angry, too, at his own absorption in other matters which had made him forget all about the automatic problem presented by a boozy old Scotsman suddenly planted on shore. He could just see Henderson in a People's Restaurant, wobbly on his feet, but standing up to shout: 'Boy here! Double quick, chop, chop!' In Henderson's hey-day in the orient, you clapped your hands and got service at once, if you had a white skin. And he had shipped under that flogging skipper. The Chinese had their reasons for not loving us much. We grabbed hold of their Customs Service after the Tai Ping rebellion, and ran it with great efficiency to our own advantage. The tow-headed boy from these streets didn't have to dig too hard to come on what was the tap root of the revolution out here, a sense of helplessness in the face of superior strength. The Chinese had shaken off that feeling of helplessness and they had no intention of ever experiencing it again.

'Sir, there's something else.'

'What, Haslett?'

'It's weird. They put the old chief in jail and ask us all to a party. The whole crew of the *Maree Tarn* has been invited to go on an overnight excursion to Nangking. We're to be given a meal in a famous restaurant there, or something.'

'When did this good news arrive?'

'While you were away. That little interpreter came in beaming all over his head. I told the men not to expect they'd be going.'

'Why?'

'I didn't think you'd feel particularly like a junket just now.'

'Look here, Haslett, we're not in mourning for anything. The whole crew of the *Maree Tarn* is planked down in what is now undoubtedly the dullest city in the orient. There isn't a woman or a decent drink available in the place, at least not to us. If this junket, as you call it, means the crew get off their backsides for a couple of days and see something besides this damn hotel, then of course they must go. All of them. Under your command.'

'Me, sir?'

'I'll have to stay here in case anything crops up with Henderson. But the rest of you clear off. Have fun if you can.'

Haslett stood up.

'Is that . . . an order, sir?'

'I want you to take the crew to Nangking, yes.'

.   .   .   .

John slept. He woke up with his head into the pillow, almost face down into it, the bed-clothes twisted under him. His dream hadn't included China. He turned his head to one side for air. There was a knocking on his door.

You couldn't switch on a light from the bed, you had to pad across the room. He hitched up pyjama bottoms and walked around the table in the dark, his return to consciousness blurred. The knocking came again before he could turn on the light.

'Yes, yes!'

It was chewed ear.

62

'Well?' John said, surly.

The man seemed to stare at John's muscles, almost a tribute.

'You put on clothes. You come.'

'Where?' In Chinese.

The man's eyes showed surprise.

'To see the prisoner.'

'I've been told I can't.'

'It's now allowed.'

'Isn't that nice? A change of heart.'

Chewed ear waited while John dressed. He didn't hurry. He even stroked his chin, contemplating a shave, but remembered the tap marked hot which was a lie. They went down to the street together, into total emptiness, and John looked at his watch. Two in the morning. An odd hour for an interview with a prisoner waiting trial.

In the car John smoked but chewed ear did not. It was the same police station, slightly less humming with activity, but by no means deserted. The place must have been extended since the days of its European use as part of British Shanghai, for they went down a long passage lit by naked bulbs, then a stair, then another long passage. A grilled door with an attendant stopped them only for a moment while keys turned.

This was where the prisoners were. You could hear them. None of them seemed to be sleeping too well. There was moaning and a pair of hands clutching a door grille. Chewed ear flicked at the hands with what looked like a dossier he was carrying. The hands withdrew and a cry of pain brought on a little crescendo of wailing, a mass protest of innocence.

The turnkey opened a cell door. At the back of it, on a stone slab with no blanket, Henderson was lying stretched out, quite motionless. He might have been taking up space in a mortuary the way he lay with hands folded on his stomach, as though he hadn't heard the door open at all. But his eyes were open, staring up at a bulb in the roof.

'Hello, Chief,' John said.

Henderson didn't move. His clothes were surprisingly neat, as if there had been no rough house. John walked across the cell, making a shadow across the recumbent body. And then he saw that the old man was crying. He was just lying there with

63

slack tears running down a seamed and living-battered face. His lips moved.

'They've got me. They've got me in this damned place!'

'Shut up, shut up!'

John didn't like total collapse, he didn't like seeing it. And this was no drunk's remorse. The alcohol had long since worked itself away.

'They wouldn't let me see anyone.'

'Sit up!' John rapped it out.

He heard chewed ear move in close behind him.

'I don't want to. I'm not . . . I don't feel . . .'

'So help me, Henderson, if you carry on like this I'll clonk you one. And you an old man lying your back.'

The eyes widened, a real reaction. Slowly the man's legs moved on the slab, coming over its edge, and he pushed his body up like a terminal senility case obsessed with the idea that the world didn't love him any more. He sat humped over, bringing the back of a hand under his nose. John pulled out a handkerchief and handed it over. In a moment the chief looked up, red-eyed, into the glow from a bulb.

'I'll never get out,' he said.

'Listen to me. I've cabled the Company. I've talked on the phone to the Embassy in Peking. You're not alone and forgotten. Everything is being done that can be. It isn't as if the ship was sailing tomorrow. We're all stuck here. And we all know what's happened to you. You can count yourself lucky in some ways.'

'Lucky! You can say it.'

'I'm not going to ask a lot of questions, Henderson. Because I can find most of the answers for myself. But where did you get whisky?'

'In the hotel. From one of the waiters.'

'Not true,' chewed ear said.

'It *is* true. I keep telling them that. And they won't believe me, John. They won't believe anything. They keep saying I killed a man.'

'Well? Do you remember hitting him with a bottle?'

'No! I swear I didn't. I swear. It never happened. It couldn't have happened.'

'Henderson, remember that time in Ceylon? It couldn't have happened, either. You didn't remember a damn thing the next morning.'

Hands came out, as though to clutch at John.

'Look . . . I didn't do this! I know I didn't do it. They've framed me, that's what they've done. They'll frame everything. What chance have I got with this thing hung around my neck?'

'No chance at all unless you keep your nerve.'

'Give me a cigarette?'

John handed over a Chinese stink and bent with the match, not checking on chewed ear's reaction. He was looking into the old man's eyes, getting nothing in response. Henderson's trembling fingers pulled out the cigarette after the first long sucking inhalation. He looked down at the floor.

'I've been allowed to see you,' John said. 'That's a good sign. I think it means there's been a policy change somewhere. It could even mean that you'll be held until the ship's ready to sail and then allowed out.'

Henderson shook his head.

'I won't get out. Not for any ship.'

'Have they ill-treated you?'

'What do you mean? Hit me or something? They just asked questions under a light.'

'Even our police have been known to do that.'

'You don't know what it's like to be in here. In China.'

'I can guess. Can you eat the food?'

'I dunno. I haven't tried.'

'Well, try next time. I don't want to be playing nurse all the way to Singapore.'

'If . . . if I thought I'd ever see Singapore again, I wouldn't want anything more in my life. That's the truth!'

'You'll see Singapore.'

Chewed ear tapped John's shoulder and made a sign towards the cell door.

'I've got to go now, Chief. Close your eyes and get some sleep. Remember we're working for you. And don't pity yourself. It's not a pretty sight. At any age.'

65

CHAPTER FOUR

Sergei Dimitri Roduschev sat listening to Tchaikovsky coming from his portable hi-fi, the 'Pathétique'. He was waiting for the thin strain of the love theme which had such a sharp parallel in his own life, with Anna, and also with lost, terrible, beloved Russia; that lament of fiddles recurring and woven in, briefly offered in all the movements and only coming as a momentary flash in the finale which was man's disillusionment and ultimate despair and death. As a youth he had found Tchaikovsky sentimental, but now at fifty-four he knew that sentiment is the core of spirit, the thing on which are built the fictions which make the act of living endurable. And the end would be like this, the fictions without real substance, a segment of a dream, a last flash before the dark.

The fictions had no real substance now, even at this stage, which could be some time before the end. There were tears in Sergei's eyes, and they were for himself. There was no one else to weep for him and there could never be. He was totally alone in a room where a box made sound for him, flinging out echoes of old pain that were received in passivity, by a grey shell.

'I am dead,' he thought.

Throughout Russian writing, in Tolstoy, Dostoevsky, Turgenev, were the dead like him, the great hollow men, in a torment of their emptiness, lost and with the agony of knowing it, souls devoured, bodies left.

66

'Like my body,' he thought.

Perhaps soon he wouldn't be able to cry. The anaesthesia might reach that point, like the drugs used in the dreadful new humanity. He would not then want to listen to the box at all. Already the impulse was weakening.

'I wish I was now nothing,' he thought.

His stomach rumbled.

He plucked at a bunch of small Chinese grapes on the table beside him, grapes that were almost yellow in colour and brought a puckering bitterness into the mouth. Like so much that was eaten in this country, they were actually inedible. As their few wines were undrinkable. He thought of the wines of the Caucasus with light held in them, and the faint sweetness which went with the Russian palate and was meant for caviar. Caviar, God in Heaven!

As Senior Directive Assistant at the Polovin Research Institute near Baikal he had eaten caviar. Even in that wilderness, in the unending weariness of a country man would never tame, he had been a Russian, listening to Russian voices, eating Russian food. Now, in China, he was a grey dog living on the offal that was still their top-level ration, and with some luxuries that made little narrow eyes smart with greed when they were delivered.

'My masters,' he thought, spitting out grape pips.

He was in China because of his weakness, because of the dying which had begun years before, started by the knowledge of mental limits, of this natural wall around ambition. He was lucky to have become Senior Directive Assistant simply because, as a scientist, he was not creative. He hadn't in him the capacity to push out beyond the bounds of the calculated experiment into any unknown. Others did that while he helped. And the role which had been assigned him in Russia was what he had earned, no more and no less, a niche that looked important and which gave him priorities in the state pattern, a good house, a car, food better than his juniors, but for all that walls close about. It was to break through those walls that he had come to China as an adviser on the development of some aspects of atomic energy, and, when the big recall came, made him decide to defect.

He was now Chinese. He called himself Professor Baikal here, ludicrous irony, because his real name twisted their tongues. Also, he wanted to get rid of it. He had wanted to get rid of Senior Directive Assistant Sergei Roduschev once and for all, assuming as Baikal the new identity of eminence.

The new identity fooled neither himself nor the Chinese. He was the best they could get, so he was in charge of this research. But if a better man suddenly became available, through an agreement with Russia to share atomic secrets, Baikal would be out. He didn't see that this was likely to happen, but it was a continuous threat to be lived with.

In China Sergei was never able to forget what he was, the journeyman suddenly given a master's authority. He could copy faithfully, and improvise, but he could not innovate. The bomb he had worked on here in the mountains of Yunnan near Ta-Li was merely a logical continuation on a course plotted by others. It was an ingenious adaptation, nothing more. And the firing device, not Sergei's field, had been a source of great trouble and delay. This had now been perfected and in the main not by Professor Baikal but by Li Ta Ling, trained in America, who had returned home also to improve his status as a scientist. Li Ta Ling expected, and before long, to take Baikal's place. He was a beloved son in Peking, who would become a hero of the Chinese Republic. Baikal would not.

The Tchaikovsky came to an end. There was a click, then silence. Sergei realized that the last movement had left him unaffected. He got up and went across the small room to a window, double-glazed against the terrible mountain winds, opening one half in, the other out, then stepping onto a small balcony.

The mountains round about went up to eleven thousand feet, but without any sharp drama of peaks, instead slow, massive ridges, warted like the long spines of dinosaurs. The great lake which gave them the water they needed never went blue under a clear sky, it retained a metallic greyness always, like a cold, secret sea. There were no trees, in spite of almost tropic latitude, as though height had pushed this land up into a permanent coldness. The sun beat on it, but shadow came quickly to refrigerate the valleys, and on Sergei's balcony, high up, the temperature could drop as much as thirty degrees in only minutes after the sun had gone.

It was healthy. You breathed a thin, germ-purged air, with few people to use it. There was no place to put people in these valleys, and the city of Ta-Li itself had been a nothing of stone buildings until it became the dormitory town of the Institute. There was now a good road to it, and roads in the area, but all of them came to a dead end against stone cliffs except the old donkey trail to Kumming which had been widened enough to take jeeps and the occasional aggressive lorry. It was the air-field that put them in the modern world, not much more than a strip, but long enough for jets, with a river beside it and a sharp dangerous ascent needed through thin air to clear humped dragon spines.

This was Sergei's view. He hated every mile of it and the feel it gave of mountains for a prison. He had never asked for leave to whatever flesh-pots of living China had left, kept back from doing so by the fear that his imprisonment would be officially indicated by a refusal. Here he was held to work and die, in luxury by Chinese standards, with his records, the sour wine, and freedom to walk in the valley. He could walk to Burma if he wanted, two hundred miles up and down knife ridges until these quietened into the jungles of the Irrawaddy's central plains. It was a walk that no man could take and live.

Sergei put his hands on the balcony railings. His laboratories and quarters were isolated from the main complex of the Institute, all of eight hundred feet above them, the approach by a winding, but wide and carefully engineered road that had a smooth tarmac surface as though this was essential for the loads that might be needed. Part of his laboratories went back into rock caverns that were now concrete-lined and celled for a half-damp troglodyte existence, a reserved area Sergei didn't use, but which was there. There was also tunnelling back into the hill-side from the main Institute, and a cave store that at the moment was still almost empty. This valley might not be a total secret from the West, but it would be hard to destroy. The sucking blast of a vast explosion might crater it, but the deep caves would still be left. Sergei was frightened to think

69

of what it might mean if they were ordered to move into the deep caves. He didn't want to think about that. The ventilators were already at work, he knew, circulating air to an emptiness.

China was still weak. She would never dare, not for many years at any rate, to challenge the giants. Not in his lifetime, probably. The bomb they had was small, and the step beyond it, to the vast power-explosions, was not a step he could take. Or Li Ta Ling either, whatever Peking might think about that. Their hero of the Republic was a small man, too. And there was no one outside who would be willing to give a potentially big man the needed training.

This was a vast country of peasants playing with modernity to a marching song. The death of the Leader made it less of a threat, too. The new man hadn't his character, and millions of people welded into a unity didn't count any more. It was easy to destroy millions. America could do it, or Russia. Even Britain.

'I'm destroying nothing by my work,' Sergei said to himself.

He watched a plane coming over the mountains, circling at about twenty thousand feet, an insect being careful about its landing place. The descent began, curiously fascinating though often seen, a process of cautious attention to sudden violent thermals. The turbulence in these parts would make an interesting study, something scarcely charted or properly assessed and difficult to do. The hour made the difference, full sun bouncing heat from stone into invisible upward cyclones that rose like challenging defence columns. He watched the plane tip and swerve, a four-engined jet, and big, but helpless-looking now, tentative, feeling its way. He felt the sun on his hands and the back of his head. The drone of the plane was loud, with an uneasy pulse-beat of engines through it.

How clear the air was, in movement the whole time and violent even when without wind, but this resistance of place to intrusion was something the eye could never see. There was nothing to be seen at all but the vividly edged mountains gone vermilion-black in their shaded areas. The Ta-Li valley seemed to offer very few intermediate days, and when the sun wasn't shining it was usually lowering cloud with rain. Sergei's view allowed a few alternatives only, a snow scene, a sun-hard

70

wilderness, or downpour. There was something infinitely depressing in this lack of gradations, as though rigidly limiting to the compass of a form of sensuous experience, making the captive feel more so.

He went back into the room, shutting the inner door, and stood there in the twelve by twelve of his living space, a place with mostly fitted furniture done by a Chinese carpenter to a foreigner's design. The result was something that the foreigner hadn't meant at all, the Chinese triumphant even under orders, with doors that opened the wrong way, or cupboards with sliding panels making what was behind almost inaccessible. It was not his room. It was on loan for his use, defying any imposition of the personal from the occupant. It might have been a leader's room at the administrative headquarters of a farm commune.

On impulse Sergei pulled open a sticking drawer and took from it the album of photographs which was all that was left of his life with Anna, twenty years stuck down with flaps, of the unreal in rigid poses. There wasn't a good picture of his wife, for the camera made her nervous and she grimaced to it, or applied a forced composure which suggested the idiot. Even little Kolya, who had died in Leningrad at seven after a mastoid operation, looked out from these pages, many pages, in a kind of plump caricature of childhood. Here were Anna and Sergei together, just before they left for Siberia, both of them looking as though they had been sentenced to the salt mines when it was actually a long hoped-for promotion. And here was Anna in China, in a little round, garden arch, finding the frame silly for her solid fleshiness. It was the last photograph before she had gone back to Russia with the other wives, not knowing that she would never see her husband again.

He wondered if she would have minded if she had known? Their marriage had begun with the love theme all right, this defined and clear on strings, dominating and recurring. But it was a theme lost before they lost each other, and would never have been recaptured. He had not stayed in China to end his marriage, that could have been done easily enough at any time, but his marriage had not been a serious factor in the final decision.

71

And yet the theme was there because it had once been, waiting perhaps for a final, thin sound piercing through the louder orchestration of death. The thought brought tears to his eyes and a remote pleasurable warmth of anticipation. The young can never understand how the old can sometimes want death and may even be able to meet it in a moment of that desire. To a godless man there is comfort in the thought, and Sergei's god lay only in his profanity which flowed from him easily to alien ears.

'Anna,' he said out loud, and closed the book, weeping for the finale which had not yet come.

The phone rang. He turned slowly to the central table on which he did a good deal of his work and ate the canteen meals. It was How Chi, Director of the Institute. Sergei knew the voice at once, a voice in a chronic state of perturbation, perpetually geared for crises and actually soundless or faintly squeaking when they occurred. It was squeaking now.

'Baikal? Baikal?'

'Yes, I'm here,' Sergei bellowed, suddenly a full-chested Slav. 'What is it?'

The squeaking made no sense for a minute. Then he caught the word 'Leader' repeated in a breathless chant.

'The Leader? What about the Leader?'

'He is here! By airplane!'

'Oh, yes,' said Sergei, the stiffening of his body not in his voice. 'Is it an inspection?'

'Chairman Liu Fa Tsu has come to see you!'

'Oh, yes. Very well. When?'

'Now, now. Soon. Any time.'

Which *meant* any time. It meant Liu Fa Tsu's pleasure, almost certainly. Sergei had never met the man and had never expected to. He couldn't decide whether he was excited or not. It might, of course, mean many things, or nothing, just a routine inspection of a pet project that was almost the Central Committee's only hobby. Various other high dignitaries showed up often enough, including a few times that celebrated Sha Li Tsao, head of propaganda, who was now reported dead as the result of a heart attack. This, to the informed, meant a bullet, though one could never really know about these things.

72

It was best to contain a small curiosity and never let it leak into words. Especially for a Chinese by naturalization who has nowhere else to go now.

It was nearly two hours later that a black car started up the slope to the Institute annex. Sergei was well warned by his staff who had been busy sweeping and polishing. He came down wooden stairs to a reception area in which there was now a large ornamental pine in a pot which certainly hadn't been there before. Nor had a scroll-painting of stylized mountains which didn't suggest these mountains. There was also a new mat down and new uniforms in evidence everywhere.

Sergei's own uniform was standard, buttoned up to the neck, and specially made for his size because there was no suitable issue available. He was six feet tall and suggested, though not to himself, a long lank skinniness of something gone to seed. It took him some time to decide where to stand, outside on the steps, or just inside behind glass doors. He decided finally on the steps where his colleagues were all busily engaged in jockeying for precedence. He took no part in this struggle, going down one step so as not to appear to loom.

The car took its time. A little wind had got up which poked through summer tunics, and the head laboratory assistant had an embarrassing bout of sneezing which he was hissed at to control, but it ran its course. Then the tired car poked a snout up onto their level, and trundled along to a stop. There were two men in the back, and one was Liu Fa Tsu. He did not emerge until a following car had vomited forth a guard, and an armed one, a considerable display of military might. The guard lined the steps and one of them butted Sergei back up onto the general level.

Liu Fa Tsu stepped briskly down. Behind him was a bunch of flowers left on the car floor and poor How Chi, bright pink and shaking. The Chairman gave a salute which was sparing of muscular activity and took the narrow steps one at a time, looking down at them. Then he looked up, at Sergei.

'Ah,' he said, like a man at the end of a quest.

Liu Fa Tsu flicked his hand indicating that Sergei was to precede him inside. Perhaps he didn't want his own stature measured against a Russian giant. This was often the case.

73

'Comrade Chairman, Liu Fa Tsu, this is our Professor Baikal.'

How Chi was hopping like an alarmed canary.

'I can see! No introductions. Come, Baikal.' He swung back to How Chi. 'Office!'

'Certainly, indeed, yes. Certainly, at once. This way please, Comrade Chairman.'

The three moved across the reception area, leaving a packed huddle at the door who looked like guests at a Royal Garden Party who haven't been smiled on by a High Personage.

'Two of my guards,' Liu said. 'One on the door.'

'Certainly, Comrade Chairman. At once.'

But the guards knew their job and were in attendance already, the guns at an angle, very obvious, a slight comment on the gnarled pine and stylized mountains.

'No one is to come in,' Liu said. 'See?'

'Certainly, Comrade Chairman. Would you wish tea?'

'Yes. A guard will bring it in.'

The office was never used. It had that air, a stage set, decorated with chairs not meant to be sat on and a conference table that had seen no decisions made across it. Liu went to the far side of the table, looked briefly around the room, which only had the one door, appeared satisfied, and sat down.

'Sit, Professor,' he said in English. 'You understand English, I believe. You speak it well?'

'I can speak it.'

'Good. There's no fool here who does.' He looked at Sergei. 'You're happy in China?'

'Yes, Comrade Chairman.'

Liu smiled then. It seemed to put humanity into a mask, but only for a moment.

'Not very happy, Baikal, not very. But we need you. Is there anything you want here? For yourself . . . that you haven't got? A woman, perhaps? She could be accommodated in Ta-Li. A Russian if you like. I understand they can still be found in Shanghai. A young Russian girl, eh?'

'I no longer feel the need, Comrade Chairman.'

'Then you should see a doctor. For a course of injections. I can have a specialist in these matters flown here.'

74

'I think . . . it isn't necessary.'

'We want you reconciled, Baikal.'

'I'm content.'

Liu stared across the table, as though that word didn't please him much. Then there was a knock on the door and a guard came in with tea in cups Sergei didn't know the annex possessed, gilded cups of delicate blue and white with a gold dragon. The guard poured twice like a well-trained servant. He had left his gun outside. Liu Fa Tsu sipped, a sucking noise of appreciation.

'Our tea,' he said, 'isn't really liked in the rest of the world. Like most other things in China. How fortunate for us. We can keep them for ourselves.'

He laughed. The door closed again behind the guard. Liu's face became the mask.

'Baikal, you know why I'm here. You know my interest in Project Seven. Well, I've news for you. You'll be overjoyed. I'm arranging to test your little bomb.'

Sergei felt that he had been kicked in the stomach. A test of his secondary device had somehow never seemed on the agenda and he had been quite happy about this. It was a scientific project, an offshoot of the major tests, simply an attempt to produce a reduced atomic reaction that might have some distant, but still theoretical, use as a field weapon.

'You don't look so pleased, Baikal.' Liu's face tightened. 'Isn't your little bomb ready to be exploded?'

'Yes. It could be ready.'

'Then what's the matter?'

'Our Institute has heard of no plans for a test, Chairman.'

'For a very good reason. This is not a matter for someone like How Chi. Is he always as silly as he has been today?'

'He's a little nervous.'

'A little? He reminds me of my old aunt in Shensi who spent her whole life being frightened of mice, most of them imaginary. She ended up mad. The man who is on the jump the whole time is on the road to mental derangement. It's better to be like you phlegmatic Russians, eh?'

Sergei looked at the brocaded table-cover for a moment.

'There's a point I must raise, Chairman.'

75

'Raise a dozen if you like.'

'Even an underground test of this device would be impossible to keep from the world. The West would know at once. It would be another indication of our nuclear progress, and, much more than that, an explosion of limited force would suggest the line of our research. There could be no secrecy.'

'Baikal, why were you put in charge of Project Seven?'

'To produce an eventual tactical weapon of limited power.'

'Ah,' said Liu. He pushed himself back in his chair. 'And at this stage you don't think it's important to test your eventual tactical weapon?'

'I would say it was premature.'

'Would you? Even when the thing is ready to explode? This seems to me an odd scientific attitude!'

'Chairman, in these days laboratory work can carry us to the point of absolute certainty.'

'Can it? Well, I haven't heard the little bang or seen a film of the small mushroom cloud, Baikal. I'm a simple man and this is what I want! Do you understand?'

'Yes, Chairman.'

'I'm exploding our eventual tactical weapon now. To see that it works at this stage. It can be adapted later. And to ensure secrecy I'm setting it off in Antarctica.'

Sergei stared.

'Your mouth is open, Baikal. Do you use it to help you think?'

'But Chairman . . . Antarctica. For us!'

'It's a long way off, eh? And we in China are a primitive people without boats big enough to take us so far?'

'That's not what I meant. There are many technical difficulties.'

'Ah, once again your triggering device? I've had Li Ta Ling in Peking. Did you know?'

'No, Chairman.'

'Excellent. The security here is better than I would have thought possible under that jumper from mice. Li has been with me for two days. I know something of your problems. You can't set off your little bomb from further away than a forty-mile maximum as yet . . . isn't that it?'

76

'Yes. And in uncertain climatic conditions like Antarctica the triggering ship could easily be affected by radioactivity. It isn't what you might call a clean bomb, Chairman.'

Liu laughed.

'Such a charming phrase . . . a clean bomb. The Americans invented it, did they not? As a gesture to the world to prove they still kept their humanity. Democracies labour under great handicaps, Baikal. They have to think of the reactions of their people, nearly all of them idiots. We don't.'

'Chairman . . . as I said, no ship would be safe. It might not be able to get out of the danger area in time. The air currents in Antarctica could prove totally unsuitable for the test. They're swift-moving, I know that.'

'It's why I'm using a submarine.'

Sergei said nothing.

'I seem to be astonishing you frequently, Comrade. China is catching up on the world without you being quite aware of it. We've two long-range submarines, not the most modern, perhaps, and certainly not atomic. I'll expect you to make me an engine for China's first atomic submarine. Or is that beyond your skills?'

Sergei looked into those mocking eyes.

'It's beyond me,' he said.

'Well. I see we'll have to persuade some other people to become Chinese, too, eh? Carefully chosen, of course. I've had it in mind for some time. And it can be done.'

'Are they Russian submarines, Chairman?'

'They were. And the crews were trained in Vladivostock during a phase of close friendship with our brothers in your original country. A phase that is coming around again, I'm glad to say. I'm sure it warms your heart to hear this?'

Sergei stared at the table-cover.

'Yes, Comrade Chairman.'

'Good. I'm glad about my part in it all. The last thing I was able to do for our great Leader. His dying wish, you might say. So we're now all brothers together again, eh? We'll soon be exchanging confidential atomic information with Moscow, and you may well live to get the Order of Lenin from your late country.'

77

Liu laughed again. Something in Sergei shrivelled, as though seared by sudden heat. Perhaps it was hope.

'It's a long way to Antarctica,' he said.

'One of our submarines has been to the coast of California with a circular sight-seeing tour around the Hawaiian islands. Perhaps you would be interested to see the film taken from them? We were close in enough to see the swimmers at Waikiki, and no one any the wiser. It was shown to me at a private viewing in Peking. We're not such bad underwater sailors, it seems. It's all most encouraging. China creeps towards the twentieth century. I'm kicking from behind to make it go faster. You see?'

'I see, Chairman.'

'Good. The American tracking satellite may pick up a record of that small explosion and no doubt a small radioactive increase will be detected. But Russia will be accused. Or the French, being naughty again. Or the Jews in Palestine conducting a little experiment. Or a development from Nasser's refugee camp for Nazis. Who'll look at China with her clumsy bomb and no ships for world travel? I think we'll still keep our secrecy about Project Seven, Baikal. And you'll have the satisfaction of proof of how well you're doing. That's what the scientist lives for, isn't it?'

Sergei said nothing. Liu took out his cigarette case for the first time and lit up without an offer across the wide table.

'What do you estimate the area of total destruction with your dirty small bomb?' Liu asked.

'About a mile and a half radius from centre. Secondary destruction up to five miles. Blast damage of great seriousness up to twenty. The blast effects of this bomb are what you might call a . . .' Sergei paused, as though looking for the English word.

'A feature?' Liu suggested gently.

Sergei cleared his throat.

'What might be called the secondary effects are in this case part of the essence of effectiveness.'

'You people dislike simplicity in anything,' Liu said. 'Particularly language. It, of course, adds to your mystery.' He leaned forward a little. 'When you are in fact, aside from your

78

specialization, little boys. Isn't that so? H. G. Wells, that great English prophet, made one big mistake. Have you read Wells, Baikal?'

'No, Chairman.'

'You should. He was a most intelligent man. A Marxist who hid the fact well. For his society. But he made one great mistake. He saw the scientist as a whole man, in all directions. This has in fact not proved to be the case. The scientist in our time has remained the servant of the man of action. He always will. You understand?'

'I think I do.'

'You see this in yourself?'

'Perhaps.'

'You're interesting, Baikal. Modest, also. I hope it is not because of a true estimate of your own abilities, eh? But that's unkind.' Liu smiled. 'Another question. What results would you foresee in the explosion of your bomb on the surface of the water?'

'The blast secondaries would most certainly be vastly increased.'

'Ah,' said Liu. 'Li tells me that the bomb will be carried harmless to the target area, in the ship we mean to destroy. Unprimed, I think you call it. It's then primed and becomes ready for the trigger device from our submarine. Correct me if I'm wrong. Once primed, the bomb is ready for triggering by remote control—if not too remote—at any time.'

'That's correct, Chairman.'

'So it ought to be possible for one man to be trained to do both jobs. That's to say . . . first to prime the bomb, and then to withdraw from the ship to be atomized to the safety of the submarine, where he can, at the right time, trigger the explosion?'

'Yes, Chairman.'

'And you think almost anyone could be trained to do these two jobs. Any one man? Someone without atomic knowledge?'

'I'm quite sure he could be trained.'

'How long would it take, Baikal?'

'Well . . . a matter of a day, perhaps.'

'Li said hours. You're more conservative. But then you're

the older man. Baikal, you're going to train this man, you and Li. Here. I want this done at once and the man will be sent to you. Only Li and you are to know what his true function is. Is that clear? If there's any leak on this point, even to someone like How Chi, the two of you are responsible. How Chi can guess what he likes, and the others, too, but none of them must *know*. You understand?'

'Yes, Chairman.'

Liu relaxed. He smiled across the table.

'As the American Secretary of Defense has pointed out, we're greatly handicapped in China as a Nuclear Power by a lack, as yet, of ballistic missiles for delivery purposes. Still, Baikal, a limited tactical weapon that no one knows about is an interesting challenge. It's rather like being presented with a bow and arrow to use against a machine-gun. But it's a fact that a well-hidden archer can kill the gunner, and the more effective weapon is thus useless, eh?'

'You could put it like that.'

'It's my problem,' Liu said. 'As the man of action in this case. We'll go into training with our bows and arrows, eh?'

He laughed.

'I'm sorry you don't want a woman, Baikal. It would do you so much good.'

CHAPTER FIVE

Henry Malthorp stood in China still, at the railway bridge with the narrow road beside it, looking over into the New Territories. He saw the reception committee waiting for him on the other side, soldiers in uniform, an officer, a clump of civilians, a nurse, and, from their cameras, reporters, some Chinese, some European.

'I didn't want this,' he said peevishly to no one in particular. 'I didn't want . . .' His voice trailed away.

They were waiting for him over there, after his seven years in China, all ready to receive a man who had left a third of his weight and all his living in a cell. They were waiting to be kind and noisy. He couldn't stand noise.

'No,' Henry said. 'I'm not going. I'm not going over there!'

'You're free,' the guard said, bored.

Only one guard, that was all they needed for him. One guard and no ceremony. Two peasants with permits, old and useless, part of the trickle who got through the official frontier post, stepped onto the bridge. There was a thin cheer from the other side. Henry Malthorp watched the two walking over the bridge, the man slightly ahead of the woman who carried the heaviest bundles. They reached the middle point of no return and suddenly the old woman started to run, crying out something. She dropped one of the bundles but didn't stop for it. The man, fussily, picked up the bundle. He staggered a little under the additional weight. The old woman was shrieking.

The reporters kept their cameras down. This happened every day and they weren't wasting film on it. They were waiting for a European back from the dead, a British businessman coming from the other side.

'Jenny would be there waiting,' Henry thought. But Jenny was dead.

He saw the British officer step forward, as though the delay irritated him.

'Go,' said the guard. 'Go!'

The guard had a train to catch. Henry wanted to be with him on that train, in the safety of a Chinese train, packed in, bolt upright on a hard seat with Chinese breathing all round him, and Chinese smells. It would be noisy on the train, but he wouldn't mind that kind of noise. It was safety. This was danger.

The guard took his arm. Henry felt the weight of his small case on his other arm, a sort of numbness from that weight, stretching from his fingers right up, as though his arm was slightly paralysed. It was the guard who led him onto the bridge, his feet suddenly docile and obedient since he was being led. It was after the push into independence that his feet seemed to freeze, leaden, an effort to lift one past the other.

'Come along, Mr Malthorp!' It was the British officer bellowing. 'We're all ready for you here.'

They were all ready for him! Malthorp turned his head. China behind him looked different, the same hills broken by an artificial unseen barrier, but different. The guard shook his fist.

This was no man's land, a place to die. He couldn't go back. He was afraid to go forward.

'Mr Malthorp!'

Henry remembered how he had dreamed of this once, long ago. Then he had stopped wanting it. He didn't remember when it was he had stopped wanting to get away, but it was a long time. Another man had wanted to be on this bridge, walking towards the loud voices. Now it was terror.

The British officer was coming out. He was a big man, very big. There was a revolver in his belt, like a guard. He was on duty, like a guard. It wasn't the man there waiting, but an officer under orders. Like a guard.

82

'Mr Malthorp, sir!' A hand was out, like a man, like a friend. It was silly of him to put his hand out. There were no friends. It was an old word, without meaning, not wholly remembered, just there.

'I'll take your bag, Mr Malthorp. Welcome to freedom.'

'Don't shout at me!'

'What? Oh, I'm sorry, sir. Just come this way. We've got a nurse waiting.'

'I don't want to be fussed over. Send those men with cameras away. Send them away!'

'I can't, Mr Malthorp, I'm afraid. You see . . . the world is interested in your story.'

'The world? The world! No! No!'

'Mr Malthorp, please. Nurse.'

The woman was coming now, crackling with starch.

'Oh, Mr Malthorp,' she said.

A lover, that's what she sounded like, a lover. He was an old man, wasn't he? Forty-eight. That was old in China. Young still when he was put away, or thinking himself young, but old now. He'd lost front teeth, too. You couldn't have a lover with no front teeth.

'Don't touch me!' he said to the woman.

The cameras came up.

'Leave me alone, all of you. Leave me alone!'

'You'll be alone in a minute, Mr Malthorp. In the ambulance.' The woman's voice was as soft as the sound of a wet cloth sloshing away on concrete floors.

'Where's the damn thing then? Get me into it!'

'This way,' said the officer. 'Make room please. Please make room. Mr Malthorp can't talk to anyone. He's not well. Can't you see that?'

'Mr Malthorp,' a voice shouted. 'What are your first reactions to freedom?'

'Mr Malthorp, how does it feel? Were you ill-treated? Have you been brain-washed?'

'Mr Malthorp, look this way, please. Just one second.'

'I . . . I . . . Damn you! Damn you all!'

They got him into the ambulance and closed the door. It was better in there, like a cell, only the woman was with him, smiling, her voice like that wet cloth he'd shoved up and down passages.

'If you'd like to lie down, Mr Malthorp. It would be more comfortable for you, I think.'

'Stop talking! I don't like talk, do you understand? I hate it.'

'Just on the stretcher. Go on.'

'No!'

She sat still, her hands in her lap. A long soft bumping began, from gentle springs. It shook the woman's cheeks, playing with her understanding smile.

After a minute he said:

'Where are you taking me?'

'To the hospital in Kowloon.' She seemed heartened by his curiosity. 'And then, after a few days rest, you'll be flown straight home to England.'

'I'm not going to England.'

'You don't want to go home, Mr Malthorp?'

'I have no home. My business is in Singapore. I'm going there.'

'You won't be ready for business for a *little* while. In England you'll find everything you need.'

'Oh, shut up!' Henry said.

She was like a great sensitive cow, with her loose fat cheeks. Kindness, that's what this was. He wasn't used to it. He didn't want it. Couldn't they understand that? Couldn't they stop being so bloody kind when it was the last thing he wanted? What were they to him, all these people?

The nurse was doing something with a little box. She had taken a syringe out of it. She didn't look at him as she broke the ampoule and filled the container. She didn't even look at him when she said:

'I know you don't want this, but I wish you would let me give it you. It's just a mild sedation.'

'I don't need anything. There's nothing wrong with me. I just don't like voices.'

'You won't hear them. If you let me give you this.'

He wouldn't hear the voices. He sighed.

'All right,' he said, like a child.

.   .   .   .

Armitage looked at the man in the bed, a neat parcel under a hospital cover. His eyes had been open for some time. He seemed unconscious of anyone in the room with him. But the intrusion had to come.

'Malthorp?'

No movement of the head at all, but the eyes blinked.

'Malthorp, do you remember me? Armitage?'

'No.'

'I think I know what's troubling you,' Armitage said. 'You mustn't let it. It's what we expected.'

The head turned. Eyes that Armitage scarcely recognized were looking at him. He smiled.

'What did you expect?' Malthorp asked.

'That you would talk to them. Spill the beans. We know how it happens. There's nothing much to be done about it. Unless you use a pill. Did you lose yours?'

'I don't know what you're talking about.'

'Malthorp, I don't think you have amnesia. But you've got your defences up and I'm not surprised. The thing is this . . . you weren't all that big a fish. We used you because we'd no one else to use. That's all. Anything you told them doesn't matter now. It's long ago. I want you to take that thought and let it give you some peace. We're not entirely cold-blooded, you know.'

'Bloody kind,' Malthorp said.

'It's meant that way.'

'I don't have any need of kindness.'

'We all do. Even spies.'

Malthorp moved under the covers. He made a sound that might have been meant as a laugh.

'If you knew how bloody small that sounds. Me. Spy. Small. Tiny. Get it?'

'I think I do. Anyway, it's not important.'

'I think it's important,' Malthorp said.

'To you. But not to us. That's what I want you to realize. It's long ago and doesn't matter. With you we took a long chance. And remember we didn't push it on you. You wanted to do it. There wasn't all that much enthusiasm with us for the proposition. Because you weren't really trained, Malthorp.

85

While you've been away there's been a policy change. We don't snatch at the casual opportunity any more. It doesn't pay off. We can't integrate casuals properly. Would it help to tell me what happened to you?'

The head and eyes turned again.

'It wouldn't help, but I'll tell you. I got the water treatment. You know all about that?'

'Yes.'

'Every day. I don't know how long. I gave your name, Madge's name, Herrick's name, every bloody name. Do you hear?'

'I said we expected it. Madge is dead. I'm in the Middle East. I only flew out here to see you.'

'Thanks. Did you have a good trip?'

'Bumpy over the Burmese mountains,' Armitage said. 'Listen, Malthorp. You've had a nervous breakdown. That's been given out. You'll stay here until the doctors say you're ready to go home. We'll get a private section on the plane for you. You won't have to talk to anyone. From London you'll be taken into Sussex.'

'Taken? Security nursing home? Lovely. Only I'm not going.'

'So I've heard. I think it best that you do.'

'I'm going to Singapore from this bed. And if you don't let me, I'll raise hell. The kind of hell the reporters would like. I don't owe you anything. You don't owe me anything. Go away. Catch a plane.'

'I don't think you'd find it easy to start up again in Singapore. Walcott is running your business. There's money, of course.'

'That's nice. I'll have to learn what it means again. Money. You can live without it. Funny, isn't it? A lot of people live without it.'

'Malthorp, I can't order you, but I beg you to come to England with me. We think you can be of help. In an indirect sort of way.'

'I'll be no help to anyone. I'm going to Singapore. You'd have to arrest me to stop me. Or you could do one of your kidnappings, snatch me from here in the middle of the night. Like to try?'

'We won't and you know it.'

'Too many watching, eh?'

'That and other factors.'

'I could, of course, be found dead. From a heart attack.'

'It was not in my mind, Malthorp. Or anyone's mind. Though it might have been if I thought you were important. You're not. Let that sink in. And get some sleep. Natural sleep. You'll feel better after it. When you want to see me, you've only got to ask.'

'I won't ask. I don't want visitors, with or without grapes. Just leave me alone. I've got a Chinese nurse who doesn't talk. They were scared to put her on because she was Chinese. But she's all right. Her mother's in China. Her brother's in their army. She doesn't talk. She has her reasons, too. Get out!'

Armitage got up and walked out into the corridor without looking back. He didn't give any sign to a man who was sitting out there in a tipped-back chair. He walked past the man, down to the stairs. He didn't like what he had seen and heard. It troubled him.

.   .   .   .

Four from the *Maree Tarn*'s crew were allowed into the spectators' seats at Henderson's trial. John Lownie had chosen three others besides himself—Haslett, Deacon the bos'n, who had seen the chief back to ship after many a sticky night ashore, and Potkin, the assistant engineer, a young man from Lancashire so pale complexioned he looked as though he had never once come up on deck in the tropics, preferring to cultivate a crop of pimples in the womb-safety of the ship's guts.

John took the outside of four chairs provided and they sat in an empty room for a time, with unlegal sounding noises beyond doors. At the top of the room, furthest from them, was a long table, covered with the inevitable cloth, with, behind it, three chairs. There was a little pen for the prisoner which looked like a big nursery fire-guard and was now shoved against the wall. There were two other tables and some odd seats. Otherwise the room had no trappings to suggest the majesty of the law, unless a portrait of the late Leader, not yet replaced, and the Chinese flag beneath it could be considered an adequate reminder of this.

Haslett, hating China, sat very straight next to John. Deacon scuffed his big feet back and forth, clearly wanting a cigarette, and Potkin longed for his engine room. Possibly he was thinking seriously these days about the possibility of his being in command down there and wondering whether he had the resources to meet a new responsibility. John, looking at the man, rather doubted this. He could recall Henderson shouting:

'My men are good oilers. But that's all they are. I pity a man who never knew steam.'

'Captain?' It was a hoarse croak from Deacon.

'Yes?'

'Are we going to be asked to speak for the old chief?'

'I doubt it.'

'Well, who's going to? I mean, they've got to have somebody speak for him, don't they?'

'No. But I'll perjure myself over his character if I get the chance.'

'Do you think they'll give him a stiff sentence?'

'I can't guess, Deacon.'

'The bastards,' Haslett said softly. It was a surprise from young lips.

'They at least let us in,' John said. 'I believe it isn't usual. Special privilege.'

'To see the old boy crucified?' Deacon croaked again.

'To report on Chinese justice, Bos'n.'

One of the doors opened, admitting voices and a few shouts. Then there was a shout inside the room, in Chinese.

'Get up!' John said.

They all stood. A man in a buttoned up tunic with a fat face and shaved head came first. He was followed by two more tunics, also with shaved heads above stiffened inner collars. The three seats behind the table were occupied, and the rest of the empty room filled rapidly with what was apparently a press gallery to one side, men with notebooks who had to stand. The public prosecutor had a seat and a table and a folio of notes which he began to arrange carefully in front of him.

88

It seemed slightly ominous that his opposite number, clearly the defence counsel, appeared to have no notes at all. The clerk of the court had a seat but no table.

And then they brought in the prisoner. This was announced by a clumping outside, then the appearance of two men with slung automatic rifles who were big enough to screen the chief sandwiched between them. They pulled forward the fire-guard and pushed Henderson in behind it. He stood there like a man who couldn't be expected to stand for long, his eyes straight in front at first, then making cautious sorties around the room, to the wall portrait, the faces under it, and finally the body of the hall.

John smiled. Henderson seemed to stiffen a little, but he looked old and worn, as though the weight of his terror was something that he couldn't adjust his frame to hold. He put out his hands to the front of the pen, but was shouted at by a guard.

The start of proceedings was totally informal. The prosecutor rose and bowed briefly to the judges as though his respect for them had limits. He then began to read a long indictment at a very rapid rate. The speed went rather ahead of John's capacity to assess the gist of the accusations, and in the end he had to be content with words here and there.

There were solemn words—'deliberate crime', 'assault on the honour of China', 'foreign felon', 'English spy'—but the action which had brought the accused to this moment seemed somehow sped over, as though the affront of a European being here at all was in a way the main issue. 'Free to roam the streets', John caught. 'Trying to revive old Shanghai vice'.

It wasn't, however, in any sense a show, no cameras, and the reporters had the look of journalists anywhere whose assignment doesn't rate as hot news. They were not going to make a propaganda parade of Henderson's sentencing, which could just mean they didn't want great publicity about a verdict that might have to be damped down later after an official change of heart.

But this small comfort couldn't reach Henderson. He was staring at the back of the prosecutor's head, as though in a desperate bid to extract from tones alone some hint of what was being said about him. But there were no tones in that voice at all, just a racing monotone to which the judges gave no impression of listening. One of them was playing with a pencil. The central figure burped from time to time, and, when this happened, his face was suffused by change, a kind of dreamy reminiscence of the meal which had produced these eruptions.

'Foreign drink,' the prosecutor said.

This slightly interested one of the judges who turned his head to look at Henderson again.

'What's it all about, Skipper?' Deacon's noisy whisper.

'Later!'

John found himself staring at a paralysing fear totally transcending any norm of pain and stress, unable not to watch. Henderson was caught in stark terror that he hadn't the moral strength to face directly. He was now pushed right outside the circle of experience with which he could cope, into an area of desolation in which death was only one of the attendant horrors.

He looked as if he might drop at any moment. And you can't muster courage on weak legs.

The prosecutor sat down. The monotone was cut off suddenly, like a hungry minister's too long sermon. Then it was revealed that the court had an interpreter, quite a loud voice.

'The prisoner may now speaks to his own case.'

Henderson's eyes darted about, seeking guidance. Then he pointed at the prosecutor's back.

'I don't know . . . what he was saying!'

The interpreter was most helpful.

'He is accusing. So you speaks I am not guilty.'

'What? What's that?'

'You tell comrade judges you are not doing.'

'Oh. Well, yes, that's quite right, your honours. I didn't do it. I mean, I couldn't have. Look at me. I'm not that sort of man. I couldn't have killed anyone.'

John looked at the floor.

'I'm not saying I didn't create a disturbance. I'm not denying I can't be a nuisance when I've got drink in me but . . . I'm an old man. Don't you see? I'm an old man.'

John couldn't look up.

'I never meant him any harm. Whoever he was. I never saw him. Not that I remember.'

'Silence, now!' called out the interpreter.

'Captain, you tell them . . . !' Henderson shouted.

John stood.

'No! Visitor sitting at once. Peace in court, only. Sit! Sit!' A judge waved his hand. John sat again.

The defence counsel rose. He spoke very slowly, as though to fools, using extremely simple words and yet somehow, possibly from a legal training in the old China, what he had to say was in a curious way elusive. It was also an odd defence, in that, in spite of the prisoner's recent statement in open court, his counsel admitted that he was undoubtedly guilty of a wilful and possibly even premeditated attack on his innocent comrade victim. His client had, bearing his foreign intoxicants with him, descended on a place of public resort full of shift worker feeders, and treated the establishment as though it was one of Nationalist rebel China's notorious brothels, shouting out his filthy decadent desires to pure-minded young female workers of the new regime. It was in defence of one of these females that the dead man had admonished the prisoner, warning him not to imagine that his licence to enter the New China permitted him to import, with himself, lewd Western practices. His client had then moved to the attack with no provocation at all, and, according to fourteen witnesses who had all been interviewed previously by this court, looked like a madman, waving his bottle and baring his teeth.

The latter point made John sit up slightly. Old Henderson's teeth, issued by the British Health Service, were not one of its more outstanding achievements, and the upper set were prone to fall onto the lower during ordinary conversation, let alone teeth-baring. In fact it was totally impossible to imagine the old man with many teeth showing, they would simply fall out on the floor. It was also interesting justice which used witnesses for the prosecution out of court, and made no effort to produce these witnesses for cross-examination by either side.

The appeal for clemency was a surprise. But apparently

there were valid grounds. The dead man, it had been found on later examination, had died from a heart attack, so that it was quite possible that a bottle broken over his head was only a contributory cause of death. To John's astonishment diminished responsibility came into things as well. Everyone in China knew, the defence counsel said, that alcohol made in Scotland resulted in large numbers of decadent Westerners in both Europe and America going around in a chronic state of whisky insanity. He submitted to the court that this man Henderson was so debased as a result of his own unspeakable habits that he couldn't be considered an ordinary human being at all. It would probably be a service to mankind to liquidate such a specimen from the world, but it might be enough to ensure by a ruling from the comrade judges that he never again threatened to contaminate pure China.

John felt he could now see the way things were going, but Henderson couldn't. The prisoner hadn't enjoyed being pointed at by the defence, which had occurred several times, a forefinger shot out from a passive hand, jerking all eyes to the dock. Indeed, as a defence counsel, the man on his feet had done an excellent job for the prosecution, as sometimes happens in the West also, but rarely intentionally.

There was no jury, and when the defence was over all that happened was a slight scrabbling on pads from the judges, one of whom didn't even attempt to look interested. After only about five minutes there was a lull in court, and the central judge read out his sentence which certainly hadn't been arrived at during the consultations.

'Twenty years penal servitude,' John heard, and held his breath.

'What is it?' Henderson shouted.

The interpreter obliged at once.

'Twenty year to the prison.'

The Chief's reaction started as a whisper, growing louder.

'No. No! You can't. Tell them . . . tell them I'm an old man. Tell them I . . .'

The blubbering was hard to bear. John heard Haslett say softly:

'I could kill them! The lot.'

'I'm an old man . . .'

John was on his feet. He said in Chinese.

'May I speak for the prisoner?'

'Down! Silent to you! Down! All made to go from court. Judges is not finished. Wait.'

John sat down, suddenly noticing that the reporters weren't even bothering to use their pads, apparently totally unaffected by the tensions of the moment. And the judges had, indeed, not finished. The middle one, as though a row was quite a common occurrence, was placidly reading something from the prepared brochure in front of him, and in quite a low voice. John could just hear.

The New China was all mercy. Outsiders told wicked lies about the New China, lies instigated by the rebels in Formosa, who were in the pay of American Imperialists. So the truth about China was never heard. Her few friends in the West had their tongues cut out or there was the noise of capitalist laughter to drown their words. Even a religious man, with a great and high position in his own country, had returned from a visit to China to be made a thing of scorn with pointing fingers from capitalist press liars. But China was unmoved by the noise of liars. Her judgements were from a kind heart still. And today great mercy would be shown.

Henderson had no hint of great mercy. He was now weeping. John saw him use a sleeve under his nose.

The judge droned on. The prisoner's sentence, because of his great age and head-sickness from alcohol, was to be commuted to banishment from China for life.

'You are an export!' shouted the interpreter, who must have learned his minimal English in East-West trade.

'What's that? What did he say?'

'You're banished from China,' John called out. 'That's all.'

No one seemed to mind the interruption. Everyone was looking at the prisoner.

'I'm . . . banished? From China? That's all? I'm banished from . . . I'm banished!'

'May he come with us now?' John asked.

The interpreter nodded. The court had lapsed into total

informality. The middle judge lit a cigarette as though he had been needing it, and passed over a light, but not his packet, to one of his colleagues.

.   .   .   .

In the launch Henderson insisted on standing up, looking about him, the weakness in his legs apparently quite gone. John stood beside him.

'Tell me, Chief. Are you sure you can't remember? Did you or did you not hit that man with a whisky bottle?'

Henderson stared at the engine coaming.

'I hit him,' he admitted. 'That's why I was so scared. I knew I'd done it.'

They came under the looming bulk of the *Maree Tarn* which was anchored again in midstream beyond the Bund, with new paint just visible above the Plimsoll line forward.

Henderson stared at the lowered gangplank and then his eyes lifted to faces lining the rail.

'Oh, God in Heaven!' he said.

John smiled.

'We've a conversion on our hands,' he told Haslett.

CHAPTER SIX

Hagerson, the Singapore agent for the Tarn Lines, was a Swede who had become a citizen of Malaya with a view to furthering his own and the company's interests. He had no intention of ever retiring to Europe, his thinned Norse blood making him cringe from the thought of seeing snow again. He was, in fact, a child of the sun, in his lean sixties, baked mahogany over still tight muscles, preserved by the thing he worshipped in an odd contraction of flesh under skin which suggested a process of mummification. His once fair hair was now quite white and only Meissen blue eyes made any statement about his origins. The blue eyes may have been warmed by compassion on occasion, but they weren't this afternoon.

'You delayed sailing on your own initiative, Captain Lownie?'

'Yes, for two days.'

'Your ship was in the river again, ready to leave, and you missed tides that could have taken you out?'

'Four to be precise,' John said. 'Four to give a member of my crew the kind of support I thought he needed.'

'That was a personal matter. The facts are that you delayed a loaded ship which had already been held up for almost a month. You put your duty as a captain second to your feelings about a member of your crew. And, I may say, a member of your crew whose services could have been dispensed with and probably will be.'

'To say nothing of mine,' John thought, looking at a man he had always disliked.

'I am bound to put this into my report to London,' Hagerson said.

'Of course.'

'It will not be necessary for me to make any comment to London on Chief Engineer Henderson's record with the company. That's already well known. I may tell you in confidence that Henderson's position with the Tarn Lines was already in jeopardy before this incident. This man, wilfully, and with no justifiable reason, created a situation which threatens all our increasing trading interests with the Republic of China. The *Maree Tarn* is now a marked ship as far as Shanghai is concerned. As you know perfectly well, it's not a question with our company of simply shifting her to another route. Our cargoes make our routes, Captain Lownie.'

'I think you're taking a prejudiced view of the situation.'

'Indeed?'

'The Chinese have accepted full responsibility for the delay to the *Maree Tarn*. We had to return to Shanghai for repairs because we struck a sunken wreck which should have been notified.'

'I'm not questioning your performance of your duty on that occasion,' Hagerson said.

'Like hell you aren't,' John thought.

'This is in no sense an inquiry, as you know well. My role is to forward the facts to London. There may be an inquiry there. Indeed, I think there will be.'

'The Chinese are holding one of their own.'

'That doesn't concern us. What does is a valuable bottom kept out of trade for one month. Our insurance companies will be concerned with that, too. And I can assure you there will be no compensation paid for a two-day voluntary delay to the ship for which you're responsible. That's a loss that will have to be borne by the company. And it's your responsibility.'

'I stand by it.'

John was sitting in a comfortable chair. There was a bogus air of relaxed informality at the interview. Hagerson watched

what he said. It would never do to have it reported in London
that the local agent had put a Tarn Line captain on the mat, on
his own initiative. John leaned forward to crush out a
cigarette.

'Have you any questions, Captain?'

'There has been no word from London about my command?'

'I don't understand?'

'It did occur to me that I might be relieved of it. Here.'

'Certainly not. At this stage. You'll take your ship to
Glasgow as soon as there's Singapore clearance.'

'Then we sail tomorrow? Or tonight?'

'No. The *Maree Tarn* is being inspected here before you
put to sea again.'

John was very interested. There was no British authority in
Singapore any longer which was empowered to concern itself
with a British ship using that port, except in the sense of a
Lloyd's survey. And this, somehow, didn't sound like that.

'You ordered this inspection, Mr Hagerson?'

'It's being done under my authority.'

'It oughtn't to take long. The damage was to the hull. There
was no real penetration.'

'You'll be notified when you can sail, Captain.'

John stood and picked up his cap.

'Your crew can be given routine shore leave for the next
two days, Captain. Except Henderson. It's my wish that he
remain on board.'

'It'll be his wish, too. Did you say two days? For an inspection of damaged plates?'

'I said two days, Captain. Good afternoon.'

The company had quite tidy premises, with secretaries at
typewriters. A Eurasian girl looked at John and smiled as he
went through the outer office, which reminded him of Mabel
Tlani Nakhon.

.   .   .   .

The Rose Arbour was rather an old-fashioned establishment, now a restaurant under the new morality codes, in that

97

you could eat there at one of the tables out in front. But then, you'd always been able to, if you were hungry. John didn't sit down at one of the tables, he walked through, not looking at the patrons. The raised area at the back, where the girls had once sat on a stage of sorts, sewing, or reading, or, rarely, deliberately displaying what they had to sell, was now fitted as a snack bar with an Espresso machine. The attendant in a white cap had only coffee to sell and knew it. John went through a door which could have been to the kitchens but wasn't. He continued down a passage to another door, opened it, and saw old Mother Ching.

She looked exactly like a lot of other old mothers in her trade, run to fat in retirement, but still keeping up personal illusions by a massive use of make-up. She had been reading the papers and smoking a cigarette. Her lips opened, the cigarette still adhering to the lower one, held on by thick pink gum.

'Johnee!'

'Hello, sweetheart. Where's Mabel?'

'Johnee, you not come here and open door and say: "Where's Mabel?" You drink Tiger beer with Mama.'

'Delighted,' John said, and sat down on her sofa, which was hard. 'Where's Mabel?'

'She fix up,' Mother Ching said. 'I tell. We got a new frig box for much ice.'

'The restaurant business looking up, eh?'

Mama laughed. She went out with a separate circulation of buttocks. John stared at the floor. So Mabel was already busy at seven-thirty in the evening? He hadn't come early enough. He didn't like to think about that. He had never been able to see Mabel as a whore somehow, a sailor's sentimentality, from fantasy living out at sea. Mabel never made any pretence. It was his personal fantasy, home-cured in a heaving cabin.

Mama came back with two tall glasses of the yellow beer.

'Oh, I'm so thirstee,' she said. 'You thirstee, Johnee?'

'Parched.'

'You look tlouble. Tell Mama?'

'It's nothing you could sell on the open market, dear. Just a personal sadness.'

98

Mama smacked her lips and looked at him.

'I wish I meet you, Johnee. When I'm good girl.'

'Round about 1930,' John said.

'Eh?'

'Nothing. I wish you had. But what would you do with a babe in arms?'

'I like babies. Sure.'

'Don't let's get indelicate. How long will Mabel be?'

'Soon. I fix.'

'You can always do that,' John thought. 'You old cow.'

How much of Mabel's money did she get? A third? Maybe more. None of them would talk about the trade commission rate. And the house belonged to Mama, together with all the fitments, including the Espresso machine.

'American cigarette, Johnee?'

'Don't smoke 'em. Trying to cut down on smoking.'

'You think it kill you, eh? You think it kill me?'

'Nothing could kill you, beautiful. You'll be here forever.'

It looked as though he was going to be, too. It wasn't the first time he had been forced to wait for Mabel, very far from the first time.

A bell rang in the passage. John knew what it meant, his clearance. He got up and Mama nodded.

He shut Mama's door. No one had to tell him where to go or what sounds not to listen to. He climbed a flight of stairs and went along another passage. It was the kind of Chinese establishment that presents a narrow façade to the street, a modest frontage of sun-peeled stucco, and then goes back forever in rooms suspended above dank-smelling courtyards where there are cats and people cooking. There is invariably the sound of music, too, Chinese jazz from transistors or a hand-crank gramophone.

He knocked on Mabel's door. She was sitting as far from the bed as possible, whores always did. The bed was very tidy. So was everything in the room, her lair, cluttered but tidy. In non-working hours there was a kind of intense personal domesticity in here, almost a terrible innocence. He had seen this functioning. Mabel liked to cook.

99

'Damn the way she looks,' he thought, looking at her.

Mabel had one comfortable chair. She sat in it with no display at all, her legs crossed, but that wasn't advertising. They would have been too thin legs but for the boning, the legs of a little jungle deer who has to use them all the time because she is so tasty. Her body was slim, too, very small, with thin arms and hands made for holding cups of good porcelain, with long oval nails she never lacquered. Her face came to a point at the chin and rose from here to wide cheekbones in which were set eyes that were too small, far too small, Chinese eyes without the intriguing slant. Her eyes warred with the rest of her face, out of line with it, an outside comment, like her hair.

He knew her hair was dyed, it wasn't nearly as red as she made it, but the copper tints were there. It was thick hair.

'Hello,' he said.

'My Johnny!'

She meant that. In her own way, she meant it. He had come into the room not wanting to be touched by her, but now he wanted it. He wanted the way she ran to him, arms out.

She smelled of scent. She always did. He bought the scent.

'Oh, Johnny. You were in China so long!'

He lifted her head, swallowed, and then kissed her, tasting first her mouth. The hunger always made him forget, almost at once.

'Johnny.'

It was a lot of fun loving a whore.

'How long are you staying?'

'Two days.'

'Come,' she said.

The bed always came into it damn quick.

'No. Not just yet. Mabel, I want to talk to you.'

'Sure. You talk, Johnny. I like you to talk.'

She didn't get a lot of talking. She suffered from deprived social instincts.

'I sit on your knee.'

That was all right, too. She loosened his collar and kissed his neck. It wasn't something women did a lot, but he always shaved carefully for Mabel. He put his hand under her blouse on a small breast and held it there, his fingers massaging the nipple. She could twist her reaction to that, so soon.

'You're not talking, Johnny.'

She brought her hand up to his face, touching it lightly, then lifting his lips.

'Open your mouth first, so. And don't keep teeth shut. Waggle your tongue. That's talking.'

'So it is,' John said. 'I was thinking about how to tell you.'

'Tell me what?'

'About changes. My company are going to give me the sack, I think. But I've got quite a bit of money and it's all in Singapore.'

'Johnny, what is the matter with your company?'

'They want older men for captains. Full of sound business judgement, the bastards.'

'Johnny, you're angry!'

'Yes, I'm angry.'

'Johnny, your face is like a stone.'

'Sorry. It's not to scare you.'

'But I *am* scared. You're a captain. I thought captains were safe.'

'No one is. You think everything's fine, that you're set for the rest of your days, that you've got all the money you'll need for the next forty years. Only you won't need money. You've got a fast cancer.'

'Johnny, don't! Don't say these things to me. Please!'

'I'm telling you there's no way to be safe.'

She shook her head.

'I can be safe.'

'How?'

'Money. When I've money I go to Singora. I get a little house in Singora. It doesn't cost much to live there. Not so much. I don't need so much. But I know what I need.'

'And in Singora?'

'There are no men coming, Johnny.'

He took his hand off her body.

'Not even one?'

'No. Not one.'

'Mabel, I love you.'

'Johnny, don't. Don't say that!'

'Do you hear it so much? From your customers? Here?'

She turned her head away.

'Do they still say it here, Mabel?'

'Yes, they say it. Yes, yes!'

She got off his knee. She went over to a mirror, peering in at her face.

'What are you trying to do to me, Johnny?'

'I meant to give you a house. Somewhere in these parts. But not in a city. And only one man coming.'

She went on looking in the mirror.

'No.'

'I'm coming back here, Mabel. In a month or two. I'm going to live out here. I might get a job in coasters, and we could have a house in Singora.'

'No.'

'You'd miss the bright lights?'

She turned. She leaned back on the dressing-table, her hands holding onto the edge of it.

'Four men,' she said. 'All kind, like you, Johnny. I can choose them.'

He got up and went to the door, looking at her with his hand on the knob.

'There's no use calling you a whore, is there?'

She didn't move.

.   .   .   .

For a city that has been purged of contemporary sin, like the big dance halls, Singapore still has quite a few attractions to offer. John walked, looking at them, not tempted. He wasn't tempted when he came to the mouldering plaster theatre down by the *Padang*, an 'Opera House' it had once been called. There were lights in the entrance, and posters, too. The town must be having a shot of culture.

He went over to sniff at it. The posters suggested a certain timidity, the print small.

By Co-operation with the Government of Malaysia
and
The Arts Council of Great Britain
Henry Maton
presents
THE GARRICK PLAYERS
In a season of Contemporary English
Drama
For three weeks only

There were pictures of the players. All the men except one looked as though they had only to pull forward their long hair to be quite ready for a change of sex. The one who didn't look like this was obviously along to play daddies. Two of the girls were pretty, one very. John stared at her.

He looked at the prices above the box office and then down to a woman who was tempting him forward with an exhausted smile. He had meant to eat somewhere, but he went over to the window.

'I'm afraid I'm late.'

'Oh, it doesn't much matter, Commander. You won't have missed a great deal.'

'You've got the uniforms mixed. The navy wouldn't let me in.'

'Heavens! I can't see why. Were you thinking of a stall?'

'Yes.'

He paid in Malay dollars. A girl taking casual employment without much hope for the future led him forward and supplied a programme. He hadn't been in his seat for long before he became conscious of an echoing in the hall, from emptiness. The acoustics had been designed to bounce sound off bodies, not seats without them. A persistent smothered cough somewhere was almost reassuring.

On the stage were three people, two men and a girl. It took him some time to recognize her as the pretty one from the posters in this setting, which was a kitchen. There was a sink on the back wall. A young man in a chair was working hard over a soliloquy which seemed to consist mainly of variations on a six-letter word. He was allowed to relax with a cigarette as he did it, but this didn't seem to make it any easier for him. There was no audible prompting, just a young man unhappy with his art form.

When the girl turned to the sink to wash dishes it was just possible to see, in spite of what she was wearing, that she had a good shape. John watched the slight movements of her body. She didn't have any lines to say, so he couldn't hear her voice. Suddenly she swung around and shouted:

'Oh, go to hell, both of you!'

She went off stage, one wall of the set shaking from a slammed door. Listening to the boys who were left made John feel that the girls in this company were almost certainly lonely.

In the interval after the first act he discovered that the play was one which had run in London for a year and a half, following this up in New York with another glittering triumph for British drama. As a comment on contemporary attitudes in the Old Country, it rather confirmed his own impression that the whole thing was coming apart at the seams. The discipline which is the essential ingredient of any ordered and progressive society was totally lacking at almost all levels and probably these bleating pansies were pretty fair specimens of the bulk of their generation. They were obviously in deep sympathy with the play over which they struggled with visible sweat, in fact the thing might have been written for them. In John's view the leading man could have done with a sound walloping on his sensitive bottom. You couldn't clout that boy, it wouldn't be fair.

On the way out, John loitered in the lobby which was totally uncrowded by an emptying audience. He looked again at the girl in the poster. She had a good nose, enough of it but not too much. She was fair, which pleased him. He hadn't the towhead's strange obsession with an incipient dark moustache in his women. There was a lot to be said, after all, for a kind of matching.

It wasn't difficult in an old Opera House to find the stage door. This was unattended, as though no one had been even faintly nervous about an uncontrollable rush of fans with autograph books. He found himself in a passage and hadn't gone very far down it before a faint smell of perspiration was noticeable.

A door opened. In sudden, harsh light was a woman who could have played Little Red Riding Hood's old granny. Her make-up couldn't begin to conceal the gouges of time.

'Oh, my God!' A hand clutched at the neck of the wrapper. It was an almost archaic, stylized modesty. 'Who the hell are you?'

'A stage-door Johnny.'

Granny stared. Then suddenly she laughed.

'Well, you're not after me. Who is it?'

'Miss Gerda Lane.'

Granny's plucked eyebrows lifted. She looked back into the dressing-room.

'Dah . . . ling! Come out here.'

'What?'

'I said come out here. *At once!*'

'I'm all creamed.'

'He'll see through it.'

'Who?'

'From another age, love. I knew them once.' She looked at John. 'I did.'

'You don't have to tell me.'

'And gallant, too! All they ever do these days is slap your sit-upon, and then go for a drink. Gerda, come here at once!'

Gerda was all creamed, right up to the roots of her hair.

'Nannie, shut that door!' she said, pushing back.

'Don't mind her, dear,' Grannie said. 'She's never managed to get used to the easy *camaraderie* of the theatre. Neither have I, after fifty years.'

She shut the door, bringing herself into the corridor with it.

'I play bits,' she said. 'And, in my capacity as a failed character actress, I also function as chaperon. Our backers like it. The steadying influence and that sort of thing.'

'I'm sure I've seen you in London.'

She looked at him, stretched unfashionably red lips over teeth which hadn't been the ones used in youth.

'I doubt it. You're not a boy, but you're still not old enough. Though I did have a part in a film once about which a critic was kind enough to say I was as good as Athene Seyler. I didn't believe him. Neither did anyone else. Recently, that is, for thirty years, I've been playing in rep. Do you ever go to rep?'

'I don't get the chance.'

'Nicely put,' said Granny. 'Are you wanting to take Gerda out for a bite of supper?'

'It was my idea. Won't you come, too?'

'I shall swoon. Young man, my role as chaperon is nominal. I mayn't be a very good actress, but I've never made a three-some. You can have the girl on your own, with my blessing. My name, incidentally, is Annette Colleridge. Don't pretend it rings any bells. You've already worked that line charmingly. But, of course, you're a sailor. You have time for women because you never see very much of them. Have you a car? If so, go out and wait in it. I'll send Gerda to you.'

It was curious how often it gave an old woman a kick to act as procuress.

'I'll get a car,' he said. 'Quickly.'

.   .   .   .

Up in a Chinese roof restaurant, Gerda Lane looked very English. Her blonde hair was smoothed down, and flared up again just above her shoulders. It was cut almost like a bala-clava, low in the forehead, only essential features like eyes, nose, and mouth remaining out in the world. What was exposed showed a very good-looking girl who apparently had no interest in the food she was eating. He had ordered care-fully, and was surprised by a total lack of curiosity over what went in her mouth. If he said it was sliced 'mouse-breast' in Chinese aspic, she would murmur 'Oh?' and continue to look out at the lights.

Pretty lights, pretty night. But all nights here were. It was a special feature of the place, stars that a sailor could put to such practical use now arranged purely as decoration, faintly blurred in competition with the neon glow.

'If the old girl hadn't pushed you into it, would you have come out with me?'

'Yes.'

'Why? Do I look reliable?'

'No. But I'm sickeningly bored. I hate this place. Not that I've seen it. But I still hate it.'

'It's practically my home town.'

She looked at him.

'It may be all right for a sailor, of course. What you want easy to find.'

'Not as easy as it used to be.'

'Still easy. Why bother with the stage-door?'

'I like blondes.'

'A commodity in short supply? Give me a cigarette.'

'What is it you hate especially?'

'Playing to an empty house. You don't know how it feels. Just draughts out there in front of you.'

'A good thing,' he said.

She was about to suck a light. She stopped.

'And what do you mean by that?'

'I'd say it was a good thing for the white man's interests in the Far East that more people didn't see that muck.'

She smiled.

'So that's what you thought of the play? You marine boor.'

'Do you enjoy acting with fairies?'

She put both hands flat on the stone table.

'I don't give a damn what sex an actor is. So long as he can act. I admit our boys wear big learner-signs. But we all have to.'

'You'll never be allowed to take yours down,' John said.

She took the kind of breath which pushed out her breasts.

'I'm sitting here eating your food. But I could slap it in your face.'

She looked at him then, and, still doing it, reached for the highball that shouldn't have been there with a Chinese meal, but was.

'And why will I always wear the learner-sign?'

'You were saying the words some writer put in your mouth. That's all.'

'It's a bit difficult to work up cold country tensions when

you're sweating at ninety-five under lights. And from back-stage comes a curious, permanent smell of drains.'

'It's not drains, it's Singapore.'

'It could never mean much to me as a place.'

'Do you know what you're doing, bringing plays like that out here?'

'What *I'm* doing? I'm not doing a damn thing except worrying about perspiration coming through the grease-paint.'

'You're telling people in the Far East that the West is all washed up. That it's reached the nasty stage of decadence. Your play is confirmation straight from the horse's mouth of the Red propaganda which pours over these people all the time. You should cut prices a bit and circulate some of the local university clubs. Anti-imperialist, anti-colonialist, anti-capitalist propaganda. A sensitive intelligent play about people who are so feeble they can't even piss straight any more. A riot in London and New York with every delicate liberal conscience.'

'I'd go back to my flea-bitten hotel,' Gerda said. 'If you didn't interest me. Just a very little.'

Her stare wasn't meant to be returned. It didn't make John uneasy.

'Where were you born, sailor?'

'In Shanghai.'

'By whom out of what?'

'I thought there were horses in your background.'

'My father is Sir Preston Lane. Does that mean anything to you? It won't. He's a Permanent Under-Secretary.'

'Your family ought to look to its blood-lines. Something is happening in this generation. In fact it's happened.'

'We think so. We're awake. Tell me about Shanghai, Captain Lownie.'

'My mother was poor but honest. My father poor.'

'Are you really British?'

'I'm really a sailor. On a ship I have a world with sharp edges. I like that. I don't greatly care for shore at either end, except perhaps this town. Now ask me what I think of the world situation?'

'What do you?'

'I think the strong and the disciplined will win, Miss Lane.'

'I'm not hungry any more,' she said. 'Shall we go?'

She probably said the same thing in the middle of eating at the Dorchester, which wouldn't reduce the charges to her escort any.

The hired car was American, roomy, with a one-piece front seat. John had paid extra for this feature. Gerda sat looking at the Riouw Islands under a rising moon. There had been a storm somewhere, and the noise of sea bullied a still air, a whiteness crackling on deep swells far out, then turning to diamond glitter where the waves broke in a terminal anger of surf. The city was a fire-glow behind them, through gently mourning *casuarinas* and the stiff palms. A tanker moved down the straits with a kind of obese dignity, the new ship, all belly and no grace. What Hagerson would call a bottom.

'That's Indonesia over there,' John said. 'Close, isn't it? They can see everything that comes in and out of Singapore.'

'So that could be enemy territory overnight.'

'Yes. The British should have pinched those islands after the Nips were kicked out. And built forts facing south on them.'

'You're a reactionary.'

'I'm a realist. You're beautiful.'

It was so easy to get randy on a warm night. Granny Colleridge was right back there somewhere rooting for them.

Gerda turned her head.

'You're a bit old for me, Captain. There's a kind of gap in the generations. Don't you feel it?'

'Not at the moment.'

'You should be looking for a woman in the thirties. The kind who has been around more.'

'You prefer playing with sweet boys?'

'I prefer my own kind. There's safety in it.'

They all wanted safety, an obsession.

'Then I don't touch?'

'I don't want to wrestle,' she said. 'In this heat.'

Damn all blondes. He lit a cigarette. She might just be slow.

'Take me back,' Gerda said. 'Even an actress needs some sleep.'

He reached out and switched on the ignition. When they hit the main road he drove fast. She put her head on the back of the seat and the wind they made lifted her hair. She had a lot of hair, like Mabel. Granny would have been more generous, once.

CHAPTER SEVEN

In port a captain feels he has been dispossessed. His ship is invaded, there are other authorities. If there is loading, it is the mate's job to see to the stowage in the holds. The bridge, the captain's domain, is derelict, all the instruments of the brain-centre covered in canvas wrappings. All about him is noise that makes no demand on his attention, and the very harbour itself, the other shipping, diminishes the margins of his world. He is hemmed in by the stranger vessels all about, great liners, the monstrous tankers, an arrogance of glittering size. He is still captain, but, like the leader of a small country come to a conference of giants, finds himself longing for a return to a different perspective on himself, with his authority unique, surrounded only by the vast, moving neutrality of sea.

Hagerson was on his ship. The man's presence was unseen, but palpable, and it seemed to John in his day-cabin that the *Maree Tarn* lay at anchor an inert mass, waiting to get rid of the company's agent.

'Yes?' he said, to a knock on his door.

It was Ginnis, the chief steward, who on a little ship had to act as purser and controller of stores.

'Sir? Have you heard about our passengers?'

'What?'

'Aye. I see you haven't, sir. May I come in?'

Ginnis came in and shut the door.

'I don't like it,' he said. 'And that's being frank.'

Frankness had always come easily to the man. It had kept him from passenger ships.

'I mean to say, Captain. Out of the blue, like. Just sprung on me. And why wasn't you notified?'

'I don't know. Did you say passengers? More than one?'

'Three, if you please. And you know what an upset passengers is, Captain. I mean to say, this isn't a ship for them. Ye canny have women milling about our decks in the morning. And wanting chairs and God knows what.'

'Women? Are you sure?'

'As sure as I can read Mr Hagerson's signature. It came as a chitty, a wee bit paper. The thing they used to be so fond of out this way for messages. You sent the house-boy with them. Well, Hagerson sent one of his clerks. He came out in a launch about twenty minutes before Hagerson showed up himself. You'd think he could have waited. But maybe he doesn't like talking to stewards. I nearly came up to see you about it at once but I thought maybe you'd know. And I had the cabins to get on with. It's a great pity I wasn't given a wee bit more time and I could have got hot-house flowers to put in for the ladies. Or some of them damned orchids they like so much out here.'

John stood.

'Where's Mr Hagerson now?'

'Don't ask me, sir. Snooping would be my bet. For the interests of the company, you see. In case we're getting away with something on our own that won't add to the annual profit balance at the board meeting. Would you like me to find him and tell him you want to see him here in your cabin?'

It was a flat challenge.

'Yes,' John said.

Ginnis grinned. He opened the outer door, stepped on deck, then looked back.

'Bully for you, Captain. Give him hell.'

The door shut.

It was quite some time before Hagerson arrived. John was at his desk when the door opened after a token knock and the agent stepped in, smoking a cigar and carrying his Panama-hat in his hand.

'Ah, Captain, I was on my way to see you when I ran into your steward . . . what's the man's name?'

John didn't get up.

'My chief steward, Mr Hagerson.'

'You can give him his title. I don't like his manner.'

'And I don't like yours.'

Hagerson hadn't been facing the desk. He swung round to it. John rose.

'When did you decide to send passengers with us on this voyage, Mr Hagerson?'

'Yesterday. If that's any of your business.'

John's fingers folded into fists.

'Why wasn't I notified?'

'There were things for me to do before I told you. This has been a last-minute decision. Confirmed from London, I may say.'

'We haven't had a passenger on this ship while I've been in command.'

'Then it'll be a new experience for you. The captain's table and all that. Light feminine conversation to while away the hours at sea. One of them is very pretty. I envy you. More than three weeks of her company. Though, of course, she may fall for your first officer.'

Hagerson's humour was a bit weighted. There seemed to be a lot of smoke from his cigar in the cabin.

'I'm sorry if you feel you should have been put in the picture sooner, Captain.'

'Who are these women?' John asked.

'One of them is a relation of a friend of a director of the company. I had my instructions from London, Lownie. The decision was not mine.'

'What about the other passenger?'

'I did arrange that. I cabled for permission and got it. Rather a sad case, really. A man with shattered nerves.'

'What? Supposing he needs a doctor?'

'He won't. He just wants to get away and be alone. I used to do business with his firm. Still do, as a matter of fact. But not with him for many years. He's been in a Chinese jail.'

John stiffened.

'You mean a British subject?'

'Oh, very much so. Up there trying to keep his firm open under the Reds. It didn't work, of course. He was arrested as a spy, after about a year of freedom during which he had to increase pay to his staff by something like three hundred per cent. That put paid to the business. He was sentenced on a trumped-up charge, of course. The usual thing. I didn't know him when I saw him again. He's only been out of China a matter of weeks, came through Hong Kong while you were up in Shanghai. There was the usual fuss at the time, but of course it all died down.'

'Why didn't he fly straight to England?'

'What a lot of questions you ask, Lownie. His home was here and he wanted to get back to it. Now he needs a long sea voyage to rest up. He won't bother you, I promise. You ought to have sympathy with the fellow.'

'It depends on the fellow,' John said.

'Your cautious Scots blood is the dominant strain in you, isn't it, Captain?'

It was a guarded way of calling someone a half-breed. And having done this Hagerson turned away to a picture on the panelled cabin walls. It was a reproduction Matthew Smith. The agent gazed at it.

'Hm. I wonder what the original is worth?'

'A couple of thousand pounds. Or maybe more.'

'Really? Extraordinary what they get away with nowadays. Values all gone to hell. It's one reason why I never want to go back to Europe. And don't. Do look after our passengers well, won't you?'

'Before you go, Mr Hagerson, I'd like to know something about the search of this ship.'

'Search?'

'That's what it boiled down to. I've been on board. It was rather a mystery. The four men didn't even eat with us. Kept very much to themselves. And it was curious that an inspection of bow plates put in up in Shanghai should have involved the after holds as well.'

'It was a check of cargo.'

'For what?'

'I'm damned if I know.'

'Shouldn't you know as the company's agent?'

'In this case . . . no.'

'I don't understand, Mr Hagerson?'

'Neither do I. We're not supposed to understand. Do you get me?'

'I get this. I'm the captain of the *Maree Tarn*. If there was need to search cargo on board, I should have been put in the picture. All I was told was the four Europeans who spent two days on my ship were Lloyd's agents.'

'It's all you need to know, Captain. And all you're going to. Is that clear?'

John took a deep breath.

'Did they find anything?' he asked.

'I haven't the faintest idea. And now I'm off. Have a pleasant voyage.'

.   .   .   .

John went out on the bridge overhang to watch the last launch from shore come alongside. It wasn't the open boat, but something for a Thames regatta, an awning stretched the whole way over it in the prettiest striped canvas with a frill all round the edge. The feminine note already.

Since leaving Shanghai John had known the vague premonition that comes to a sailor about an unhappy voyage. The thought of women on board was a further depressant. This mightn't have been his reaction if his time in Singapore had been more satisfactory, but the fact was that he had been looking forward to getting away from women. There is undoubtedly something very soothing about a cargo ship at sea, with no dinner dances on schedule, just men doing their jobs and planning to eat well and drink a certain amount. It was a routine with easily accepted rules in which gradations of rank, never stressed, none the less contributed to a sense of order. It might well be that it is this controlled order, with minimal displays of temperament, which makes so many men look back on their service careers—apart from unpleasant action—as one of the most agreeable periods in their living, though they don't say this at home.

'Haslett?'

'Yes, sir?'

'Go down and meet our passengers.'

There was no reluctance on the boy's part. He went quickly, his feet clattering on the bridge companion-way. Milton, the second mate, looked cynical. He was a compact little man from the Isle of Wight, who came as near to having black side-burns as he dared under John's command, and at twenty-six had already seen and done everything, which gave him a smug air of complacence and a vocabulary of cynicism unenlivened by wit. If he ever reached the heights, he would make a horrible captain. Between Haslett and Milton ran a current of enmity which never surfaced but was always there in swift movement beneath a smooth sea of conventional behaviour.

'Milton?'

'Sir?'

'Have you ever considered leaving these glorified tramps and joining the Peninsula and Oriental Shipping Company?'

'Sometimes, sir.'

'In that case this voyage should give you an excellent chance to practise the charm which leads to promotion in the higher maritime spheres.'

'I understand.'

'Have you any light conversation, Mr Milton?'

'Not much.'

'Polish it up, boy, polish it up.'

It was a pretty good imitation, John thought, of the burly old sea-dog. Was he really getting to be one? He was certainly too old for a young actress. A chasm was beginning to yawn between him and the kind of girl to whom he still felt attracted, which probably meant that he should have settled down long ago, with a bungalow overlooking the river Clyde in which there was a Scots wife who would always produce the best china for her relations. He would return from foreign parts to those unspeakable high teas, where you ate fried fish and then proceeded to stuff yourself with carbohydrates. But you would be settled in life. God knew, he was far from settled.

Mr Milton never missed any opportunity for social contact with those who might further his interests. He came out onto the bridge overhang beside John, smiling.

'Our male passenger is a funny-looking bloke, sir.'

'You've seen the man?'

'Yes, I was down on the shelter deck when he came on board with Mr Hagerson. This chap was wearing dark glasses and had his hat pulled low. He never looked up. Mr Hagerson took him to his cabin at once.'

The agent had certainly made no mention of having established his friend already.

'Was Ginnis there when they came on board?'

'No, just Rafferty. He showed them the way. I wonder where they got that launch, sir?'

'Perhaps Mr Hagerson keeps it for island picnics with his lady friends.'

When Milton laughed John wished he hadn't said that.

The frivolous awning was now almost directly beneath them, bobbing gently. Beyond the milky waters surrounding the ship was a stream of pure translucent jade, as though a probe from the clean straits of Malacca. A large three-masted junk, on auxiliaries, but with its sails going up, was already moving out of anchorage on what would be the *Maree Tarn*'s course, but certainly keeping closer to the Malaysian coast in a bid to avoid the Indonesian patrols now prowling the waters to the north-west in search of small victims. You were always being reminded in Singapore of the proximity of the Indonesians, and, even as you cleared South East Asia, the vast, aggressive bulk of Sumatra stuck its dinosaur's snout out into the Indian Ocean as though to send its fetid breath in your wake. John knew that his feeling about Soekarno's empire would always be an acute distrust. China's allies were so near, playing a tune of neutrality on tinkling *gamelans* while they nursed visions of sharing what was left of the tropic east with hordes of little men from the north. Malaysia was beleaguered, there was no doubt about it, a shallow sea-frontier all along her south-west coast, and to the north only contested Vietnam, half-mad Cambodia, and the Thais who had, in their history, danced to so many tunes. Malaysia itself was a little country in which the Malays watched the Chinese, while the minority southern Indians moved warily between both lots, aiming for a balance to their advantage. If Malaysia's precarious unity ever disintegrated, there would, at once, be a roaring under this hot sun and over the green seas.

It was John's only real world, for all his transience. It was his concern and his future, too, if he had one, for he could conceive of no pattern which didn't at least bring him back to warm nights and the sound of Chinese jazz and the girls in one thin layer of cotton walking the pavements to a tune of sex. He wanted no Glasgow suburb for his roots, or an English one either, with their terrible dullness of organized safety. You couldn't starve in Britain today, state welfare wouldn't let you. And if you were even moderately good, quiescent to your union, and paid the tithes, so much else was added, television, hospitalization, even the truly full life with a refrigerator. The crime rate went steadily up, of course, in a world without economic fears of any kind, but this was something that would be taken care of by the adult-education boys, the psychiatrists, and those comfortable open prisons. You had, after all, to pay some price for progress towards total security, and the transitional stage was bound to have growing pains.

John leaned on his bridge rail and considered how he looked forward less and less each time to these returns to Britain. You came out of the sun gate of the Mediterranean, and turned north towards the ideal climate for rock gardeners, usually with fog waiting for you in the Channel, or one of those totally exceptional, but regularly recurrent, force-eight gales. Your ship docked not against a squalor teeming with life, but a chromiumed austerity of technological progress, a world without empty bellies and no need for anything to worship. You saw fur coats, and faces drawn from the only anxiety left, a competitive one for possessions. You rode on diesel trains that were late and ate canteen food at restaurant prices. There was no variety, no contrast, the people in Inverness looked exactly like the people in Ipswich, all driven by curiously automated compulsions towards nothing.

'Maybe I belong out here on a coaster,' he thought.

The party boat bumped against the landing platform at the

foot of the gangway, with Ginnis and Rafferty both down there, the chief steward now in a spotless white jacket in spite of earlier protests, and looking not unlike the head waiter at some classy swick joint. He had even applied a hypocritical oiliness and was bobbing his head towards new patrons. Ginnis would almost certainly chivvy the cooks and John wondered about the gastronomic heights towards which the *Maree Tarn*'s cuisine would stagger upwards on this voyage. It might even mean *not* tinned tomato soup three times out of four.

Bags were first, these dealt with by Rafferty who passed them to a sailor on the half-way staging. Then an enormous hat came out of the launch, a great cart-wheel of white straw, the owner reaching back to help a companion not so sure-footed. Ginnis intervened with a kind of bouncing Lowland Scot chivalry, awkward because rarely used. The two women started up the gangway stairs, neither of them looking up, the older woman first. Then Haslett stepped out into view. His words were not audible but they made the older woman stop to look up. It was Granny, alias Annette Colleridge. John didn't need to see under the other hat. He knew.

.   .   .   .

For reasons of duty a captain may miss an appearance at the first meal after sailing and John did. He missed breakfast, too, tightening his already small world to an area of bridge, day-cabin, and a section of the boat deck. By lunch on the first day out they were at a point almost half way between Penang and Pygmalion Point on Great Nicobar Island. He went down to this meal wearing a buttoned up white tunic and his braided cap. The sea was glass flat and shimmering, and the *Maree Tarn* moved elegantly through it, cutting two clean swathes with her bow, two neatly symmetrical folds of polished water. Only her wake had any turbulence at all, a white-of-egg fluff on a tarnished blue sea. Heat haze danced everywhere and there was no horizon, the ocean curving up into sky, containing them in an oval of brightness.

The doors were all caught open for no breeze, and John stepped over a sill into a small foyer where fans tried to make one. Even fairly small cargo ships these days have areas which ape the liner, and this entrance hall was panelled in a light African wood. From it led two passages to the cabins, and two doors into the large saloon which was used as a lounge when the tables were cleared. Between the doors was a settee flanked by potted plants, and above this the notice board, which was usually blank, but would now have to be titivated with reports on the day's run, a world-news sheet from the radio cabin, and other concessions to super-cargoes.

John opened the saloon door. He was late, it is a captain's privilege. So are the respectful eyes turned for his entrance. He moved down towards his table for six. At it, without consulting the master, Ginnis had put the two ladies, together with the chief engineer and Haslett. Milton was one of those demoted, and an empty chair, reserved for the man who was eating in his cabin, offered a kind of mute protest.

Haslett rose, but Henderson did not. A chief engineer has no obeisance to make to deck officers, and he now imagined himself suffering from an incipient blood clot in one leg which was the direct result of his sufferings in China.

'Fine day,' John said, and then looked at Gerda Lane. She was wearing white, and this should have diminished a blonde who isn't much sun-tanned, but it didn't. It was very hot in the dining-room, under the flapping fans, but she looked very cool.

Granny looked immensely interested, but accepted the introductory moments without any comment. This was a considerable relief to John.

He looked at the menu card and decided there would be mutiny in the galley if things went on at this rate. A hot joint and a cold. Fresh salmon! Where in hell's name did the fresh salmon come from? A treasure horded in deep-freeze all the way out from Greenock, and waiting all through the time of invasion by Chinese riveters?

'Captain,' said Annette Colleridge, 'I get the curious feeling that you would rather have a dead albatross on this ship than a woman.'

This was dangerous, but John smiled.

'We're not a liner. And really have no comforts for passengers.'

'Oh, but my dear, my cabin's luxurious. I don't wonder people become sailors. You get away from it all in such comfort. Not like my young days. I can remember in the twenties, taking a season of Shaw to Australia. We went out in something called the *Moolatiki*, I think it was, second class. Whenever I was quiet in my cabin, studying lines or something like that, the cockroaches came out by the dozen. Great juicy fat ones, too. I'd heard all those dreadful stories about them gnawing your toes. I never slept for six weeks. Perhaps that accounted for my Australian notices. There's also the fact that I've never liked Shaw much. Do you like Shaw, Captain?'

'Ah . . . yes.'

Gerda said nothing. It was clear that no news had reached his crew as yet of an earlier meeting with the ladies in Singapore. John could imagine how this information would delight Milton. It was Gerda who focused attention on Henderson by a question about his experiences in a Chinese prison. Henderson rose to the occasion with the ardour of a man who has for a long time been wanting an audience for an account of his sufferings, and John, listening, thought how quickly we all get back into our image of ourselves even when we have been kicked out of it. You couldn't, from the chief's picture, see a blubbering old man at all, only an old China hand in a jam he knew how to deal with from his vast experience of the natives.

'Were you tortured?' Gerda asked.

Henderson looked at John and then changed his mind about what he had wanted to say.

'Just by questioning. Hour after hour.'

'Sounds worse than a dress rehearsal,' Granny said.

It seemed a very long lunch. When John was released he went out onto the shelter deck which was narrow, no room for chairs or sitting, just for two men to walk abreast up and down past the square ports of the state rooms.

No one else was taking the air out there, and heat seemed to have forced a siesta hour down on a vessel which scarcely appeared to move. Even the engine vibration was very slight, just a quivering of life, no more. The surface of the sea, hazed like a cauldron of water coming to the boil, offered one of the little daily mysteries that are never quite solved, something unidentifiable out in the distance half way to the horizon. It looked like a large empty can and could easily be. Without glasses John couldn't be sure, and it wasn't worth going up to his cabin to get them.

And yet he stared at the thing, as though attention was focused from the subconscious, almost against his will. Something round, which wasn't bobbing up and down, but apparently held up from the water to a height of some inches, and, though it was certainly being passed by the *Maree Tarn*, it wasn't stationary on that windless sea to their fourteen and a half knots. If it left any wake at all, this wasn't visible in the shimmering, and how could a can be travelling out into the Indian Ocean at even half a ship's speed?

The currents? There was certainly a strong flow in the wide channel between Great Nicobar and Sumatra, but they hadn't reached this yet. And at this season the South-East Trades were pushing in from the Indian Ocean towards the coasts of Burma, so the run of the sea should be against, not with them. The can, which must be moving, was moving in the wrong direction.

John had seen some optical illusions at sea. On a day of haze the light could play strange tricks. He turned and went towards a companion-way forward which would take him up to the boat deck, and in passing the open door to the foyer was nearly run into by Gerda Lane.

'Captain, could I speak to you for a minute?'

He looked at the sea before he answered. There was no sign of the can at all.

'Of course.'

'I'm not keeping you back from anything?'

'No.'

'Because I don't want to. I don't want either of us to be underfoot in any way on this voyage.'

'Thank you. I'm sure you won't be.'

'You really are miserable about having us, aren't you?'

'No. I'm just uneasy about passengers on this kind of ship. Some of the bigger ones in our company carry twelve, and two of them twenty, but somehow I've never wanted a command like that.'

She smiled.

'When you're at sea you like to be at sea?'

'Yes, I do.'

'I notice a great change in you, Captain.'

'Oh?'

'The air of responsibility and authority. It makes you almost unrecognizable. Not Johnny at all.'

'I'm not Johnny on the *Maree Tarn*.'

'I know. That's what I mean. I don't expect you to be. And if you're worried about Nannie saying anything silly . . . she knows I'd twist her head off if she did.'

'Thanks for the reassurance. Miss Lane, why did you choose my ship?'

'I didn't know it was yours. You never told me a thing about yourself as a captain. I heard about Shanghai, but not the *Maree Tarn*.'

'Oh. You just wanted a quiet sea voyage?'

'Nannie has anaemia. It's quite common at her age. The doctor said she had better go home, and that sea might be good for her. I couldn't let her go alone.'

'What about your theatrical company?'

'They're going on to Hong Kong. Another girl is flying out to take my place. Nannie, poor thing, is dispensable and knows it.'

'You can just walk out on your art like that?'

Gerda smiled.

'I can walk out on that company, yes.'

Five minutes later on the bridge, he looked for the can. There was no sign of it.

Actress be damned! He had known that wasn't right. Years ago there had been a girl friend in rep. in Liverpool, an odd thing for her and an odd thing for him. Nothing lasting there at all, just a sailor bumping a world that couldn't in its own intense self-absorption move over to make room for him. Laurette was her name, born Laura. She was pretty and devoted to a continual consciousness of this, together with a consciousness of herself in the part she was playing that week. Beyond these two absorptions, her looks and the theatre, was a void of disinterest, and all the worlds that revolved around her in an industrial city only flicked her attention when she could identify in them a type, a character shape into which she could see herself pushing the formless ectoplasm of her personality.

Laurette. She had gone into films later, bit parts, and he had seen her once by accident in a cinema in Ceylon—Laurette being passionately someone else.

That wasn't Gerda Lane at all. The only moment in the play in which she had been at all convincing was when she turned to the boys and damned them both. There had been real heat in that. It was what she was feeling, but not as an actress.

The daughter of a permanent civil servant, plenty of money, the new generation that takes the world for its beat and—some of them—wanting to take it without drawing on family funds. At least for a time. After a while she would go back to marry the right young man and to have the right wedding-reception in a Surrey garden of ten acres. Now she was packing into her escape from the moneyed norm everything she could, including a voyage on a freighter, but, when it came to wrestling, she preferred the chaps her brother had introduced her to.

It was comforting to think that it was not only his age which put up a barrier. He hoped she would enjoy her cruise.

.   .   .   .   .

'Damn the bitch!' John said.

He got out of his bunk without switching on the light. He was sweating. He went into the shower-room, and, still in the dark, ran the fine spray, only patting himself with a towel. He put on shorts and went into the day-cabin, groping towards a cupboard, opening it. He judged quantity from the glugging of the bottle. Then he went to the door onto the deck, and, with a quick glance up to this end of the bridge to check that it was empty, took the glass to the rail and leaned there.

Almost directly north was Great Nicobar, a lump in the sea that went up to above two thousand feet, one of the islands he had passed often and always wondered about, a curiosity that had frequently taken him, in ports, to libraries. Nicobar had an unhealthy climate for Europeans, and had once been part of the penal colony in the Andamans used by British India for political prisoners and probably now used by the Indians in the same way. It belonged to India, but it was a long way from her shores, the last outpost of the real Far East, the southern-most tip of a long chain of islands that pushed up for a thousand miles towards Rangoon.

Nicobar was a forgotten island on the world trade routes. In the seventeenth century it was reported that the natives had tails, but later it was discovered this came from the way they tied their loincloths. They were not a big people, but they lived to a great age, secure in the world's disinterest, about eight hundred of them on that lump surrounded by a sea that was more often stormy than amiable, as tonight. John spent the whole of his life passing little worlds where people lived their rounds of time, not without terrors certainly, but these measurable because of only local importance. He never went by these islands without a sense of the confines of one life, and a curious longing for experience that couldn't be his in it. A boy on a place like that must have fun, though probably a boy would come down in the night to the shore to see the lights passing, sick with a longing for the things he couldn't reach.

Gerda wouldn't see Great Nicobar, she would be asleep. Pity. He could have told her about it.

He put the glass back in his cabin and went down to the shelter deck, silent in bare feet, doing what he had done often before in the tropics on his ship, making an inspection of it alone and in silence, an almost naked man using shadow for his bulk. He couldn't sleep, so he prowled in an anonymity of no uniform, the softness of hot dark against his skin. The moon which had shown Great Nicobar went into cloud and shadow didn't have to be searched for. He pushed open a door from the glassed-in portion of the shelter deck, and went down a steep ladder, turning around to do it, his hands on guide rails. The well-deck boards were still hot to his feet and the beat of the engines louder. There was a smell of paint and a hotness of used air turned out from inside the ship by venti-lators. He went forward past the stowed cargo davits, and by canvas-covered hatches towards a fo'c'sle that wasn't used for housing crew, just a store and a carpenter's shop. He went up onto the top of this, right to the peak of the bow, confident that he couldn't be seen from the bridge.

Here was only the hiss of separating waters, the engines far behind and inaudible. There was just the smallest lift up and down, scarcely more than a kick from twin screws. Beyond the established low sound it was very still, as though a great silence stretched out over a vast ocean, the kind of heavy quiet that can be a warning to sailors. He lay half out over the bows, breathing alone in a vast emptiness, feeling paint-roughened metal biting into the weight of his body.

And then he heard something else, so distant that it was a slow intrusion on awareness, but pushing in steadily. Out there, on the sea, was a beating from other diesels.

John looked for the running lights of a ship. There was nothing. The earlier heat haze had gone and visibility was to the horizon. He stood up, taking in every angle that wasn't blocked by the *Maree Tarn*'s superstructure, but there was still no light. The throbbing wasn't coming from astern either. It was out there to port, and travelling with them.

He knew what it meant. Somewhere out there, perhaps on a parallel course, was another vessel running without lights.

He turned and made for the steps down to the well-deck, using his hands on the guide rail, swinging on his arms, his feet touching every fourth step. He landed on the deck with scarcely any sound, straightening to run, and catapulting into a shape which spun away from him, thrown against the cut-back of the low bulkhead, with a scrabbling noise of hands, and a thump. He saw dimly a face, pale as putty.

And then there was a scream, a repeating reverberation. Like the wild hysteria of a jackal.

CHAPTER EIGHT

Gerda woke to the sound of feet running along the shelter-deck outside her cabin. The sheet slid off her naked body as she sat up. She put her hands on the cold brass sill of the open port and pulled herself up. A couple of ship's oysters burned dimly, but she couldn't see anything. Then there was a shouting forward.

She swung out of the berth, her feet finding slip-ons. She stood, groping in the dark for shorts and a shirt. She didn't like the flapping femininity of a dressing-gown for an emergency. Her hair had never seen curlers outside of a hairdresser's.

The slip-ons had rubber soles and made no sound in the short side-passage, or in the corridor beyond. This was brightly lit and empty, filled with a humming from the engines, and hot. She went down it fast towards the entrance lobby which was empty, too. The doors onto the deck were still open on both sides of the ship. She took the port one.

A heavy door forward was back on its hinges, and when she reached it Gerda found herself above the drop to the fore-deck well. She stood there, hearing voices, and seeing the light from a torch.

'I'm all right!' It was a shout. She didn't recognize the voice. 'Take your hands off me! I just came down here for some air, that's all. Can't I go where I like?'

'Come along, Mr Malthorp,' John Lownie's voice. 'I think you ought to be in your cabin.'

'Don't try to push me around! I'm sick of being bullied. You gave me a fright, that's all. Who wouldn't have got one? A half-naked man jumping on top of you.'

'I'm sorry, Mr Malthorp. I'd no idea there was anyone else about. Mr Haslett will see you back to your cabin.'

'It's too hot in there. I can't breathe. I'm stifled.'

'You don't get air-conditioning on cargo ships of this type.' The captain's voice was crisp. 'Have you tried using your fan?'

'I can't work the damn thing.'

The voices were coming nearer. Someone shone a torch. Gerda stepped back.

'Mr Haslett will put the fan on for you.'

The mate's voice came then, warning a passenger to watch the steps. Gerda heard a panting ascent and flattened herself in behind the hung-back steel door. A glow came through the opening, and then the panting man, followed by Haslett. Then there was the second officer whom she had not spoken to yet. The captain was holding the torch, shining it behind them. He came through the door himself. The torch went out on the palely lit deck. Then its brightness was on her, right into her eyes.

'Put that out!' Gerda said.

The man in shorts was standing looking at her. He somehow didn't need the badges of rank, with those shoulders.

'Couldn't you sleep either, Miss Lane?'

'I was woken up.'

She came out from behind the door, feeling a fool.

'By what?'

'Feet. It must have been your boys.'

'You didn't hear anything else?'

'No. What was there to hear?'

She didn't get an answer. At some distance from them, three men were caught in the light from the entrance hall, two sailors, one in uniform, the other in pyjamas, and the man called Malthorp, fully dressed, wearing a jacket and tie, almost neat-looking but for his shambling steps.

'Where was he going?' Gerda asked.

'He's had a nervous breakdown. I frightened him.'

'I know about him. Perhaps I could help? I've had some Red Cross training.'

'I don't think he would appreciate a nurse. We'll leave him tonight. See if he needs anything tomorrow.'

'Captain, what do you do on a ship like this if someone is seriously ill?'

'Put in for the nearest port. Or radio a liner.'

'And if someone in the galley chops off the top of his finger?'

'I deal with that, usually. Or Ginnis. He's quite a dab hand at accidents. We can't sew the finger on again, of course. But we can stop the blood.'

'I'm reassured,' Gerda said.

She moved away from him.

'Miss Lane?'

She didn't look back.

'Yes?'

'What was your idea in coming out here?'

'To see if I could help.'

'Why hide behind the door?'

'I felt a bit of a snooper, by that time.'

'And you're not a snooper?'

'No.'

'Good night, Miss Lane.'

There were stairs to take him up to his boat-deck, but he didn't use them, he stood waiting for her to go. Gerda walked down towards the entrance, turned into it, crossed the lobby and out the other open door. She reached the forward part of the glassed-in deck on the starboard side just in time to see Captain Lownie go back down to the well-deck. She crossed over and followed him, quickly, before he was likely to turn his head for a check. She couldn't see him down below her, nor did she hear anything of his movement. She took good care to make no sound over her own, and once down there in the total dark, found a ventilator, standing tucked against it for moments, looking towards the bows.

She thought she saw a shadow going up onto the raised forepeak and, gambling that she was right, went forward slowly to another ladder, climbing it. She didn't have to go right to the bows to see the captain of the *Maree Tarn* sprawled out over them. He appeared to be peering down. Gerda squeezed herself into deep shadow between the anchor capstan and its machinery. She watched the captain push himself up with his hands, then take a step backwards. He was listening for something. He took another step backwards, again listening, then another. After that he moved forward again, quite motionless for all of five minutes.

Suddenly he swung around and came by her, within two feet of her toes. She waited until a shape showed against the faint light of the glassed-in deck, then crept forward on hands and knees to pull herself up and lie where Captain Lownie had been lying.

At first, all she heard was the hiss of the ship's bows. Then there was something else, an intrusion on the near pattern of sound, a pounding. She dissected this out in consciousness, isolating it. It was another ship out there.

Gerda was going to look for the other ship when light did it for her, a blast of white light that bathed the forepeak in a secondary glow, forward first and then swinging to port, high up, a funnelled beam. It made a little circle on the sea, and then lifted to search wider, sweeping back and forth in little arcs until suddenly it stopped and steadied.

She turned her head. It wasn't sea held in this circle of light, but a long, black, faintly shining shape with a lump poking up in the middle. She knew what it was, a submarine on the surface at night, running on its diesels.

She thought about that. This was a well-used sea lane, but the submarine had been showing no light. It wasn't attempting to show one now.

Something was happening to that shape. There was less of it. In a moment only the lump was visible, and then that went. The spot of light held on empty sea for all of a minute, then went out.

Gerda crawled back towards the ladder, and going down it she found her hands trembling. She didn't want to think before she got to her cabin. No one was on the glassed-in area or on the open well-deck beyond it. There was no one in the lobby, or the corridor, or the side-passage. She went into her cabin, careful about the click of the lock for Nannie opposite.

It was terribly hot in here, and there was no sound of the sea. She didn't understand this for a moment until the light over the wash-basin came on.

Captain Lownie was standing there, still without his shirt.

'There's no need to scream,' he said. 'This isn't intended rape.'

Gerda's mouth felt dry.

'The others didn't notice you down there on the forepeak, Miss Lane. The interest was elsewhere. But I noticed you. So you're not a snooper?'

She didn't say anything.

'I want to make one thing perfectly plain. What you saw tonight you don't talk about. To anyone.'

Her lips opened.

'What are you going to do?'

'Nothing.'

'What about a radio message reporting this?'

'They'd pick up the signal. It's what they're expecting. For they're still around. It's a nice thought to sleep on, isn't it?'

'You mean . . . they're tracking us?'

'It looks like it. I first saw them after lunch today.'

'But why should anyone track this ship?'

'I don't know. I'm very interested. A lot of things about this voyage interest me. Including you.'

He was still standing with his back against the wash-basin. He had closed the port-hole. That was why it was so stifling. He was keeping his voice very low.

'Are you an actress, Miss Lane?'

'What? Of course I'm an actress. Why do you ask that?'

'When you were out with me a few nights ago, had you any intention of going back to England on a cargo ship?'

'I've told you how it came about. I didn't know about this ship then.'

'You deserted your company in the middle of a tour?'

'Someone had to come home with Nannie. And there wasn't a part for me in the first week in Hong Kong. They can get someone to fly out quite easily.'

'You think your company is doing well enough to afford to fly out someone from England?'

'The tour has backers, Captain Lownie!'

'Yes, it must have. Miss Lane, I don't think you're an actress. I've already said so. I don't think acting is the centre of your life at all. You do it just well enough to get by. As a cover for something else, perhaps? I'd give a good deal to know what that something else is. Though I'm a good guesser. Remember, you don't talk about what has happened. Good night.'

He came past her. She had to press against the wardrobe to let him by. There was the smell of sweat from his body.

The door opened and closed again. Gerda stood quite still for a moment, with her eyes shut. Then she went across to kneel on the berth and open the port-hole.

      .   .   .   .

Very few sailors seem to pound round their ships in an effort to preserve health, but Haslett did his two miles every morning on the shelter-deck which was the only place on board giving him a complete circuit. He was on his seventh lap when Gerda came out. She was wearing a pair of pale lavender, silk slacks and a white shirt. The first officer seemed slightly at a loss, as though no one had given him a lead on what to do about a lady passenger met before breakfast.

'You've my idea,' Gerda said. 'But I'll go the other way. I only stroll.'

'Oh, well, dash it, I've really had my exercise. I was about to pack it in and go for some ham and eggs.'

He fell in beside her and took a moment or two to match strides, even doing a little skip to put them in step.

'I think it's going to be a stinker of a day again, Miss Lane. There's that heat haze again. We should've hit the Trades by this morning. Bit of a blow. But it looks like heat all the way for us. Usually one only has to really stick it in the Red Sea. I've never been through that place when it wasn't an inferno. Is this your first time out East?'

132

'Yes. And I saw nothing. Just felt hot. So don't ask me how I liked it.'

Haslett was encouraging.

'The Med. will be nice at this time of year.'

They completed the first round in silence. On the second, she noticed that Mr Malthorp's port was open, but the curtain pulled across. She had already found out where his cabin was. On the third round, she contrived a lull in Haslett's extroversions in order to listen for sound beyond the curtain, but there was nothing, not even the whir of a fan.

'Your friend is enormously sprightly for her age, isn't she?'

'Yes.'

'I suppose an actress sees a great deal of life and all that?'

'No,' Gerda said. 'She sees a lot of theatres. An old actress can look back and remember the dressing-rooms. But she has forgotten the plays.'

After a minute Haslett laughed.

'It sounds rather . . . confined.'

The poor boy was sweating. She had spoiled his constitutional which was a solitary ritual. He was an amiable fool outside of his speciality of steering a ship. Gerda hadn't been quite sure of this before. She smiled at him and said she must go to her friend.

Nannie didn't answer the first knock. It was quite some time before she answered the second. Gerda opened a door to a little tableau against pillows of a woman of mature years facing the new day with happy resolution. Then the happiness faded.

'Oh, you? I thought it was the steward. With *chota hazri*.'

'With what?'

'Early morning tea, darling.'

'What's *chota hazri* to you?'

'Well, I thought in this area I ought to be playing the great *mem sahib*. Positively final performances after a run of three hundred years. How did you sleep?'

'Beautifully.'

'I didn't. Firstly it was hot. And then people kept doing things all night. Feet running, and doors opening and shutting ever so quietly. Then a perfectly incredible light began flashing about.'

133

'Nerves,' Gerda said.

'I thought it might be until I got up and looked out of my port-hole. Then I saw I wasn't imagining things.'

Gerda lit a cigarette.

'Did you see anything?'

'Yes. A submarine.'

Gerda blew out smoke.

'Nannie!'

'I tell you, I saw a submarine. I'm far-sighted, as the decaying so often are. And there it was.'

'Markings?'

'Well, I felt it wasn't one of ours. It didn't have a British shape, somehow. And we'd have been flying the flag, of course. These people weren't.'

'Nannie, don't say anything about it.'

'So you saw it, too?'

'Yes. And we're not to talk about it. Captain's orders.'

'Really? Did he give you this order when he was in your cabin?'

Gerda looked at Annette Colleridge. The old girl smiled.

'Darling, it's all right. Tonight I mean to take a sleeping pill. I really should more often, but I don't like to get into the habit.'

They were late for breakfast. Second Officer Milton was coming out of the dining-room as Gerda and Nannie reached the lobby. He gave them a polite greeting, but he was looking worried as he went out on deck. Gerda looked after him.

'Darling,' Nannie called out. 'There's something up on the notice board. Do you suppose it's rules for passengers?'

It was a typewritten bulletin, timed an hour ago. Gerda read it and so did Nannie, without her glasses.

EAST GERMANS DECLARE BLOCKADE OF BERLIN. AUTOBAHNS CLOSED AS FROM THIS MORNING. ONE WEEK FROM TODAY AIR CORRIDORS TO BE CLOSED TO ALL FOREIGN FLIGHTS. BERLIN IN STATE OF SIEGE. U.S. IS IMMEDIATELY DISPATCHING TWO AIR-BORNE DIVISIONS TO EUROPE. BRITISH PRIME MINISTER HAS STATED THAT A CALL-UP OF RESERVES IS CONTEMPLATED IN BRITAIN. NATO DIVISIONS TO BE REINFORCED.

'Oh, my God!' Nannie said. 'We've been getting too comfortable.'

Gerda didn't say anything. She read the bald news from the radio cabin again, with the feeling of being held in a vacuum of remoteness while a whirlwind was starting up a long way off.

'The submarine!' the old woman said.

'Nannie, be quiet!'

The captain wasn't in his seat, nor was Haslett, though there was a used plate at his place. Chief Engineer Henderson was chewing through bacon and eggs, but he put down his napkin for the ladies and stirred in his chair.

'Ah, come along and sit yourselves down. Sleep well? You've certainly brought us calm weather.'

'Just coffee,' Gerda said to Ginnis.

'Miss, just a little something else. I can give you cornflakes, grape-nuts, puffed rice, Scots porridge, bacon and eggs, kippers, or fried herring.'

'Just coffee,' Gerda said again.

'I'll have bacon and eggs,' Nannie announced. 'Since we're probably going home to rationing.'

Henderson looked up.

'Eh? Oh, the news, you mean? Och, just a bit of a flurry. Battledore and shuttlecock, that's what it is. Like the old Japanese game played by those geeshas, or whatever you call 'em.'

'Berlin is never a game,' Gerda said. 'It's a lot of people in one small place.'

Henderson sipped tea.

'You know, my dear, if I've any criticism of your generation, it's that you're all so damn gloomy. Sitting around in cellars with guitars and singing about death. When you're twenty! My God, I wasn't thinking about death when I was twenty.'

'Probably you didn't have to, Mr Henderson.'

'Now look here, Miss Lane. I was too young for the first World War . . . just. But I did my bit in the second. Convoys to Narvik and the Middle East. I've known what it is to be gloomy. Perhaps the real thing makes you not so jumpy over this kind of nonsense.'

'Perhaps.'

'It's always the same. The Russians try it on. We have a nice long time of cultural exchange with their ballet leaping around in London, then . . . wham! A new move on the chess-board. I don't see why everyone gets in such a flap. We should just have another move ready to push back at them. If it was the Chinks, now, that would be different. I admit you could scare the pants off me with the Chinks. But not Russia. And this was bound to happen in Moscow. New man at the top testing out his wings. Wants to look a big boy. So there's old Berlin sitting there waiting for a good crisis, and he has a crack at it. He can't do anything else.'

Gerda said:

'If they don't let planes in, we can't have any air-lift this time, can we? But we've got to go in. With fighters as escort.'

'Did you read that thing properly? They've given a week's grace for the air corridors. Time for talks. They'll talk. They always do. They don't want an atomic war. Who does?'

Gerda didn't say anything. She lit a cigarette and drank her coffee. It was impossible not to have a slight feeling of sickness, perhaps because she belonged to the generation that had never seen war, never known what it meant, except as a slight inconvenience of early childhood.

She went up on deck when she could, up amongst the boats, but back from the bridge. The *Maree Tarn* was moving steadily towards Europe, and she seemed to be going faster, leaving the Far East behind. Gerda stood in the shelter of a davit and looked out at the haze on the blue sea. The hot air, scarcely stirred even by the movement of the ship, was salty, you could taste the salt on your lips.

Henderson was his generation, when a war, however terrible, was still conceivable, something that could be fought by men and nations who might survive. The chasm between the age groups was simply a refusal of the older ones to see the totality of the thing hanging over them, too. They went on, being tight-lipped about what they had endured, lost in a kind of glory of their recollections, in campaigns of misery and horror that nonetheless were as much things of the past, and totally remote, as the trenches in France, or Lawrence of Arabia, or that Boer fighting. The death camps of Burma and Borneo and Buchenwald were yesterday. Yesterday, yesterday! It was today now, the hot tongue of fire a band of death around the world.

And a submarine was tracking the *Maree Tarn*. It didn't mean anything, it couldn't. But she knew it did.

The world was run by old campaigners, that was the trouble, yesterday's boys, like Daddy. Like her respected parent, who had taken his war service towards a K.G. in the Honours List, and whose life was meeting other old boys in one of his two clubs. He would be taking his furled umbrella to the office today as usual, looking like the ex-colonel he was. From a long line of ex-colonels, a stray into the civil service from them because the family money had run out a generation back.

God, there was a chasm all right, a great yawning gulf, between a world in which it still mattered that you really had your roots in the country and only called on people you'd known for at least twenty years and of whose financial position you had a very sound idea. John Lownie and his talk about blood lines! He was right. That was what counted still on the other side of the chasm, blood lines and money lines. And they couldn't understand it when their young wouldn't always tag along and play by exactly the same rules. After all, those rules had worked for hundreds of years. The sensible girl kept her eyes peeled for the son of a marquess. That's the way you got on if you were a woman, and a pretty one. Damn them!

'Did you sleep all right?' John Lownie said behind her.

She turned to him, looking in his eyes.

'No.'

'Neither did I. It was too hot.'

'If you'd stayed, Captain, I wouldn't have screamed.'

It wasn't her own voice saying it, or real feeling. She saw him put out a hand to painted metal and hold on. His Adam's apple moved when he swallowed.

'We'll skip that, shall we, Miss Lane?'

'Oh, for God's sake call me Gerda. I'm scared this morning. Are you?'

'Yes.'

'What did that thing mean last night?'

'I don't know, Gerda.'

'Whose could it have been?'

'I don't know that either.'

'You don't think it was some kind of accident? I mean out on an exercise or something?'

'No. We were being shadowed. Gerda, tell me why you're on this ship.'

She put her hands on the rail.

'Is it to watch Malthorp?'

'Please don't question me, John. Please!'

'All right. But leave the snooping to me. I think it could be dangerous.'

She knew when he had gone, without hearing his feet. It was something real gone from her, something living. Her hands tightened over the rail.

.   .   .   .

On the fourth day out from Singapore, Henry Malthorp came to claim his seat in the dining-room. He did this at lunch, arriving to surprise, and then the kind of mildly congratulatory atmosphere which greets the bad traveller on a first tentative attempt to make a stand against seasickness. The captain stood up, with a concerned half-deference, and Ginnis was bustling.

'Ah, there you are, sir. Just sit down and we'll see about a bite to eat, eh?'

No one asked Malthorp if he was feeling better. His presence was an announcement of this. He was very pale amongst burnt skins, Gerda now with a honey tan, and even Nannie allowing herself twenty minutes each morning without a hat on the boat-deck. Malthorp's fingers trembled a little with the cutlery, but he seemed to have a modest appetite.

'I hear the news is bad,' he said suddenly, in an almost loud voice. 'The world news, I mean.'

'It'll all blow over,' Henderson said. 'It always does. No one's going to really light the fuse. There are fewer madmen about than we think. And most of them are locked up, eh?'

He laughed. He seemed to be thriving on the tension that hung over the ship, that waiting for the bald news bulletins tacked up twice a day, morning and evening.

'Berlin, isn't it?' Malthorp asked. 'Berlin? What's happening?'

'There's a blockade,' John Lownie told him.

'But not in the air,' Henderson put in quickly. 'The planes are still getting through. A lot of them. I ask you, are the Russians going to give us a week's grace to fly in supplies and men if they really mean war over Berlin? It would just be damn silly strategy, that's all. This is another big bluff. The climb down will come at the last minute. The eleventh hour.'

'We can have one eleventh hour too many,' Gerda said.

'Oh, dear,' Nannie complained. 'Can't we just put this out of our minds for a little? Here we are on a ship in the middle of the Indian Ocean and we're all behaving as though we were sitting in the middle of Berlin. If we're going to be blown up don't let's be morbid about it in the time that's left.'

'Hear, hear,' from Henderson. 'I couldn't agree more. We're the old fogies, Miss Colleridge. Take life while you've got it. Even what we've got left, eh?'

'You've had a lot more of it than the young,' John said.

'Listen to the Captain. He's for the young now. Me, I'm for the old. We don't get much attention these days. We ought to band together, eh, Miss Colleridge?'

'I don't know,' Nannie said, not much liking the suggested alliance. There were moments when she remembered she had once been employed in support of Sir Laurence Olivier's Shakespeare, as a maid-servant.

Malthorp lifted soup to his mouth, a bit precariously.

'It's rather strange,' he said. 'Coming out from a Chinese jail to this. You don't hear about the world in jail. Nothing. It doesn't exist. Only four walls. And the noise of the door opening when they bring you food. It's taking me a little while to get used to things again. Ordinary things. I can't look at anything too big. Isn't it odd?'

'It's not surprising,' John said.

Henderson looked at Malthorp.

'You and me in a Chink lock-up, eh?'

Gerda crumbled bread. There were times when she hated the chief engineer. She looked at Malthorp briefly when she could, the grey face fleshy for someone who had been under-nourished, with the kind of curious drained pallor that marks patients recovering from a heart attack, as though they had been granted a reprieve from death, but only on a tentative basis. The trembling fingers interested her, too, for there were moments when this stopped completely, his hands quite steady. It was almost as though periodically Malthorp remembered something again which brought on the shaking.

He might have been good-looking as a younger man. There was about him a relic of arrogance, as though the world had been on his plate once, with women and money. Whatever his future might be he could look back with retrospective confidence on his past and she found herself wondering if growing older was this, a credit balance of favourable experience which can be drawn on to keep going when the trembling begins.

Henderson had it, the old days on the China coast, never to be forgotten, lost, but still there in a fund of yesterdays, the white man automatically big in an alien world, even if he was only a bottle-opener. He had been able to walk streets in an arrogance from skin colour, putting between him and the different violent patterns a thin screen of generous patronage, the gift of superiority his heritage.

Gerda knew that her own family, both the men and the women, had moved like this, less blatant from their breeding, but also more isolated by it, one a governor of islands, another an administrator in Delhi, conscientious, hard-working, but removed. They had all followed the patterns which had been established, never trying to break through, or even considering it. Gerda could remember as a little girl the thin high voice of a great-aunt, a matriarch, terrible in pearls, saying: 'We never allowed the Indians beyond the veranda, of course, except servants. Never!'

The chasm. The older ones couldn't really feel the change that had happened in twenty years, they saw it, but it wasn't acceptable and it was put away, relegated to a corner for the unpleasant. Even Nannie, who had no securities to hug from her past, just bad parts in bad plays, didn't want to think about Berlin.

Wogs, kaffirs, chinks, nips, and niggers. It would never have occurred to the safe ones that the world's doom was breeding in their hands.

'We've got an iced pudding,' Ginnis said at her elbow. 'Cook's special. I don't mind telling you, miss, I wouldn't have believed he could do it.'

'All right,' Gerda said.

She looked up to see John's eyes on her.

CHAPTER NINE

Armitage found thrillers a total relaxation from his work as a professional spy. They were also a boost to his ego in that the fictional spy was nearly always a helluva chap, precisely the kind he thoroughly enjoyed being in fantasy. He knew he wouldn't have liked it much in fact, the tempo was too fast for one thing, and this was likely to have a terrible effect on your blood pressure even if you did have muscles of steel.

High blood pressure was something that quite a few real spies had to contend with. One of the best Armitage had ever known, an American, had lived through two coronaries, and was expecting a third at the time he directed a very curious operation into the island of Hainan, which it was suspected, and rightly, the Chinese were using as a main base for their probes into South East Asia. The coronary subject had landed on that great lump in the South China Sea with a party of seven and had lived concealed in the place for three months, all the time having to watch his fat intake against the danger of another clot, a much more personal threat than a Chinese bullet. He was also, as is often the case, an eminent man in his public profession which was something as highly unromantic as entomology, and he had returned from Hainan with a lot of useful information about underground hangars for long-range aircraft, together with twenty-seven bottles of choice pickled local insects.

The plain truth about spies was that, without special training, only a little concentration, you could pick them out at any cocktail party, particularly in those areas where they were thick on the ground. That newly arrived personnel manager for an American oil company, with his clean executive look, three-hundred-dollar suits, attractive wife, four bouncing kids, and a Cadillac, was a dead cert. You could rule out at once the myopic British archaeologist who knew seven Semitic languages and was busy on a little mystery out in the desert together with an aggressively intellectual Oxford lady in amber beads whom he had married, apparently in a moment of aberration. That character was interested in Babylon and nothing else.

The contemporary spy blends into the tones of his background and invariably has an economic reason for being where he is. The peripatetic globe-trotter, hurled out to trouble spots by a Chief sitting behind seven secret doors, would at once gum up the local organization and could only expect to be shot immediately on landing by colleagues who had to protect themselves. There are little things, too, like language barriers which don't make your globe-jumper too effective, for an agent doesn't do his best work through interpreters.

Armitage hankered for, and never got, those periods of lull neatly placed between the thunder of action. The fictional spy tends to pass these in bouts of frustrated alcoholism, no doubt earned, but the real agent never seems able to complete a single job in this total manner, probably because he always has six jobs on the string at the same time. For Armitage, leave in England wasn't a lull—as a correspondent for a London Sunday newspaper he had to see his editor. He had hopes of taking in some Test cricket by way of recreation, but no hope at all of a well-curved blonde. Behind him wasn't any total success in the Middle East, no major Russian defeat, just routine which someone else was dealing with, and almost certainly without any feeling of loss that the master mind wasn't around.

Armitage walked from Fleet Street and an interview with an editor who was a gentleman, towards the Embankment and a meeting with a former policeman who certainly wasn't, and couldn't care less for the label. England may be run by old

Etonians, but the old Etonian has so far been intelligent enough to make use of the trained outsider, which is why the little island isn't as much of an exclusive aristocracy of birth as it sometimes seems. Armitage had not been in the least nervous of his meeting with the editorial gentleman, but an imminent second encounter this morning had his heart thumping just a little.

He turned into one of those streets which run down to the Thames, and which, for all the towering of new sky-scrapers beyond, contrive to keep themselves little oases of Victorian London. It was narrow, flanked by bay-windowed buildings retaining a sedate charm, a good many of them now hotels with basement kitchens from which came up the distinctly British smells of plain cooking, a solid menu with no French nonsense. He passed two of these and turned into the third, which was large, a couple of buildings knocked together.

The lobby had a residential air, a discreet porter, the lady behind the reception desk no flightly chick, the lift just slightly creaky. He pressed a button for the eighth floor, the top, and went up slowly, movement a decorous gentleness not likely to raise a fluttering even in the most aged stomach. He got out into a passage not expecting to see anything more sinister than a chamber-maid, and didn't even see her. The door to the outer room of the suite wasn't locked.

He knocked and went in. This sitting-room had been converted into an office, but only partially. It retained an air of a setting for afternoon naps, and a slight mustiness of indifferent ventilation. Behind the desk was a gaunt woman in her fifties, with breeding in the background, one of those who are reluctantly adapting themselves to a changed world. It was outrageous that she should have to work for a living, but since this indignity had been forced on her she was determined to do it rather better than anyone else. She had a cold eye for all visitors, and obviously didn't believe that 'S' Branch was saving the United Kingdom from anything.

'Mr Armitage? You're a little early. Three minutes. Please sit down.'

She had done the flowers on a central table herself. No one else could have got quite that effect of a contempt for all those three months courses on how to put blooms into a container. Miss Belling had dropped hers in, stirred them slightly, and then sat down.

She used a typewriter while Armitage waited, turning to the contraption in anger, and battering at this mechanical intrusion with ruthless efficiency. In exactly three minutes—he timed her—she stopped what she was doing, flicked a lever, and said:

'Mr Johnson? Your next appointment.'

Angus Johnson was a Lowland Scot from Lanark, who had come into the world expecting nothing, and had set out early, via the London police, to beat it to pulp. On the pavement he had been a rough character, in Scotland Yard only slightly less rough, and now, in exclusive isolation, had developed a kind of horrible charm which he used with contempt on all whom he considered nor worth bothering about. This was a formidable list which included a number of Cabinet Ministers.

He didn't smile at Armitage. He used an aggressive burr which proclaimed him a paid mercenary of the English.

'Sit down then. How's your particular hell-hole?'

For nearly an hour they talked about the Middle East, and all the time Armitage was conscious of small jet eyes watching him from under heavy brows that were an exuberance of growth on an almost hairless head. Quite suddenly, cutting across an account of Sheikh Al Menin's flirtation with the Russians, Johnson said:

'Your trip to Hong Kong was just a damn waste of money, I suppose?'

Anger flicked at Armitage. The breakdown of the Far East chain, through Malthorp, was something brought about by a direct ruling from Johnson. It was also waste, waste of men who had been properly established, with knowledge of Malay and Cantonese, and the loss, too, of a net spread out, an elaborate spinning over a long time.

'Still blaming me?' Johnson asked. 'It was a gamble. I took it. It might have been worth it. It could have worked for longer. Another six months.'

'And that would have balanced the wreck?'

'Yes,' Johnson said flatly.

145

You didn't argue with this character. And you weren't paid to like him.

'Taking a holiday now are you?'

'Well, six weeks. I'm in time for the Test Match.'

'God in Heaven! You know this, the Englishman's preoccupation with battering balls about could lose us the Cold War.'

'What about the Scots and golf?'

'I never played the bloody thing. I was too busy hammering laddies bigger than me at my school. I went into training early.'

He grinned. He had lost half his teeth and never bothered to replace them.

'We've got a better organization in Hong Kong now than yours, Armitage.'

'Thanks very much.'

'Not that you did so badly. The main thing about you is that you're a linguist plus. Most of them are linguists minus. When I hear a man's good at languages, I don't want him near me. You're an exception.'

'You mean I can be moved about, not sacked?'

'Aye. Just what I do mean.'

Johnson picked up a pipe from the ash tray and put a match to the dottle in the bottom.

'He's a bastard,' Armitage thought. But this didn't let you underrate him. The man's potency lay in an unassailable simplicity. Security, with Johnson, was a matter of practically never putting anything down on paper, using your brain for a file. What was in his brain could never be twisted out of the living body, though his death would leave chaos. Everything he knew was portable, and he wasn't desk-bound, quite a traveller in his way, and this with a flourish, turning up to stay in embassies and to meet top people, as blatant as the head of Soviet security accompanying one of their top politicians.

Johnson had taken this job over on his own terms years before after some unnerving failures in British security had shaken the world. It had been a panic appointment at the time, quite out of the pattern, and further failures in security had happened after it, but these rooted in past organization, not his. He now had things his own way, stripped to essential bones. His greatest strength lay in the fact that he had no stake at all in the Establishment, and no time for it. It was improbable that he was even a patriot in the English sense of the word, he was far too much a realist. But he had got this job and he was keeping it by stark efficiency. Once a Scotsman is really dug in, there is no moving him in this life. The whole of England is full of irritated Englishmen who have come to realize this too late.

'I've news for you, Armitage. You're going to miss your Test cricket. To meet that ship called the *Maree Tarn*. It's your own fault I'm sending you. You poked your nose into this business. You didn't have my authorization to follow Malthorp to Singapore at all. And I understand you were on board the ship there?'

'I was.'

'Not really trusting your successors in the Far East Branch? And what did you find?'

'Damn all.'

'So I understand.'

'We hadn't the equipment to do a better job. No proper detectors.'

Johnson smiled.

'It could be that the Chinese just repaired the ship. What were you looking for?'

'A nuclear bomb. Or opium. There simply wasn't room between the double bottoms for the kind of nuclear device the boffins tell us the Chinese have. And they hadn't built a little annex onto the hull. It wasn't stashed away in the cargo, either, we made sure of that.'

'So you concentrated on the old bogey, opium?'

Armitage felt heat coming back.

'It could be the new bogey, too. The mass drive to send Chinese drugs to the West is a fact. And we're the natural target for a new effort simply because we've the smallest narcotic problem in Europe. They might want to make that one of our big problems. They may have the set up for it at this end all ready. Plenty of Chinese resident in Great Britain these days . . . to control retail distribution.'

147

'So they fit out a ship on regular service to them as a bulk-carrier?'

'Could be.'

'And Malthorp in all this?'

'I think now it's improbable he's concerned. Much more likely crew members in the racket.'

Johnson knocked his pipe in the ash tray, and then, with a certain reluctance, took out his pouch for a refill, which he tamped down carefully.

'Aye, I've been checking up on that crew. I'm not greatly taken with the Captain's background, for one thing. Russian mother, father a disreputable Scotsman . . .' Johnson showed those few teeth. 'There are a few. Mostly in London these days. Then there's the chief engineer who's a drunk, and a second mate who had a wee spell in a boy's reformatory before he found himself on the high seas, as you might say. Two of the oilers have also served time. God save our Merchant Navy.'

Johnson struck a match and sucked.

'There's another thing. Interesting, in that it fits in with your opium. The Chinese population in Britain has gone up three thousand in the last four years, a hundred and seventy per cent. increase over the previous like period. It seems we're developing a taste for chop-suey. Aye, we'll keep an eye on the *Maree Tarn*. If anything out of the ordinary's been happening, you can find out at Suez from that girl. If I'm going to have the ship searched when it gets to Gourock, I'll need to twist a few tails for permission. Can you get into Egypt?'

'Walk in.'

'Disguised as a plump Egyptian?'

'They're not plump in Port Said these days. The place has gone limp for tourists. No real night life. Everyone is lean and purged.'

. . . . .

Sergei Dimitri Roduschev wasn't listening to anything. He was sitting forward in a chair, staring at the floor. An ant had somehow got up to his high room and was walking along a crack in the boarding as though on the edge of a canyon, stopping to measure the distance down to whatever crumbs were there in an accumulation of fluff, then deciding against descent at this point and hurrying on.

Sergei saw the ant, he saw the boards, and he saw beyond them into hell. In his hell there was only fire, and it was man-made.

He got up, but as though the view was unbearable to him, turned his back to it and stood, still with his hands clasped, staring at the built-in fitment made by a Chinese carpenter. His coffin would be made by a Chinese carpenter, if he had one.

He had listened to the news from Peking on his radio, and at once there had been a flashing recognition of evil, something so immense and dominant that all his training as a rationalist couldn't contend with it, and he was left the frightened child, but with no one to hear his crying.

For weeks there had been a question in his mind that he kept pushing back, trying to cover it over with the debris of routine. It had seemed half-smothered until now, until this terrible shouting.

Why had Liu Fa Tsu trained a European to set off his bomb?

There had been half an answer, and he had tried to make it whole. Treachery was planned. The European was to be destroyed with the bomb he set off. The man Liu Fa Tsu had sent was no scientist, just someone who could be trained to do a job that needed specialist knowledge. Such a man could be written off.

But this answer made no sense, it never had. There was no need to write off a man's life in the experiment. And even if there was, would Liu Fa Tsu hesitate to spend one Chinese life this way? The Chinese fought their wars by throwing thousands against guns, and then sending thousands more over heaped bodies. Would Liu go to the trouble and risk of training a Westerner to save one of his own people? The answer was a shouting, too, and it was 'no!'

Yet, for a day, a European had been here, a man who scarcely spoke, totally withdrawn. He had walked here, and been instructed here, in an aura of that withdrawal, and it had been somehow frightening to watch.

149

'He was like me,' Sergei thought. 'He had sold himself.'

But there had been no spark of real contact between them. Then the man had gone away, Li Ta Ling with him. And today the news had come on the radio. There was a whole answer at last.

'It's no test,' Sergei said out loud. 'They're going to use Project Seven.'

A man could go mad in an empty room talking to himself, unable to do anything. What could he do? Could he walk over the mountains to Burma? He knew the answer to that, and how far he would get. There was no contact-line out, either, for a man who had sealed himself off by his own wish and become Professor Baikal. No way to Russia, or the Americans, or anyone.

One man from the West had been totally responsible for Project Seven, and another man from the West was going to set it off. Against the West, certainly. What was the difference between the two men? Was there any? The other's motives might have been his own, the need to escape from the confines of littleness, of being small and a nothing, knowing this all your life. You became something by turning yourself into a servant of hell. God, you became something!

His radio had brought the truth out from all recesses, setting it before him. There was only one thing more needed, for the phone to ring and a voice to confirm the imminent desolation. All morning he had been waiting for that phone, unable to go down to the laboratories, saying that he was feeling unwell. They had offered a doctor, the elderly Chinese trained at Harvard, who didn't use herbal remedies. A good man, but unable to prescribe for a final explosive crumbling of the spirit.

If the phone rang with that message, what then? Did he just acquiesce? Another case of the scientist bowing before the man of action, allowing the thing he had made to be taken from his hands for practical political application? He would be hidden in history, together with that other who pressed the button. He might even go on living for years if the bigger bombs didn't fall too heavily on China.

Sergei sat down again, his head in his hands. He remembered the tunnels into the hills, the cavern rooms, and the drill for movement back from the vulnerable buildings in the event war loomed. That moving was bound to be a time of chaos. And he knew where the new radio rooms were, the equipment installed and waiting now as a reserve. He might be able to get to those rooms and a short-wave sending set. He would need no more than that to reach Burma.

There was still this open to him, the thin chance that he might get word out. But he was a small man, his courage ingrown and small, too. Terror would hold him back. He knew it.

The phone rang. He couldn't touch it for more than a minute. And then the bell on that private line seemed to get louder and louder until it had to be cut off.

'Yes?'

'Comrade Professor Baikal? The Red plan! The Red plan is now effective. Priority orders from Peking. You are to take the necessary steps as from now. Is that understood?'

Sergei said nothing.

'Is that understood, Comrade? The Red plan is now in operation!'

'Yes,' Sergei said.

Into the cave tombs.

.   .   .   .

The *Maree Tarn*, doing her all-out speed with a light bulk cargo, nearly sixteen and a half knots, was just through the break in the coral chain of the Maldive Islands and twelve hundred miles south-east of Socotra at the entrance to the Gulf of Aden. She was ahead of schedule, putting around four hundred nautical miles a day behind her, but John was holding this speed for the time being, even though Henderson might mutter that his engines needed an overhaul and shouldn't be asked to put up any maiden performance. The vibration on board had increased to the point where you were continuously conscious of it, and everything loose rattled. There was still no sign of the overdue south-east trade winds, just a breeze this morning which faded towards noon and might get up again after dark. John couldn't remember the Indian Ocean so calm.

Even without wind there was usually a heavy swell, distinctive long undulations of sea that were unlike a swell in any other waters, and which put a ship into a leisurely, almost somnolent groaning of her plates. A sea without deep movement over a vast area made a sailor uneasy.

He pulled his desk-chart forward to mark in their latest position, and the day's news sheet slid over the top of heavy white paper. He read it again:

RED CHINA ATTACKS QUEMOY ISLAND IN FORCE. MASS LANDING OF PARATROOPS AFTER CONCENTRATED AIR BOMBARDMENT. NOW ESTIMATED THIRTY THOUSAND CHINESE ON ISLAND. BEACH-HEAD ESTABLISHED AND SUPPLIES REACHING FROM THE MAINLAND. U.S. PRESIDENT ORDERS PACIFIC FLEET TO FORMOSA CHANNEL. CHINA ON FORMOSA THREATENS COUNTER-INVASION OF MAIN-LAND. PHILIPPINES STATE NEUTRALITY. U.S. AIR-LIFT TO OKI-NAWA ISLANDS. RUSSIA ANNOUNCES NUCLEAR ROCKET ALERT. NATIONAL ALERT IN UNITED STATES. BRITISH V-BOMBER FORCE MANNED AND ON PATROL. U.S. PRESIDENT TO SPEAK TO THE NATION ON QUEMOY AND BERLIN. BRITISH PRIME MINISTER SAYS WAR NOT INEVITABLE, NO TIME FOR PANIC. CHAIRMAN SOL-VONOFF AFFIRMS RUSSIAN SOLIDARITY BEHIND RED CHINA. INDIA NEUTRAL. JAPANESE PRIME MINISTER HASHIMOTO SUG-GESTS TOP-LEVEL MEETING TOKYO BETWEEN U.S. PRESIDENT, LIU FA TSU AND SOLVONOFF. BRITISH PRIME MINISTER PROTESTS AGAINST ANY TOP-LEVEL MEETING NOT INVOLVING ALL NUCLEAR POWERS. ANTI-WAR DEMONSTRATIONS IN LONDON AND EUROPEAN CAPITALS. POPE APPEALS FOR MODERATION AND CALM.

ACTOR RICHARD LEVINE DIED IN HOLLYWOOD TODAY AGED 64.

YEMENI TRIBESMEN REVOLT AGAINST CENTRAL GOVERNMENT. SANA ACCUSES BRITISH.

SKIRTS TO BE LONGER SAY PARIS FASHION HOUSES.

U.S. SECRETARY OF DEFENSE ANNOUNCES THIRTY-SEVEN POLARIS SUBMARINES NOW ON ACTIVE DUTY THROUGHOUT THE WORLD.

ANGLO-FRENCH AIRLINER 'CONCORD' HAD FIRST TEST FLIGHT TODAY FROM MUESSAY-SUR-MARNE AIRFIELD. FLEW FOR TWO HOURS WITH FULL PAY-LOAD AND REPORTED TO HAVE BROKEN THE SOUND BARRIER OVER BAY OF BISCAY.

152

The Radio officer hadn't forgotten women's interest. John wondered just how concerned Gerda was about the new skirt lengths. This sheet had gone up at noon, the first one to be posted in the middle of the day, and lunch after it had not been one of the better social occasions on board. Even Henderson had kept his mouth shut.

John switched out the desk light, got up, and went over to a cabinet from which he took a bottle of whisky. Then he put it back again. A drink wasn't a pleasure these days, it seemed to play on the wrong nerves. Henderson was on the bottle again, which wasn't surprising, but had to be watched. Haslett clung to his routine, more punctilious than ever, pounding round the decks and spattering the bridge with deferential 'sirs'. He was probably thinking about his family at Farnham. There were times when no one to think about made it a lot easier, and what John wanted, and wouldn't get, was now on this ship.

He went out on deck. As he stepped over the sill, there was a slight jarring, then the *Maree Tarn* shuddered. The vibration stopped altogether, and he felt a movement of the ship, as though she had changed course. He sprinted for the bridge. It was Milton's watch.

'Is an engine out?' John called.

'Yes, sir. Starboard. The line to the Chief is pretty hot.'

It was. John announced himself, then listened. The old man was remarkably profane, reaching new heights.

'An engine,' he bellowed, 'is not just a thing! Blast and damn all upper-deck scabs.'

'Cut that out! You're talking to the captain!'

'Gawd give me strength! Where the hell would you all be without us down here, eh? Steering damn all, that's what you'd be doing. I warned you not to try this caper of sixteen and a half knots. And if there's a report to the company, you can tell 'em I warned ye!'

'I'll tell them.'

'Sixteen and a half knots out of this old floating cow! You want the impossible. And you'll never get it again from me. Do you hear that?'

'How do you know that your engine wouldn't have gone at fourteen knots?'

153

'Because it wouldn't, that's all. Overheating's done this.'

'Are you sure, Henderson?'

'I can't be sure until the thing's cool. We'll probably have to strip her half down. Here . . . what are you getting at?'

'The main door to your engine-room is always open in these seas. It's just two decks down, easy to get at. I've stood on that grille above your moving pistons and thought how easy it would be, literally, to drop a spanner in the works.'

'Are you saying . . . ?'

'I'm not saying a damn thing. Only keep your eyes peeled when you're doing the stripping. For anything you don't understand.'

'Have you got secrets from me, Captain? Or are you still thinking about that sub?'

'Never mind what I'm thinking about. I'm telling you what I want done. What speed can we expect from the port engine?'

'About six knots.'

'Is that all?'

'It's all I'm risking on one engine.'

Plenty of time for a submarine to catch up. John put the receiver on its hook and looked at the shining, empty sea.

CHAPTER TEN

Aft on the *Maree Tarn*'s boat-deck an awning had been rigged
and there were wicker chairs, with a bulkhead oyster for light.
Ginnis had produced two of his plants, which offered no hope
of flower but were hardy enough to stand sea-air and constant
changes of climate.

He stood on the edge of the party with his tray, not quite
knowing whether he approved or not. A little gaiety on ship-
board was certainly all right, but the girl was setting the pace
tonight, putting back whiskies at a rate the paternal in him said
was too fast. It was all right to want to break the gloom that
hung over the ship, but good cheer from a bottle is a temporary
effect with a kick waiting. He knew. He was teetotal himself,
but he hadn't always been.

Gerda looked up and smiled at the steward.

'Another round please, Ginnis. Four whiskies.'

'Four?' he repeated, before he could stop himself.

She seemed to be making a slight effort to focus.

'Yes, four.'

The steward turned away. This kind of overtime was not
part of his routine. He hated passenger ships for their high
population of the idle, who appeared to make this their profession in life and lurched from one bar decorated for idiots to
another. He had once done six months on a cruise liner, and
the experience had shaken him to the roots of his moral being.

'What's wrong with the man?' Gerda asked.

Nannie blinked.

'He sees in you, darling, the child he has never had. Those who haven't been parents have a little red book full of rules for the young.'

'I don't have any rules for the young,' Henderson said. 'As far as I'm concerned they can go where they're going anyway.'

Gerda raised her glass.

'To the young,' she said. 'God bless us all. It's a trying time.'

Malthorp drank deeply. His hands weren't trembling these days. He was even prepared, on occasion, to be social, and seemed totally immune to the frigid gloom which hit everyone else twice daily with the news sheets. He was a neutral, immunized by personal experience against mass terrors, and with a certain visible contempt for them.

'How about a song, eh?' Henderson suggested.

Nannie looked pained.

'I've no voice. This kept me out of musical comedy. Together with my knees. In my young days, the psychological distresses that can be traced to knocking knees were not fully understood. No one ever thought of straightening them. My parents least of all. I come, you see, from an old theatrical family. The one good thing about an old theatrical family is that it tends to die out rather more quickly than other families.'

'And you always resisted marriage, ma'am?' Henderson asked.

'It always resisted me. I go back to the days when the stage wasn't respectable. If you had the money likely to interest a pretty woman as a wife, you didn't look for her behind the footlights. A few Gaiety Girls may have become peeresses, but it wasn't the general thing.'

'Some man missed his chance,' Henderson said.

'Are you being charming because that engine is working again? But you're wrong. I should've made a trying spouse. I'm too intelligent. Intelligence can be a handicap to an actress, too. It's not the way to get under the skin of a part. It's better to have a pea brain that lets you wallow in someone else's creation, however bad that creation may be.'

'Can *you* sing, Miss Lane?' Henderson asked.

'Yes.'

Gerda sang *Greensleeves* in a competent, just slightly thin soprano given body by the warm night. During the applause for this, Ginnis showed up with the four whiskies which he put on a central table. He was wearing the expression of a man who is not in any way affected by music. He turned and walked off.

'I'd like *Bonny Mary of Argyll*,' Henderson said. 'Do you know it?'

'Yes.'

She sang that, too. After it, the chief engineer blew his nose.

'Aye, that fair gets me. Every time.'

Gerda opened her hand-bag.

'I'm out of cigarettes. I won't be a minute.'

Malthorp pushed himself forward in his chair.

'Have one of mine?'

'Thanks, but I like my tips.'

The *Maree Tarn* wasn't rolling, but Gerda swayed, just slightly. She went along past the boats and down to the shelter-deck. The moon wasn't up, only stars put white specks on a black sea. She went into the lobby and down the full length of the corridor to the cabins, taking a look over her shoulder before turning into an aisle at the end of it. The door to Malthorp's cabin wasn't locked.

It was large, bigger than hers, with two square windows, both shut, one to port and the other looking out aft towards the ship's poop. She pulled heavy green curtains before putting on the light. Then she was quick, opening drawers, her fingers moving in them lightly, seeming to disturb nothing. She opened the wardrobe and checked in there.

Under the berth was a single suitcase, locked. She pulled it out and set it up on the coverlet, her hand-bag alongside. She opened this and produced from it what looked like soft wire set in a handle. She worked this into the lock, pressing hard, and there was a click. The other lock was slower, but came back, too.

Malthorp was using his suitcase for soiled linen, but the reason for it being locked was in the handkerchief sack, a small, new Colt automatic. It was loaded. There was also a box of

157

cartridges with the seal broken. She was checking the gun when a voice behind her said:

'So you wanted tipped cigarettes?'

Gerda didn't turn. There was a click as a berth light came on and another as the ceiling light went out. The cabin was now softly lit. Malthorp switched on a fan. Gerda felt a warm draught beating on her back before she swung around with the gun in her hand.

Malthorp was smiling.

'Are you going to shoot me, Miss Lane? I dare say your orders were to select the right opportunity. But I don't think this is it.'

He looked almost happy.

'It might be my opportunity, though. I said good night up there. A man wanting his berth to sleep off just a little too much alcohol on a prison-weakened stomach. Next time, if you have one, remember to check when you set out to get a man drunk and incapable that he isn't sitting in a chair right back against a deck-gutter. I watched you poisoning one of Ginnis's prize plants with your whisky.'

'Stand away from that door,' Gerda said.

'And if I don't? Have you ever shot anyone? I doubt it. You're just an apprentice, aren't you? Out in Singapore pretending to be an actress. Ingenious. An attachment to a touring company that can go anywhere without arousing suspicion. They're getting smarter. An agent backed by the Arts Council of Great Britain. It opens up charming vistas of British ballet in Peking, the chorus dotted with spies.'

He took a step towards her, just one step. Gerda jerked up the gun, feeling almost a fool. It was like being in the middle of a stage with suddenly no lines remembered, a desperate waiting for the prompter's voice.

He took another step, his hands lifting just slightly, the palms open, fingers out. It was his hands she watched. He kicked up with one foot. The gun went up and then clattered on the floor, sliding under the berth. Gerda had a stinging wrist.

'An old trick,' he said. 'Don't they teach it to females? I suggest you make room on the berth and sit down.'

Gerda sat. She might be able to reach the gun with one foot. Malthorp took out a packet of cigarettes and threw one over.

'Untipped, I'm afraid. Would you like my life story, Miss Lane? As one agent to another? And since I'm your assignment?'

He leaned against the wash-basin, struck a match, then tossed her the box. There was no trembling about him now at all, of the hands, or that slight shaking of his head which had been noticeable earlier in the voyage. He was fit enough, in spite of that dead greyness.

'My wife died when I was in a Chinese prison. They were working on me at the time. They thought the news would help them, so they told me. But it had rather the reverse effect. I held out for a little longer. You see, it was good news. I hated my wife.'

Gerda looked at the floor. She had to.

'I went to China as a volunteer for my firm because you couldn't take wives along. She had to wait, dutifully, in Singapore. I think I was quite a good agent in China, but our superiors don't agree with me. I committed the sin which makes you a bloody nuisance, I was caught and I talked. My talking did a lot of damage. They don't like me at all, Miss Lane. From their point of view it's a great pity I ever came out of China.'

'I don't believe that!'

'Don't you? In a Hong Kong hospital I was visited by my former chief in the East. He wanted to know why I hadn't taken the pill. You know what the pill is? I see you do. He asked me if I'd lost it. I hadn't. I just preferred to cling to life. Even with torture. Torture is a strange thing, you know. I mean what it does to you. It isn't any intensity of pain on one occasion, not really, just the thought of it going on and on. Not the water treatment itself, just the prospect of recurrence. Tomorrow and the next day.'

'I'm sorry,' Gerda said.

He smiled again.

'You're in the wrong business for a gentle heart. Agents who become a nuisance to their own side are killed. By their own side. It's considered necessary.'

She looked up.

'Do you really think I was sent on this ship to kill you?'

'No. But then they hadn't much time to organize things. They thought I was staying in Singapore. It would have suited them. It's a violent city. A little bit of extra violence would scarcely be noticed. Instead I nipped out, but a friend I relied on must have talked. I'm angry about that. He may live to be sorry one day.'

Malthorp sucked at his second cigarette.

'Armitage whipped you out of your touring company, didn't he? I know he was in Singapore, to keep an eye on me. He could scarcely come himself. So he had to use you, and the old woman.'

'Nannie has nothing to do with this!'

'I wonder? She's intelligent enough. And if she was such a failure on the stage how has she lived?'

'Scraping along. Not much more.'

'The fool! When there's so much you can take by just picking it up. That is, if I believe you.'

'Mr Malthorp, I'm certain of one thing. No one wants to do you any harm. I'm sure!'

'My dear, you should use a tear or two with a sentiment like that. And you don't know what's in the minds of our masters. I've a much better idea than you. I'm not walking into a trap by going to Britain, either. I've some things to do before I go back East again. And though they think they've got me nicely bottled up in this ship, I'm not a fool. They'll find they're mistaken.'

He dropped the cigarette in the wash-basin behind him.

'I've told you a lot, haven't I, Miss Lane? It just might be in my mind that you wouldn't ever listen to anyone else. You could have come to a dead-end right in this cabin. It would be very easy. There's no moon tonight. And a door onto the deck almost beside us. I wouldn't use a bullet. I'd break your neck.'

Gerda thought that if she dropped down suddenly she might get that gun.

'A black night. A girl who got drunk. Witnesses to testify to six whiskies in an hour and a half. You could so easily have fallen overboard, coming down for cigarettes. No one could have seen you in the corridor or you wouldn't have come in here . . .'

There was a sharp rap on the door. For a second, Malthorp's tenseness held. Then he relaxed. The handle turned and Ginnis stood there with a thermos jug in his hand.

'Your milk, sir.'

Malthorp smiled and reached out for the jug.

'Oh, thank you. Our little party continues, Ginnis . . . on milk.'

'Yes, sir.'

The steward looked straight at Gerda, then closed the door quietly.

'I'd forgotten about my nightly milk,' Malthorp said. 'And Ginnis has changed the situation. You'd better go! But remember this, I'll be carrying my gun from now on.'

Gerda locked her own cabin door. The trembling she hadn't shown for Malthorp took her now, like the start of a chill. She sat on the one chair and held her hands against her jaw.

Nannie's voice sounded from the corridor.

'Are you all right, darling? I wondered when you didn't come back.'

Gerda lowered her hands. She forced the words.

'Yes, I'm all right.'

.   .   .   .

Ginnis quite enjoyed his little reports on the aliens, their passengers. He was making a good story out of this.

'Six whiskies in an hour and a half?' John said. 'I don't think she'd be on her feet.'

'There's girls that can hold it. And she's one. Pouring it back, that's what she was. And fair stottin'. She couldn't look at me right.'

'What do you mean by that?'

'Well, it was the way she talked, too. Thick, like. That's a fact.'

'And how did she look when you saw her in Malthorp's cabin?'

'She was just sitting there.'

161

'Sitting on the bunk, you said?'

'Aye.'

'Still looking drunk?'

'Well no, not then, sir. When I think of it.'

'How did she look?'

'Maybe a wee bit frightened.'

'Where was he standing?'

'Over by the wash-basin.'

'You didn't feel, Ginnis, that you'd interrupted a closer contact?'

'No, sir. I just knocked and opened the door. I didn't wait. I didn't see a light. There wouldn't have been time for a . . .'

Delicacy lost Ginnis his words. John supplied them.

'A quick break?'

Ginnis accepted this with a nod.

So it wasn't romance? John hadn't thought this likely anyway. Caught red-handed probably, not drinking as much as she pretended and then taking a quick nip down to have a look round the cabin of the man she was shadowing. An agent's work. And Gerda didn't seem to have scored any professional triumph. He wanted to laugh.

'Thank you for telling me, Ginnis.'

'I feel I'm sort of tattling a wee bit sometimes, Captain.'

It was a shaky protest issued straight from self-conscious rectitude. Ginnis had always been an upright man, never pinching from the ship's stores, or never caught at it.

'You're carrying out my orders!'

'Yes, sir.'

When the steward had gone, John put his feet up on a second chair and pushed his body back. He was on cigarette rationing again in spite of world crisis, and now looked up at the ceiling wanting nicotine. A drink didn't do anything to help the craving, it just made you want a cigarette even more. So he was really taking an ascetic's control of his own body, fending off lung cancer and alcoholism with the same effort of will. It ought to be a greater satisfaction than it was.

What he really needed was a woman. It was becoming a chronic condition. He thought about Gerda sitting on the edge of Malthorp's bunk, and was still thinking about her when there was another knock on the cabin door. The place was becoming like the duty doctor's room in a night casualty ward.

The radio officer looked untroubled as usual, though these days he was a kind of contact-point with disaster. Leslie came in and shut the door.

'More news, sir. I thought you'd want to have it tonight.'

'Quemoy?'

'Yes. It's surrendered. The Chinese air force has sunk two loaded ships trying to get away from the island. The Americans are picking up survivors and have come close in-shore to do it. As yet, no one's fired at them. Formosa has bombed Amoy though. And they got it back, China has bombed Taipei and Keelung. Though they don't seem big raids, any of them.'

'What are the Americans saying?'

'From now on, they're going to shoot down any Chinese aircraft seen over the Formosa channel. That was announced by the U.S. Secretary of Defense.'

'What has China said to that?'

'She hasn't said anything . . . yet. But Formosa seems to be preparing for an invasion of the mainland. And one commentator says America may decide to back this with more than just arms.'

John pulled out his cigarettes and lit one. Leslie didn't smoke.

'Heard anything from Britain?'

'Our Prime Minister has called for an immediate conference of America, Britain, Russia, China, France, and Germany.'

'To talk out our little problems around a conference table, eh, Leslie? Do you have my feeling that it may be getting past time for that?'

'Yes.'

'Well, don't sit up all night listening. It won't do any good. Do you ever go to bed, boy?'

Leslie's face, protected from tan by his occupation, took on a flush. He was young enough to hate having his youth thrown at him.

'I only need four or five hours.'

'We ought to have an assistant operator. The company profits would stand it. Only the board of directors don't think so. Their bottoms have to be crewed as economically as possible. I hate those bastards. Like a drink?'

'No thanks, sir.'

The boy drank bottled fizz, quantities of it. He wanted to get back to his earphones. The air was alive for him, but nothing else.

.   .   .   .

Gregory Hartshorn opened a drawer in his desk and pulled out a German volume which was a translation of *The Principles of War* by Wu Ha Hang, of the ninth century, a work of which there was not apparently—according to the National Library—an English version available. The book had been printed in Berlin in 1913, an interesting date. Certain passages Gregory had translated himself into English, inserting sheets into the text. He took one of these out and read his own handwriting slowly.

'Prudent practices in war do not permit any reliance on an ally beyond a certain point. The ally is of military value for a specific purpose only, and the wise general will always remember that the purposes of another general can only accidentally coincide with his own, and this only for brief periods. Therefore, use your allies with total wariness always, for the immediate end to be gained from this alliance, and with no thought of any permanent union of forces. The wise tactician may, when this is feasible, use the association to undermine the strength of his temporary friend, perhaps even to subvert his armies. To strike an immediate blow against your partner in a military objective as soon as that objective has been achieved is sound policy for the man who would be strong. True strength tolerates no rivals, and any efforts towards permanent unions are only a sign of weakness.'

Eleven centuries had done remarkably little to change the basic thinking behind military alliances. It might be interesting to send a copy of this to General Haufmeyer in the Pentagon as a memento of a two-day row over whether the

164

Polaris base ship was to be tied down or not. Gregory smiled. He pulled out another sheet.

'The adder strikes low, at the leg-supports of the enemy, bringing down the giant in pain and terror to the ground.'

This, too, was a beautiful thought. It was scarcely surprising that Wu Ha Hang, on these principles, had become the military dictator of a larger area of China than any of his immediate predecessors. And the interest felt in this oriental tactician by the Prussians wasn't surprising, either. Wu's doctrine made the later Western colonial principle of 'divide and rule' seem rather feeble, as indeed it had proved. You destroyed and ruled instead, and destroyed like the adder when you could.

Liu Fa Tsu was an educated man, grounded in the Chinese classics, and no doubt these days even a student of war. People like Lugworth would accept that China's new Leader was a traditionalist at heart. And Liu had certainly made deft use of his allies over Quemoy. Was he stopping there? Wu Ha Hang wouldn't have done.

His secretary told him that the car was ready. He went down to the black Humber which took him to 10 Downing Street, but had a considerable wait for the Prime Minister. Gregory sat listening to the gentle patter of rain and wondering what motivation lay behind the crowd which always gathered here in crisis times to watch the comings and goings. Was it a feeling of helplessness in life and death matters totally shaped by others? He had never really looked at one of these crowds before. They seemed to include young and old, the bowler-hatted citizen and the tight-trousered girl with unwashed hair. These shared a solemnity in the rain, and watched the occupant of the official car because there was nothing else to watch in the quiet street. It was a thinner crowd than a few days ago, possibly because of the sudden international agreement to hold the Lake Garda talks.

Gregory had no illusions that any of them out there recognized him. The man in the street knows his Prime Minister and possibly the Foreign Secretary, but everyone else at Cabinet level is just another face. And certainly the face of the professional politician is rarely distinctive, unless he marks it by a spectacular hair style or specially cultivated eyebrows.

Gregory had been going to light one of his cigars, but didn't. A Defence Minister should look relaxed, but not plutocratic. The reporters out there would know him. And a man who can send an old woman's son to his death fighting Yemeni tribesmen oughtn't to look as though he was enjoying his own life too much.

He was still troubled by responsibility, and the statistic made suddenly personal in an illiterate letter from the bereaved. He had the sedentary's almost mystical respect for physical action in war, and a tendency to overrate its dreadful splendours in the imagination. Since he had taken office, a border skirmish was something seen from reports in the camera-eye of his mind, terrible in colour, and he wondered how the planners in major war could have risen daily to their task which inevitably meant the death of thousands. Yet he was Defence Minister with his country quite near the edge of final cataclysm.

The policeman stiffened to partial attention. The fan-lighted door opened and the Prime Minister came out, raising his own umbrella, then trotting under it down to the car. The chauffeur took the umbrella and folded it down, popping it on the floor at the back for certain future use.

'Sorry to keep you waiting, Gregory. And it brings us into peak traffic. But it can't be helped. I'm getting a head-cold. When I get this prickling I know it's something that's going to hang round me for ten days. I'll be taking it to Garda.'

'Couldn't a doctor help?'

'Have you ever met a doctor who could cure a Prime Minister's cold? Or anyone else's cold?'

The P.M. broke off to wave to the crowd. He sent out of rain-spattered windows the smile of confidence the country expected. He was fond of his crowds and really rather enjoyed a mass attendance at his comings and goings. It had to be a crisis before he got this, however, the norm seeing the crowds attending long-haired boys with guitars. Even Royalty weren't getting the turn-outs they once had.

'Well?' said the P.M. 'Have you something for my ear alone?'

'Not exactly. I find myself preoccupied with China.'

'Ah. Your premonition of evil?'

'I'm not an old spey-wife!' Gregory said, nettled.

'My God! What do you think I was playing at with your appointment? A premonition is a perfectly valid form of experience. It's a process of the subconscious and nothing else. A computer eject from brain areas where conscious thought isn't a factor at all.'

'All right, James. My premonition of evil.'

'I've a premonition about this conference at Garda. But I'm damned if I'll tell you what it is.'

'You don't expect total success?'

'I'm not such a fool as to expect total success in anything. It never happens. Certainly not to a politician. Certainly not in foreign affairs. Damn compromise, that's all you get. And anyone who rejects compromise in our time is putting the ultimate dissolution under his world and lighting the fuse. That's what they call me, you know, the mediator, the planner of devices to achieve apparent unity. I do it in the party, I do it in the country, and I'm trying to do it in the world. And the leader who doesn't do it in the world is a bigger threat in our time than Hitler was in his. And I don't care what his nationality may be. Democracy is a process of patching. It has never been anything else and never will be. We patch and alter because there can never be anything cut to cover adequately for a generation, even for a decade, a free people. The fools who think that the free world has nothing coherent to offer overlook the fact that our patching is a continuous process. And a creative process. We are not ruled by dogmas and I've never accepted them as man or a politician. Life changes every day. And there's no dogma that can be made to fit this inevitable change.'

'Make that speech in the House some time,' Gregory said.

'I never speak well in the House. It's one of the great handicaps to my career. I believe I'm a little awed by the place still, by the echoing of dead voices. What have you to tell me from your China-watching?'

'Nothing, really. Though I've been wondering if perhaps Liu Fa Tsu is playing a double game with the Russians.'

'Well, it's pretty obvious that Berlin and Quemoy were cooked in the same pot. And it's landed us back again into the old horrible position of striving for containment. I couldn't say it in public, Gregory, but the plain fact is now that we have to hope Quemoy was *all* the Chinese wanted. And that the Russians will slow down on the blockade. We have to negotiate from this position and it's too much of a compromise, even for me. It makes me sick to do it. You know this, I'd die happy if in my time in office the West was able to blow containment into outer space. If only we could get our hands on something real to use against it. To bash at it from unassailable strength, without blowing up the world.'

'Are you thinking of a real and final split between China and Russia?'

The P.M. leaned back against the cushions.

'The thought is almost too beautiful to contemplate. Do you mind if I have a little nap? I need one before all that talk tonight.'

CHAPTER ELEVEN

All the way up the Red Sea, the *Maree Tarn* had moved by day through a shimmering, hazed heat climbing to humid temperatures which made breath a thickness in the lungs. Nights came with no breeze at all, only the little currents created by the ship, and these almost painful to endure, like ripples on the steaming surface of a too-hot bath. You sat on deck or lay in bed in an only half-animate torpor, news from the world reaching just a partial consciousness, your real attention focused on a body wasting in sweat. Land was never seen, just sensed, Arabia on the one side, the deserts of Nubia on the other, worlds which might have been habitable once but were now burned out by a killer sun. The ship cut through a heat-sterile vacuum which seemed reluctant to permit its passage and allow the animate to escape.

Here in the Suez Canal Gerda could feel a blessed stirring of living air against her skin. She had a sense of being convalescent from an ordeal, though what she looked at was still a hard bright nothing of sand. She wore shorts, shirt, and sunglasses, and her hair had gone the colour of white corn. She was also wearing a large ring left to her by her great-aunt, an Indian ruby of considerable size surrounded by emerald chips and set in heavy gold which caused a slight dampness under it. A trophy, a kind of loot, burning with its own fire.

The Suez Canal may be an engineering miracle, but it is very dull. The Egyptians have found it relatively easy to keep digging the sand out and leading strings of ships through the water passageways; they would be decidedly incompetent if they couldn't. No pilot on that stretch ever got a coronary from the tensions of his job. The *Maree Tarn* was one of a row of more impressive vessels, a twenty-thousand-ton P. & O. liner in front of her, and a thirty-thousand tanker astern. All moved at precisely the same speed, like downtown traffic controlled by tyrant cops.

The chief engineer leaned on the rail beside her.

'Well, Miss Lane, the Med. next, eh? Glad to be getting away from the East?'

'I don't know. Yes, I think I am. I don't believe I could ever live there.'

'Maybe it's a part that gets into your bone-marrow when you're young and have to take a big dose of it. Me now, I feel that everything goes tame and old after here. I don't like a tideless sea. Used water.'

'It's very beautiful around the Greek islands.'

'Aye, so I've heard. But you're in a bottle, that's all it is. Europe's sun-trap. They don't know what sun is. And everything that ever happened in the Med. is down in the charts. The canal is a gate into a back-yard. Are you thinking about going ashore at Port Said. Maybe the captain would let you for a couple of hours.'

'We asked, and he said no.'

'Did he? Oh, well, he probably didn't want any trouble. The place isn't what it was. And they still don't like the British. They hacked down that Frenchie's statue, too. The one that built the canal. Weren't going to have any Frenchman presiding over their ditch. Feeling their oats, the Gypos. I can remember when we wouldn't have let one of them near the canal. They couldn't even spit in it. Changed days.'

'Yes.'

'Are you still worrying about the international situation? Didn't I tell you there'd be a conference? Maybe this one will even be important. I can remember a few that were going to be. Usher in a new era of peace and all that. Like Locarno. Does that mean anything to you?'

'Not much.'

'I think that one was going to end war.'

He laughed.

She saw a little boy on the canal bank, with a dog. He seemed to have come from nowhere, remote from any village, but leading his dog carefully on a length of rope. They had pets here, too, in the desert. It was an odd sentimentality of man, a universal inclination. A dog, with his tongue-lolling, tail-wagging dependence was a boost to the ego. However small you were, a dog was smaller. Gerda could remember her two dogs, one from childhood, loved passionately then. She couldn't have one in her present life.

'The Locarno Pact,' Henderson said. 'No, I can't remember what it was all about. But the world was facing destruction then, too. Long ago. We all thought about nothing else. I was young.'

Gerda's hands were on the rail. She was conscious of Henderson looking at the ruby ring.

'Nice piece of ready cash that, Miss Lane. Diamonds are for the cold countries. A ruby's for the sun. You've got to stop worrying, you know. Everything will work out all right. No one's going to blow up the world. It's just what I said. The Russians aren't going to try anything.'

'And the Chinese? Now?'

'Well, they've got Quemoy. It's what they wanted. You don't think the Americans are going to send their navy in there to take it back again, do you? I tell you, the Chinese are coming to that Lake Garda conference feeling very pleased with themselves. They'll make a noise about Formosa, maybe, but they won't try to grab it. They take what they see they can get. It's as simple as that.'

'I wish I really believed you,' Gerda said.

'Well, you can. No one used the bomb to stop the Chinks getting Quemoy. So they're feeling good. And don't forget, they tried to grab Korea and only got half of it. Burned their fingers badly.'

'So did we,' Gerda said. 'My brother died there. He was twenty-one.'

'Oh, my God! I'm sorry.'

'It's a long time ago.'

'Aye, but it's something you remember.'

A jeep came down a road edging the canal, running smoothly like a toy on the carpet, going the way of the little boy, now lost, with his dog.

.   .   .   .

Port Said lay in a white glare that could have been a setting for new arrogance but only pointed up old dilapidations, the large buildings oddly uncertain-looking, as though the sand beneath them had already set a limit on their span. The harbour offered bright blue patches between anchored ships, the Norwegians, Danes, British, American, Japanese, French, German, a whole world held here under orders that would have seemed startling only a decade ago, a new courtesy offered to the formerly ignored because it had to be, but given with a kind of contempt even yet. Port Said didn't stand up well to the glitter of ships which waited on her pleasure. She was like an ancient whore appointed commissar after a revolution, clutching at new dignity in feverish self-consciousness, but still wearing the tawdry bangles of her past.

The bum-boats wobbled about the harbour, loaded to within an inch of the water with bright junk for rich travellers, clustering around huge hulls. A still air was loaded with the shouting of salesmen. The *Maree Tarn* had only one of the little boats, a vast cruise-liner from New York nearby offering a much better potential market.

'We used to throw pennies,' Nannie said, peering down. 'But now they don't want them. No doubt that's progress. Do you fancy a souvenir of Egypt, Gerda?'

'No thanks.'

'You can sometimes pick up bargains. I once met a man who got a good emerald here. From a man selling rings. Everything was glass except the stone the salesman was wearing himself on his little pinkie. So my acquaintance took that and paid for it, after quite a struggle. It was in the old days of colonial pride, of course. What's that man offering? Is it watches?'

'You don't want anything, Nannie.'

'My dear, like those who have always been deprived, I want

172

everything. I wonder if those cameras are Japanese? And hide bags of some sort. In one's final decline, it's so nice to be surrounded by reminders of the full life one once led. Actually, a little rug would be rather nice.'

'It'll be rubbish.'

'If we went down into the well-deck, that ruffian could throw a rope up quite easily. And he's signalling. I remember ... you tie the rope and they swarm up it, bringing a nice selection with them.'

Gerda went with Nannie, telling herself that she was only doing it to see that the old girl didn't fall on steep steps. And she caught the rope on the second throw, making it fast, looking up as she did so for disapproving eyes from the boat-deck. There was only a pair of feet propped against one of the lower rungs of the railing. They looked like Malthorp's.

Nannie's ruffian was certainly agile. He made a careful selection from his stock, putting this into a vast bundle which he tied over one shoulder, then he came easily up the rope, hand over hand.

'Good things for ladies here. Sure.'

The bundle opened out. The contents didn't seem all that good to Gerda. The one 'oriental' rug said loud things about chemical dyes which denied all the dealer's talk about Kurdistan.

'Like silk,' Nannie said, stroking it. 'Feel.'

'Watches? You like ladies' watches. Pure Swiss. Three pounds. In England, twenty pounds.'

'I do so like this little rug,' Nannie said. 'Portable for lodgings and so cosy to get out of bed on.'

She moved down the deck a little distance, to lay it out flat and stand back, gazing down. The dealer held out a portable radio.

'Japanese transistor,' he said. 'Four pounds ten. Fifteen pounds in England.' Then his voice went low. 'But a free issue to you, Miss Lane.'

.   .   .   .

The Atlantic was grey, a force eight gale killing even a

173

recollection of flat tropic seas and sun. Short-troughed waves smashed at the *Maree Tarn*, and she took water over the bows, geysers of it shooting up to half-mast height and then slapping down into the forward well-deck, which was awash. They were making poor speed, beating into a northerly, and the ship lost way every few minutes when twin screws came right up out of the sea. When this happened, there was an earthquake vibration, metal plates jarred to a ruthless testing of rivets.

John Lownie was half enjoying the storm. It restored him to total command, giving him escape from his passengers. The role of host to unwanted guests had become an increasing strain, and he had bankrupted his small talk even before they were into the Mediterranean, the captain's stories all told, the last ones out of the bottom of the barrel smelling a bit high as they were pulled up. The only real alternative to nautical anecdotes had been what was happening in the world, and in combating this gloom John had felt at times like a too-healthy warder escorting a batch of the condemned to the death chamber. Even Henderson's belaboured optimisms went out like a light just south of Malta, as though suddenly he had read one bulletin too many. Haslett was no use at all, only once rallying to his social duties by rigging up a deck-quoits net behind the funnel, and forcing a little extrovert exercise as an antidote to morbid self-communings.

Gerda, too, had tried. She managed sometimes at table to be quite funny about the theatre, but Nannie, who should have taken this as a cue to move in, just sat and appeared to be contemplating desolation. John noticed, though, that the old girl still continued to eat, almost with dedication. It could be that three square meals a day had never been a total certainty in her long life, and it was almost instinct to eat when the opportunity was there.

In the dining-room, which was really the only time he met Gerda, John was very conscious of her sitting just beyond his right elbow. As the only two real workers at maintaining a fiction of the social norm, they had this in common, a kind of bond in effort which developed its own ease between them. But for the captain the ease was something applied, and under it remained a whetted appetite for sex. Once or twice the cover he had put on this slipped, and he knew perfectly well that she had observed lust without any discomfort, indeed the half-pleasure of a woman who has provoked it as a regular thing and will be quietly grieved when she is no longer able to. With her deep tan Gerda was very nearly beautiful, but beyond the very marked effect this had on John he was aware of something else, a continuing core of caution. In his experience, which wasn't limited, the prettiest women were not the best in bed, as though they assumed, quite wrongly, that nature had automatically presented them with all they needed in every direction and there was no special effort called for. It was in fact that special effort which was memorable, remaining in recollection long after a face had been forgotten.

John was handicapped, too, on this voyage by more than the authority and dignity of his position, both barriers which in other circumstances might have been broken down. But tension hung over them all, putting them in a waiting-room with two doors, one back to the known, the other opening into almost certain darkness. There was no lasting escape from the reality of this, even at sea, for when they reached the Mediterranean portable radios began to buzz a replacement to those daily typewritten bulletins, and in the Atlantic reception was almost as good as on land. On board the *Maree Tarn*, they were spared only television coverage of the arrival at Lake Garda of the American President, the British, French, and German Prime Ministers, Solvonoff, and Liu Fa Tsu. The United Nations, as usual in a moment of real testing, had been gently by-passed, and the inevitable noisy protests about this from the emergent nations wasn't even commented on. There was music between crisis items, and it seemed put out as sedation, less pop, more gentle Haydn. Religious broadcasts, too, had been stepped up, and probably people were filling the churches again, ready to try even prayer in an acute emergency, just in case God was still available.

Milton, on his watch, was standing directly behind the helmsman in the shelter-bridge, the young man with his arms folded across his chest, small, compact, and alone, almost a Napoleonic contemplative. And his comment on imminent war, only half a day old, stuck in John's mind, together with a recollection of the sour tone used: 'Why the hell does all this have to happen as we're coming *back* to Europe? It might just as easily have been when we were heading for Singapore.'

The second mate hadn't enlarged on this theme. But it was clear that Milton didn't see himself as expendable along with half the world. And to another sailor there was a certain logic in this, at least to one with no roots on shore. The only real world was a moving ship, the rest a series of landing-stages some offering more amenities than others, but all easy to leave when the time came. It had been true for John. It probably always would be. In a personal sense he had no stake at all in what happened to Europe, or America, or Russia for that matter.

The radio officer came up onto the bridge with the forecast. John read about a predicted continuing disturbance between two low-pressure areas which were bringing rain and high winds to the southern portions of the British Isles. Further north it appeared to be calmer, with some touches of coast fog, but the *Maree Tarn* was still a long way from any ironing out of the sea.

Two of the passengers were prostrate, according to the reports from Ginnis. Nannie lay in her bunk, at first letting out yips of terror between sessions of using the tin attached to her berth holding-board, but finally quiescent and exhausted, mostly sleeping now under pills the steward had found for her. Malthorp was also missing all meals. Ginnis took him ginger ale and dry crackers, his fancy in suffering. Gerda still turned up in the saloon with an appetite improved by the cold air of home. She was also determined to walk on sea-washed decks, and it had been necessary to order certain areas roped off.

John came down from the bridge, needing both hands on the guide-rails, on an inspection visit to sea-sick passengers which Ginnis had prodded him into. A faint haze of moonlight let him see waves as high as the *Maree Tarn*'s boat-deck, each a looming threat until somehow it dissolved away under a rising hull. The wind hummed like a massive dynamo against the ship's resistance, and he saw the stern rise, almost flipped

176

up, making the vessel seem segmented, her extremities free in a violent, exclusive motion of their own. It was enough to make even a sailor giddy.

One of them was. Potkin stood by the rail just opposite the captain's cabin, straight arms holding his body rigid, and he was staring at those waves. John knew at once that their degree of roll had exceeded the norm for a heavy gale. It must be the light cargo. Potkin was a kind of register of the ship's movement, almost continuously happy down in the engine-room until the roll added a couple more degrees than his sense of balance would tolerate; then he came up for air. John had never seen the engineer actually sick, just a man applying his own cure for a chronic condition, breathing deeply.

'Quite a blow,' John said.

Potkin didn't move his head suddenly.

'Yes.'

'Starboard engine standing up all right?'

'Yes.'

'We're not due for dry dock this turn around. But I could insist on it if the chief still thinks it's necessary.'

'It isn't,' Potkin said, holding on.

'But when the thing went in the Indian Ocean the chief howled about an overhaul.'

'That was just him making a noise.'

Quite a long sentence from the man. It seemed to have taken a lot out of him.

'I didn't understand the report of what happened, of course. But then I never do.'

'We had a lubrication failure to a main bearing.'

'Yes. What's that mean?'

Potkin looked as though he was going to appeal for mercy. Then he took another of those slow, deep breaths.

'It's an automatic feed, on the flow principle. Like they used on some of the bigger British cars up to twelve years ago. You know what I mean?'

'No.'

'Well, you have a centre tank and feed pipes from it. One of them packed in.'

'And it took two days to fix?'

177

'We had to renew the whole length of pipe. The chief hates patching. The bearing had to be replaced, too. That was what took the time.'

'Was the pipe blocked?'

'No. Leak. Some kind of corrosion. Odd with copper. But it can happen under certain pressures.'

'Ever see anything like this before, Potkin?'

'Well, not exactly. But nothing's ever the same, is it?'

Except the reaction of certain ganglia in the second engineer's inner ear to a degree of roll beyond the point of permitted toleration. John felt almost like offering to hold the poor fellow's forehead. Instead he left.

The first passenger on the sick list wasn't in his berth. Malthorp sat on the settee under a tightly closed port from which the curtains swayed out and back again. He was wearing pyjama trousers and a cardigan. He looked gaunt and cold. His head came up quickly, though he hadn't answered the knock at all. He stared.

'What do you want?'

'I came to see how you were. Ginnis told me you were feeling this sea.'

'The sea? Don't be silly. I've never felt the sea in my life. I'm a perfectly good sailor. It's ... I get headaches, that's all. You don't know what it's like. I got them in China. I started to get them very badly. I had to go out ... I mean, they made me work. Cleaning up. I had to clean up a courtyard. With a guard following me round. He was always checking his rifle, you know ... No! You don't know. Get out!'

'I thought I might get you something from my medical kit, Mr Malthorp.'

'No!' He seemed to get hold of himself. 'I suppose it's kind of you. But I don't want your kindness. Why the hell should I?'

John went along the corridor to another aisle. Again there was no answer to his knock. He turned the handle and opened onto a heaving darkness.

'Oh, hell! Is that you, Ginnis?'

John switched on the light.

'No, the captain.'

'Eh?'

She hated that white blaze from the ceiling. He was ashamed of having used it. Nannie lay under twisted covers, her face puckered in, all fight with the years given up. He saw the defencelessness of age, a continued living without the physical equipment to make it endurable, and he knew he didn't want this for himself.

'Why did you want to see me?'

'I hear you're not eating. I thought I'd better check up and see if there isn't something we could tempt you with.'

'What do you suggest? That I put in my teeth and gnaw a chop? Will you please put out that damn spot-light, Captain?'

The soft glow put her face in shadow.

'I'm not being very gracious, am I? Sorry. But I never knew a ship could do what this one's done in the last few days. I'd have died but for Ginnis. He's wonderful. Makes clucking noises. But there's nothing I want to eat, thank you very much. I've come to an arrangement with my stomach. If I let it alone, it lets me alone.'

She seemed to be staring at him.

'Have you ever been sea-sick, Captain?'

'Not really.'

'Then you don't know what it can do to morale. Especially when you're old. I got up yesterday and hung on long enough to see myself in that mirror. You know . . . if I'd had the strength, I'd have hauled myself outside and jumped over the rail. What the hell's left for someone who looks like I do now?'

'You won't be feeling this way in a day or two.'

He had to push those words out. He was thinking of Natasha Lownie, alone, no longer able to use that covering smile, facing her moment of total emptiness.

'I'm going to get brandy for you, Miss Colleridge. Sipping it does a lot of good.'

'Really? Oddly, I've never felt tempted towards serious alcoholism. Perhaps I've been holding that in reserve.'

John wanted to get back into the storm.

.   .   .   .

Gregory Hartshorn didn't like the tag which hung on in his

mind these days, something which had popped up from the desultory reading of youth. It was a prophecy of Nostradamus, made four hundred years ago, and it said: 'Before the end of the twentieth century, the yellow men will fly over Paris.'

He was not in the least superstitious, and he didn't believe that a French Jew had been given a special vision. The idea was absurd. And yet the words remained, resisting a purging of sense. They were unpleasantly appropriate to this moment in time.

Gregory leaned back in his chair. He pulled out a handkerchief and rubbed his eyes with it, then put on his spectacles again. He looked round his office. It seemed to him a slightly absurd setting for the work that had to be done here, oak panelling, red Turkey carpet, Chippendale, and the log show-fire that was kept burning most of the year in an iron-basket grate. The whole room suggested sanctuary from the world. In his job it should have been steel and glass, with a rubber plant, a background for ulcers.

His secretary reminded him that it was time for another television relay from the Garda conference. He walked over to a cabinet, pulled open concealing doors, revealing the screen. He switched the set on.

The Garda conference was getting the largest audience the world had ever known. Pictures from the public sessions were going live to the States by the new triple-Telstar hook-up, then relayed to Japan. Every nation in Europe was watching, and parts of Asiatic Russia. A billion viewers saw a compact, smallish man rise from a carved Renaissance chair unsmiling but composed, using English with total confidence. He was the last of the principal speakers before the meetings in private began, and Liu Fa Tsu had something of the presence of an old star who appears for the first time in the last act, but for whose performance everyone has been waiting. He looked directly at the cameras, as though he had taken pains to locate the lens eyes and he almost ignored the great U-shaped table around him. He spoke rapidly in a tone that was almost conciliatory. He stressed the strength of the new Sino-Soviet alliance, but pointed out that China, having satisfied national honour by bringing her own territorial islands back under her flag, was not at this conference to make any demands for herself, but only to support her Russian brothers in their insistence on a final settlement now of the Berlin problem. Liu didn't mention Formosa or an exchange of bombing raids with that rump of Old China. He stated, almost as if holding the brief for Solvonoff, that unless the Western world was ready immediately to discuss Berlin then military action to end a totally unnatural situation seemed the only course left open.

Liu Fa Tsu was quietly committing the Russians to a stand they had been very reluctant to make themselves. And after this speech they were faced with two alternatives, a very humiliating climb-down in front of the world, probably involving an open break with China, or an invasion of Berlin from East Germany.

Liu sat down. Almost at once the cameras switched to Solvonoff who was visibly sweating. Gregory felt a trickle along his own spine. Then there was Liu again, bending to one side to speak to an aide, and even smiling faintly. He had reason to be pleased with himself. Most delicately, by accenting the fact that there was no major problem in East Asia at all, Liu had put the pressure back where it had been for so long, between the Americans and the Russians. Gregory was suddenly certain that the Leader of China had come to Lake Garda to do just this, deftly side-stepping any real involvement in that old quarrel centred in Europe. At no point, for all his avowed loyalty to ideological allies, had Liu suggested that war against Russia automatically meant war against China. He hadn't talked of war at all. The Russians had been tricked by a much older chess player, left with their crisis raging while the dove of peace skimmed happily over Oriental waters.

CHAPTER TWELVE

Gregory closed the lid of his cigar box. These days he seemed always to be about to smoke one, then deciding not to. When he saw Angus Johnson he was glad of his decision. There was nothing dramatic about the man's entrance, just a tightness that was at once communicated.

'I came myself, Minister. I felt I'd better.'

It was Gregory's second meeting with the head of 'S' Branch, the first had been brief and formal, part of the routine for a new Minister.

Johnson didn't sit down, he went over to the fire. Gregory had to turn his chair. He had the feeling that the Scotsman was not sure of himself, and knew enough about the man to find this surprising.

'We have three listening posts in Burma, Mr Hartshorn. They're not easy to maintain, with Burmese aggressive neutrality, but we've done it. You don't pick up much that's valuable on short-range signals. However, we have this time, I think. From a place called Ta-Li in Yunnan. The Chinese have a secondary nuclear establishment there. We couldn't find out what they were doing at it. We have now. Small nuclear bombs, tactical weapons.'

'You mean there's been another test?'

'No. We haven't that kind of proof. We picked up a signal from a Russian scientist working at Ta-Li. In charge of research there, he claims. He's made them a compact, medium-power atomic device. Portable. Convenient, if you can use the word for the bloody things. Technical data given as corroboration was precise, and could only have come from an atomic scientist. The message came over for seven minutes. Fortunately our chap got it all down second time round. The listening points have been alerted for further messages, but there haven't been any so far.'

'Did this man defect from Russia?'

'Yes. Name of Roduschev. We've been onto that. He's a real man. The Russians sent him to China and he stayed, after a general recall. That's been known for some time. I'm damn sure this isn't any kind of hoax or trick, though I can't prove it. Roduschev said he was sending the signal because he's now certain that the Chinese mean to use his package bomb . . . and soon. He wants to stop them.'

'How do they mean to use it?'

'That's the snag. He doesn't know. The only clue he could give was a submarine.'

'Have they any?'

'We thought just small stuff. But I've been onto Washington on a scrambled line. Their Intelligence learned of a sale a few years ago of two obsolete Zirnov-class long-range submarines to the Chinese. In spite of supposed strained relations between them, the Russians must have trained the Chinese crews, because a Zirnov was tracked off the coast of California last year. And the Russians have scrapped the class.'

'The Americans didn't tell us about this?'

'It was their pigeon. No.'

'Have you any recent information about unidentified submarines?'

It was a moment before Johnson answered that. He really looked now like a man trying to contain shaken self-confidence.

'Yes, I do.'

For all of ten minutes Gregory listened without interrupting. Then he had to.

'Johnson, I don't get that? You say the captain of the *Maree Tarn* waited until he was in the Med. before he sent a signal about a submarine following his ship?'

'Yes. The captain has a plausible enough explanation for his delay. We queried his signal, and he answered again, via Malta. He said he hadn't sent the message further east because he didn't want it intercepted by the sub. He had a feeling his ship was still being followed, so he put on speed to shake it off. But there was engine trouble, and for all he knew the sub. was there behind them again. He was most emphatic that his ship was being tracked, it wasn't just a meeting at sea. It seemed to him highly probable that the sub. was following him up the Red Sea, only stopped by the canal. And we've got to say this for the captain, when he did send his message he identified that submarine very well indeed. No doubt about it being a Zirnov.'

'Didn't your man at Port Said get anything from this girl you have on board?'

'Not much. There wasn't time for one thing. She told Armitage that she thought Malthorp was mad, which is quite probable. And she did confirm that submarine. She saw it, too.'

'So the captain could just have been covering himself when he finally sent his report? He might by then have tumbled to the fact that the girl was an agent and had been contacted at Port Said.'

'Granted,' Johnson said. 'But the fact remains that a Chinese submarine was following a British ship. The Russians don't have that type in commission at all now. Even for training.'

Gregory took a long slow breath. Then he said:

'Is there any connection in your mind between the Chinese having this new atomic device, and this submarine following one of our ships which had spent a long time in a Chinese dry dock?'

'Aye, there's a connection in my mind all right. That's why I came to you. But I'm stopped by one thing. The Chinese would be mad to try and start anything with a bomb of this type, even if they had some kind of Pearl Harbour in mind. They'd be smothered themselves in a matter of hours by the really big stuff.'

'Where is the *Maree Tarn* making for?' Gregory asked.

'Gourock.'

The Minister stared at Johnson for a moment, then he got up. The wall-maps in the office were on rollers. He pulled one down, eight feet of the British Isles and the waters around it. Johnson came over to stand beside him.

'Where's the ship now?' Gregory's voice was tight.

'About here. Somewhere around eighty miles off the coast of Northern Ireland.'

Gregory saw the funnel of the Clyde leading up to Gourock, from which point there is an octopus of sea-lochs sending tentacles of water back into rough hills. Any ship approaching Gourock had to come within a mile or two of the American Polaris base in the Holy Loch, which was on the shortest of the tentacles. And in Washington he himself had tied down that base-ship, having a fight to do it.

It was no moment for panic. The Chinese couldn't have got word of that Pentagon arrangement. It couldn't be part of their plans because the *Maree Tarn* had left China before the mission to Washington had been thought of. And yet what did this Clyde area represent? Even without Polaris, it still remained one of the world's major targets in any blast of war between Russia and America. The rockets would fall here as quickly as they fell on New York. Or just one rocket. It was now a British nuclear-submarine base as well, over at Faslane on another of the loch tentacles. Just a short way up Loch Long was a major deep-water unloading point for the world's biggest oil tankers. Russia had a permanent fix on this area all the time, to wipe it out in the first smash-attack of nuclear war.

A policy of base dispersal in the nuclear age didn't make much sense, particularly in these **tiny** islands which could be almost totally shattered in minutes. Defence strategy against this kind of situation was only self-deception. But one fact remained, of all the top military targets in the world equal to this one in importance, the Clyde was probably the most vulnerable to sneak attack. Chinese Intelligence could have spotted this, a major target which could be approached without question by any shipping at all from any place in the world.

Gregory felt sick. Johnson was nearer the map. He turned.

'Minister, this is a first target for the Russians, all right. But what could the Chinese hope to do with a sneak attack?'

'They could start World War III,' Gregory said.

'What? With their little bomb? That went off without any Radar warning of a missile approach?'

'Johnson, we've no Radar screen to the Atlantic. It could be a missile from a Russian submarine taking advantage of that fact.'

'But the size of the explosion . . . !'

'Do you think anyone's going to stop to think about the calibre of a nuclear explosion when a major military target has been wiped out? Do you, Johnson? I don't. I think the button-pushing would start. And so do the Chinese!'

Johnson was looking now the way Gregory felt.

'A double-cross of their allies?'

Gregory nodded.

'Yes. China and Russia fell out over the business of a nuclear war to further Marxism. They've patched up the quarrel. But can we even begin to believe the Chinese have changed their minds? Of course they haven't. Johnson, these people care for nothing but their own world. Did you watch Liu Fa Tsu at Garda? Did he look like a man who would change the policy of China for a new age? To me he looked like a man neatly pulling off the first stage in history's most massive double-cross. The *Maree Tarn* has got to be stopped and boarded. Now!'

.   .   .   .

Admiral Whitcomb wore a monocle because only his left eye was defective. He needed the thing, but it still gave him just slightly the air of dated caricature. He was a pole of a man, over six feet three, with a stoop from his neck which might have come from years at sea and keeping his head bent for low bulkhead doors. He waited for the rotors to cut, and then, as Gregory jumped down from the helicopter, walked forward to meet the Defence Minister with a jerky formality suggesting a parade ground rather than this remoteness of an English country-house lawn at dusk.

'This way, sir,' Whitcomb said. 'We're ready for you.'

Gregory was conscious, as often with senior officers in the

186

services, of a strict ration of courtesy offered without the slightest hint of any potential personal warmth behind it. In the Pentagon you tended to be received with an easy assumption of the possibility of friendship, whatever disillusionment on this score might be in store for later, but he had never once met this approach from British top brass. They didn't like him, they thought his appointment idiocy, and in consequence all that was issued was basic politeness.

Half way across the lawn to the house Gregory said:

'What did you think of the American President's speech, Admiral?'

'Short and tough. No negotiation over Berlin from any position of blackmail. He answered Liu Fa Tsu before the Chink spoke.'

This was true enough. The Americans were in no mood for compromise. If something had to give it wasn't going to be them, though it was becoming increasingly obvious that something had to give somewhere.

There was no small area of hopefulness in Gregory's feelings. What he had expected, on many counts, was precisely what was happening. It was as though that computer eject from the subconscious the P.M. had talked about was now putting out a printed pattern on which the moves behind them were marked and the moves ahead indicated clearly. Liu's timing had been almost perfect. He had planned to come to the conference for one purpose, which he had fulfilled, and he was now waiting for the right moment to leave Garda. It seemed to Gregory a certainty that Liu would be the first to go, withdrawing from the conference in order to break it up. And his departure could, in a very real way, be connected with the movement of the *Maree Tarn*. The Leader of China planned to be back home, or at least well on the way, before hell was let loose in the world he didn't care about. Even the timing of the conference had come from Liu, the West accommodating itself to the Sino-Russian suggestion of dates and a rather long delay. The West had been allowed to choose place.

The Admiral and the Defence Minister went towards french windows behind a terrace. The house they entered was

Queen-Anne, pleasantly set, with the gardens an order of massed bloom just visible in the last light. They went into the chintz and antique dimness of a sitting-room where two Ming table-lamps glowed, and from it to a high cool hall. Here twin steel doors had been fitted into panelling, and the lift behind them was a utility steel box lit by a single bulb. They seemed to go down in it a long way.

The operations room was vast, with a girdered steel ceiling. One wall, forty feet high, was an illumined map of Britain. Desks radiated away from this map and there were at least fifty people down here. Gregory was led up to a chair on a control-gallery. Whitcomb sat beside him.

'The red light,' he said, 'is the *Maree Tarn*. We're keeping it moving with the ship. She's covered by high-flying reconnaissance, but we don't know how long that's going to last.'

'Why?'

'Fog,' the admiral said. 'Irish Channel and right out beyond Islay there. Visibility isn't a boat length. Clyde traffic at a standstill. The *Maree Tarn* will move into that fog about Rathlin Island. That's just off the north Irish coast.'

'And what have you got to intercept the *Maree Tarn*?'

'Those two green lights,' the admiral said.

'They're a long way off!'

'Yes.'

'Haven't you got something nearer?'

'No, sir. The corvette *Hesperus* is making full speed in from the Atlantic towards Rathlin Island. The submarine *Avenger* is coming up the Irish Channel and she'll be at the mouth of the Clyde between the mainland and the point of Kintyre in about four hours.'

'Admiral, there must be something nearer! What about up-river? Gourock?'

'Launches. That's all we've got. Only one Radar-equipped. The submarine *Parthan* has just gone into dry dock at Faslane, and we could get her out again, but it would be half a day before she was down-river. All the Polaris subs. are gone from the Holy Loch. A U.S. signal says they're not available for recall. They're on patrol. If the *Maree Tarn* gets into that fog, we can rule out air. She must be stopped by Rathlin. We've been waiting for you to send this signal.'

'I can't believe there isn't something nearer!'

'Minister. The Royal Navy is thinner now than ever before in our history. Nearly everything we've got is tied up with N.A.T.O. commitments. They're all on the east. There's a fishery cruiser moving south from Oban, but I don't think she'd be much use. I would point out that it isn't the Navy's fault, we simply haven't the ships . . . sir!'

Gregory stared at the map.

'Send that signal to the *Maree Tarn*,' he said.

. . . .

Leslie, the radio officer, was the ship's recluse. He had one large room full of equipment and a small cabin off it. Usually he contrived to have Ginnis bring up his meals, avoiding the saloon. Milton claimed that the boy had undergone a traumatic experience with a Bombay tart at the age of sixteen, and certainly he was very chary about shore excursions when the ship was tied up.

Everyone knocked on the door of the radio cabin before entering, even the captain. Ginnis had his own special knock, and the chief steward kept a little separate niche of warmth for Leslie who never noticed what he ate and was a regular and tidy consumer of the ship's menu failures. Under an aluminium cover, this evening, was a last Malayan *papaya*, withered almost dry in refrigeration, and arranged beside it a hunk from a large fish originally caught off Singapore and solemnly rejected in the dining-room for three nights running even when smeared with the assistant cook's wild bid for *tartare* sauce. The steak had travelled from one side of the world to the other, then back again after dry dock, and was mutinous about not being allowed to decompose gently.

Ginnis set down the tray. He lifted the lid with a flourish.

'There you are then. As nice a little meal as you'd get at the Ritz.'

Leslie looked up through spectacles. He plucked off earphones.

'What? Oh, thanks. Ginnis, what do you make of Malthorp?'

The steward considered this.

'A bit strange, I must say.'

'A bit? I think he's nuts. I've had him in here for nearly three quarters of an hour. Came in saying he wanted to send a radiogram, so I quoted him rates and said I could get it off at once. Then he stalled, and said maybe it was too early and he ought to wait until we knew when the ship would get to Gourock. Talked about getting reporters to meet him.'

'From the newspapers?'

'Yes, it was pretty vague. I got the feeling he was snooping, the way he hung on. He knows a bit about radio, and he seemed to be trying to turn things into a social hour I didn't want. Then the weirdest thing of all. I think he was trying to bribe me. Not that he flashed a roll. But said he was in a difficult personal situation and it would be a great help to him if he knew of any messages coming in about him. To the captain. I got the feeling I could name my price for giving him a dekko at any signal to the skipper that had Malthorp's name in it. What do you make of all that?'

'I don't know, Mr Leslie. But I'll be seeing the skipper in a wee bit, would you like me to tell him?'

'No, leave it. I can deal with Malthorp.'

'Then eat your supper. Don't let it get cold.'

Ten minutes after the steward had gone, every plate on the tray was empty and ready for the dishwasher. As he swung his chair around again to the radio table the fog-horn started, and he saw himself on all-night duty as they crept through the muck, locating any other ships in the area. Even if they anchored, he still had to check to keep something from running them down.

The call sign made him sit bolt upright.

'Admiralty calling *Maree Tarn* on 275, top priority. Admiralty calling *Maree Tarn*, top priority. Over.'

'*Maree Tarn* to Admiralty on 275, over.'

He took the message down carefully and repeated it back. He acknowledged and signed off. Then he crossed the cabin to his typewriter and sat at it. He spoiled the first sheet and had to re-do it. He was a tidy man. He heard the door open and turned his head.

'Just a minute, sir. I've got a signal here from Admiralty . . .'

Leslie didn't see the gun, or hear it, for the fog-horn went again, smothering the sound of a revolver blast in the cabin.

.   .   .   .

The little tapping fingers at the base of his skull frightened Malthorp. He knew what came after the fingers, suddenly a hand clamped down on his brain, pressing it, numbing reason.

At one point on this voyage he had thought his headaches were coming under control, more spaced out, the muzzy half-delirium from them not so overwhelming. They had told him in Singapore that he needed rest and a long sea voyage to get back an appetite. He was to have no worries. God, no worries! What did they know? How could a hunted man have no worries?

The radio officer had suspected something, seeing a man blundering about his purpose, not able to conceal it with words. Words had betrayed him, as though he had lost any knack in their use. And that youth just waiting to put on earphones again had almost laughed.

Malthorp lit a cigarette. Sometimes, if you didn't give in to it, the pain went away. It threatened a visit and then withdrew. There had been moments on this ship when he had really believed he was going to get rid of it, as though his living was suddenly out on a flat from which he could see in every direction, as a whole man should. He had laughed at their jokes in the saloon, when they had still been making them. Now everyone worried about war.

He didn't worry about it. It was something far off, something he couldn't see and didn't try to. There were closer shadows, much more frightening. That girl they'd sent along to watch him, she didn't frighten him at all, the apprentice, her techniques creakingly obvious. It had been like a game dealing with her, almost an entertainment. The girl was nothing, but the men waiting for this ship to come into port weren't nothing.

There was a way out. He'd used it in that Hong Kong hospital when they thought they had him, when he was tucked away in a private ward with a man on a chair in the passage outside. He had been in a trap there, but he'd got out of it. He had threatened Armitage with the one thing he couldn't risk, reporters, publicity. That would work again.

The big London dailies all had their Scottish editions, with printing-houses in Glasgow. Even with the war-scare stories these days, the editors would be interested in a man coming back from the grave of a Chinese prison. They would send their reporters to the ship, all of them pressing for a story, crowding out the other men who would be there. Armitage wouldn't get him at Gourock either, not if he could get through to those papers.

The pain in his head was becoming more than a touch. He became helpless for hours after a real clamp down. If he was going to do anything he had to do it now, before he forgot, before he lay whimpering and helpless on his bunk.

He got up. He felt dizzy. The blast of the fog-horn didn't help. What he had to do was quite easy. There was no need to find out addresses, the name of the paper and Glasgow would be enough. The reporters would come on that, and cameramen, too, maybe. Well, this time he'd welcome them. Let them take all the pictures they wanted. The more publicity the better. Mr Malthorp returning from China. 'How does it feel to be free, Mr Malthorp?' Mr Malthorp escaping from the plain men with flat faces by publicity, a story on the front page. It would work! It would serve him for as long as he needed, get him to London where he would sell the agency over Walcott's head, and for a good price, too. Walcott had been running the business in Singapore for seven years, and made a good thing of it . . . for himself. But there wasn't so much money available. Not nearly enough for the life he wanted now, away from Britain, safe, the West Indies maybe. He would get a good price for the agency on the London market, trade was expanding out east. The new owners could keep Walcott on if they wanted. He didn't give a damn what they did so long as he got the money, enough to buy himself a complete new life. That's what he wanted. He'd beat Armitage or anyone to get it.

The reporters . . . bring them to the ship.

In the corridor, the pain caught him like a claw. He began to sway under it, using the guide-rails because he had to. There was no one in the lobby or out on the shelter-deck. He lurched towards the companion stairs leading up, and on them heard the sound of his own breathing loud in his ears. He had to take each step carefully, his eyes suddenly weren't too good. Your eyes packed in sometimes, altogether.

Someone was coming down from the boat-deck above him. Malthorp looked up into a face. He knew it quite well. It was a face he had seen often recently, but it still meant nothing to him, only a man he was passing on one side of the stairs. He began to pull himself up by his arms.

It was cool on the boat-deck, almost cold. There was a light near the bridge steps and another blurred by a curtain pulled over the port-hole of the radio cabin. He went towards the closed door and put his hand out for the softly shining brass handle.

It was then that he was put back into a dream, of China, of walking around a concrete yard alone on his daily exercise, with the armed guard standing near a barred door. But not always standing, either. The dream turned into a nightmare of a guard coming up softly behind a shuffling man to end all terrors and all furies with the small round circle of a gun pushed against the base of a prisoner's neck.

Henry Malthorp stood quite still. He felt that cold roundness at the base of his skull. And then the siren roared.

CHAPTER THIRTEEN

The fog-horn didn't put John Lownie up on the bridge at
once, he had been expecting it anyway. He knew his ship's
position, Rathlin Island three miles to starboard, their course
towards the point of Kintyre and then a sharp turn north into
the lower reaches of the Clyde. He finished a small whisky
which he needed. It was going to be a mucky night. Then he
went up.

Haslett was standing behind the Radar screen.

'I cut her to six knots, sir.'

'Right. Anything on the screen?'

'Nothing at all.'

'Sparks had still better locate all known shipping. See him
will you?'

'Yes, sir.'

Haslett went down the bridge steps. John was at the
windows, peering forward, when he heard the step beside him.
The mate's face was a weird pallor under tan.

'What's the matter?'

Haslett swallowed.

'Leslie. He's . . . dead!'

John turned and ran. The door of the radio cabin was still
back. Something moved in there. It was Ginnis coming to the
door, his mouth open.

'Look! The boy's been shot! I was coming for his tray.
Look!'

'Shut up, Ginnis!'

Leslie was on the floor, by his typing chair. He had twisted about in falling, and his eyes stared. There was blood on the floor. It looked as though the killer had used an axe in the cabin, doing a job of destruction which he understood. There was now no radio on the *Maree Tarn*. The stand-by set had got it, too.

'What are you going to do, sir? Leslie was just a laddie. I . . . I brought him his supper!'

'Did you touch anything in here, Ginnis?'

'What? No. I was going for the tray, you understand. And the door was open. I just stepped in. And then you came . . .'

'Get outside.' John turned the key. 'I'm locking the cabin. I want you to fetch the bos'n. He's to put a stout padlock on here and bring me the key. Understand?'

'Yes, sir. Oh, my God! What's happening on this ship?'

'We'll find out. Meantime keep your mouth shut. Don't talk to the crew. It'll get around, but don't push it out.'

'Sir . . . that Malthorp . . .'

'What about him?'

'He was hanging around here. Mr Leslie told me. When I took him his tray. Malthorp was hanging around for a long time. He wanted to send radiograms or something.'

John swung away to the bridge steps. Haslett was again behind the Radar screen, his curiously innocent face a map of horror.

'Come into the chart-room,' John said. He shut the door. 'Malthorp was hanging around the radio cabin. Leslie told Ginnis about it. I want you to find that man and bring him to my day-cabin. If he isn't in his own cabin, get a couple of sailors and search the ship. I'll take your duty here meantime. We're going up to Gourock tonight. Through this muck and as fast as we can. I'm going up to ten knots.'

'In the river, sir? It's closed tight. There's no visibility now beyond the ship. And it'll probably get worse.'

'I know the Clyde,' John said. 'We're going up. We've got Radar, even if no radio.'

'Are the sets hopeless? I didn't really look.'

'Yes, out. Nothing we can do about it. Milton or anyone.

The only thing to do is get to the police at Gourock as fast as we can. This is a job for them. And them alone.'

. . . .

Gregory Hartshorn hadn't left the control-gallery for more than three minutes in over three hours. Beside him was a mug of coffee. On the vast map the red light showed now just beyond Rathlin Island, moving towards the Mull of Kintyre and the reaches of the Clyde. One of the green lights was off Malin Head in Donegal and the other in the North Channel from the Irish Sea, moving up past the Rinns of Galloway towards Ailsa Craig.

All aircraft were grounded, reconnaissance from that source cut off. An admiralty launch, the *Viceroy*, had left Greenock and was probing through the fog, but it was tiny and unarmed. At Gourock twelve merchantmen lay anchored, waiting for the weather to lift, immobilized by the thick pall. The Cunard liner *Melantic*, bound for Liverpool with twelve hundred passengers on board, had signalled that she intended to anchor off Rathlin Island for the night, and had been given the puzzling order to turn back out to sea for at least fifty miles. The order had been queried and repeated. A forty-thousand-ton tanker from Galveston, Texas, a hundred miles out in the Atlantic, bound for the pumping station on Loch Long, had been told to cut speed to five knots.

Admiral Whitcomb came back and took his chair. Gregory didn't even turn his head.

'Still no answer from the *Maree Tarn*?'

'Damn all,' Whitcomb said. 'We tried to get her on everything. That signal was received, acknowledged ... then nothing.'

'The radio's been knocked out.' Gregory's voice was harsh. 'I'm getting Johnson on a scrambled line. We can't wait any longer.'

He put the call to exchange and then, waiting, finished the cold coffee. At the first burr, he had the receiver in his hand.

'Johnson?'

'Yes, Minister?'

'Those signals have been going out to your agent?'

'Every fifteen minutes since four-thirty.'

'What are the chances of her picking them up?'

'Poor. We set 10 p.m. as the listening time. But we've sent nothing until today. She mightn't listen on her last night.'

'My God! It's a wonderful communications hook-up. An adapted portable. Couldn't you have done better than that?'

'How? We couldn't smuggle a two-way set on board at Port Said, could we?'

'No, I know. Listen. I want to change the signal. It's to include an order to the captain of the *Maree Tarn*. An Admiralty order. He is to stop the ship at once, wherever he is. The Navy will rendezvous with her when she's anchored. If the captain refuses to listen to your agent, she's to stop the ship on her own, somehow. Get that?'

'Yes.'

Gregory hung up. He looked at the admiral.

'What about helicopters?'

'Can't move in this. Wouldn't pick up the ship from the air even if they did get up. We haven't coastal Radar in the area. But the captain won't push up river in that muck. What possible reason could he have for doing it?'

'I don't know,' Gregory said. 'But there might be a reason, a good one. Making the captain push on. How long before the *Avenger* picks up the *Maree Tarn* on her Radar?'

'Depends on the freighter's speed. That couldn't be more than four knots in close fog. In which case she should be in Radar range in about an hour. Maybe a little more.'

A door opened behind them. A petty officer handed a folded sheet to Whitcomb which he opened, stared at, then passed over to Gregory.

REPORT TOP SECRET. NAVAL BASE, FORMERLY SUBMARINE SUPPLY AND REPAIR, NORTH AFRICAN REPUBLIC OF GOMBI, CLOSED FROM SIXTH THIS MONTH TO SEVENTEENTH. INTENSE SECURITY PRECAUTIONS. UNCONFIRMED INCREASE OF CHINESE TRADE-MISSION TO GOMBI BY TWENTY-SEVEN MEN ON JET FLIGHT FROM CAIRO THIRD OF THIS MONTH. AIR RECONNAISSANCE

'Your second Chinese sub. could be in the Atlantic all right,' Whitcomb said. 'And trailing the *Maree Tarn* now. But one thing I don't see. The Clyde area has plenty of rain and fog, but dammit, the Chinese couldn't rely on having that kind of weather waiting for them! Supposing it had been fine? Any submarine surfacing in the river would have been spotted as sure as hell. How would they have picked up their agent then?'

'The submarine wouldn't have rendezvoused in the Clyde at all. Look, Admiral, we had that report from the atomic research people. Almost certainly this type of bomb has to be primed manually. But it can then be triggered from a considerable distance. I think this weather has hit them, too. It's meant the agent has had to stay on board until well up the Clyde.'

'Why? To see the ship as near the target area as he can risk?'

'Yes,' Gregory said.

'Then how the hell would they have worked it in good weather? Supposing a bomb could be triggered from as far away as out north of Ireland, and the agent got on the sub. there to do it . . . how would they know just when the *Maree Tarn* was sailing into Gourock?'

'From agents on shore.'

'You mean Chinese agents?'

'I do.'

'Minister, an agent on shore reporting accurately that the *Maree Tarn* was on target would be in the target area himself!'

'Yes. He wouldn't know why he had been ordered to watch a ship. He'd send in the report that was his own death sentence, too. Probably from Gourock itself. What do the lives of a few agents matter in something like this? Especially to the Chinese?'

'My God!' the admiral said.

He stared at the map with its lights.

'There's another point, Minister. That enemy agent on

board is now going to have to *estimate* how long it's going to take the *Maree Tarn* to reach target from the point where he leaves her. I'm a sailor, but I wouldn't like to make that kind of guess about a ship's probable progress up river in a fog.'

Gregory said quietly:

'Not even if you were in command of that ship, Admiral? And left clear orders on the bridge before you got off?'

.　　.　　.　　.

Gerda was sick of the trawler wave-band. As soon as the *Maree Tarn* was in the Atlantic and within range, she had kept her 10 p.m. vigil with the portable set, listening to captains and crews on their way to or from the Iceland white-fishing. These men used the air over vast distances for some extraordinary gossip, interspersed with touching domestic messages like an appeal for two pairs of heavy wool socks left in a chest at home to be forwarded by mail to Reykjavik. There was one captain whose wife apparently had short-wave by her fireside, and hubby called her up daily from wild northern seas to find out how she had spent her afternoon. But the talk was rarely uxorious, usually just plain male, and Gerda had become weary of that one verb which also does such astonishing overtime throughout the English-speaking world as an adjective. None of the fishermen or their land contacts ever mentioned world crisis, which was in itself something of a relief.

She switched on for what she hoped was the last time. With any luck, Nannie and she would be on a night sleeper from Glasgow by this time tomorrow, her miserable little task of keeping an eye on Malthorp over.

Crackling covered a distant voice that seemed to be sending a love-lorn appeal from just out of range, a strange, faded whimpering. And then loud across it came her call sign:

'Base to Eastern Star. Repeat Base to Eastern Star.'

Gerda hadn't a pencil handy, and had a moment of sickness at this incompetence. She groped in her bag, missing the first sentence, praying for a repeat as she used her own shorthand. The repeat came. And as the long message was read slowly for a second time, she found her thought entangled with an idiot bid to make sense out of what was a designed banality.

She stared at the pad and groped for a memorized code, skip the first word, skip the next two, skip three, then reverse, two, one. Her pencil stroked out the padding.

'A . . . device . . . on . . . ship . . . destruction . . . American . . . Clyde . . . base . . . war . . . navy . . . order . . . to . . . captain . . . stop . . . ship . . . anchor . . . now . . . if . . . captain . . . refuses . . . your . . . initiative . . . stop . . . ship . . . enemy . . . agent . . . on . . . board.'

For a moment 'a . . . device' stopped her. Then she knew what it meant.

Gerda burned the paper, holding it over the wash-basin, running the tap. She put on a cardigan, and, opening her hand-bag, took a gun from it, sliding this into a holder sewn onto the knitting. She opened her cabin door. Nannie's door was caught back, with a curtain over it.

'Gerda?'

'Yes? I've got to go on deck for a moment.'

'Not before you hear this. I just perjured myself for you. I hope I was right?'

Gerda pulled back the curtain. Nannie was sitting on the settee with her feet up, holding recently lacquered nails out to dry. She had returned to full make-up, including green eye-shadow, and now looked like a Récamier who has hung on for a quarter of a century too long.

'What are you talking about?'

'I wonder you didn't hear, darling. You must have had your souvenir radio on. It was that beautiful boy Haslett, but troubled tonight.'

'Nannie, I must go up.'

'Very well! All I did was say you hadn't got Malthorp secreted in your cabin. Because apparently they've lost him.'

'Lost him?'

'Well, they can't find him any place. I'd offer to help, but one can't run around being useful with wet finger nails. So you can join in. It's all very dramatic, but I'm not expecting an exciting denouement. Unless, of course, the poor fellow has jumped overboard. He's been odd again recently . . .'

Gerda went up the aisle. Out on the shelter-deck she stood by the rail for just a moment, thinking about what she had to do. There was a scuffling above her, and, after a blast from the horn, clearly voices. She went up the companion steps to stand at the top in shadow, just behind the covered canopy.

There were men down beyond one of the boat-davits shining torches. One moved back towards the radio cabin, keeping light on planking, but enough was reflected to show Gerda a padlocked door and a dark port-hole above it. She heard John Lownie say:

'He was dragged across the deck all right.'

'You mean shoved overboard?' That was Haslett.

'What else? Easy to do here. Push him under a life-boat. No rail. No lifting. Only the killer forgot about blood. Maybe Malthorp saw something, coming up here. And because of that he had to go. He could have seen the killer coming away.'

'We don't know the blood is Malthorp's!'

'Who else is missing?'

'Do you want me to check the crew, sir?'

'No. It was Malthorp all right. Were both the women in their cabins just now?'

'Yes, though I didn't see Miss Lane. But she had her radio on, and the old girl said she was in there alone.'

'You didn't see her?' John's voice was soft. 'Then perhaps I'd better.'

'You can, Captain,' Gerda said.

He shone the torch on her, as he had done once before.

'Don't do that, damn you!'

'Shall we go to my day-cabin, Miss Lane? Haslett, get back on the bridge. There's nothing more we can do here.'

The captain walked beside her across the boat-deck, through the dark area at the centre of the cross-over. Then he switched on cabin lights.

'Sit down, Miss Lane.'

She shook her head.

'Why were you standing watching us?'

'I heard something from below and came up.'

'You've been on the spot quite often on this voyage.'

'I was coming up here to find you.'

'I see. Your watching of Malthorp slipped up, didn't it?'

'I wasn't watching him any more. He was a sick man. I could see that. Eaten up with fears that didn't mean anything. Only to him. There was nothing I could do.'

'Miss Lane, my radio officer has been murdered. And I'm sure Malthorp died because he saw the killer. Have you any theories about this double murder on my ship?'

Gerda had to sit down then. It was suddenly as though John Lownie's talk of murder had made that radio message to her come alive. Two men had already died on a ship which someone was planning to use as an instrument of mass killing. And because of those two dead she could see it as something real, terror on a scale that was beyond earlier imaginings.

The siren went. During the noise of that she saw his eyes, like stones, watching her. She wanted to cry out to him that they were two people still alive in a world that could soon be for the dead. Instead, when she heard her voice, there was no appeal in it, just the flat tones of fact, her radio, her instructions, and the message. There seemed a lot to tell in this way, with no help from him, a man listening but no more, a long way off standing there, a stranger with a cold heart. She found herself at the end not even looking at him, her eyes down to the floor, like a liar with something to hide.

Gerda jerked her head up.

'It's an Admiralty order, Captain!'

'So you say. Would you like a brandy?'

'No! Listen to me. This isn't any kind of hoax. It couldn't be. My call sign and my code. And the trawler band. Everything. It's real. I know it isn't easy to believe at first, but it's happening. You've got to stop this ship now!'

'I don't take orders from passengers, Miss Lane.'

'Oh, my God! *I'm* not giving the order. You know that. Do you mean . . . you still don't believe this?'

His face hadn't changed. In his eyes was no reflection of the misery she was feeling and which she knew must show. He had only to look at her to see that she was telling the truth, but he continued to stand like a man who had been listening with no growing feelings of conviction at all. There was no sign of any reaction to what she had told him. It mightn't even be a surprise to Captain Lownie that there was a nuclear bomb on his ship.

'I think you'd better go back to your cabin now, Miss Lane.'

She stared.

'What do you mean by that? You're not going to stop at once?'

'I'll do what I think best.'

She couldn't look at him any more. She remembered the last part of that message, which she hadn't told him about, that was personal to her. They were her instructions in the event of the captain not being convinced.

'Don't think, Miss Lane, I'm not taking action on what you've told me. I need a little time.'

'There isn't time!'

'I'm still taking it. Now please go back to your cabin. It would be best if you stayed there. Don't wander round the ship.'

He was polite. Damn him, he was polite!

Gerda got up. She walked towards the door, but she didn't open it. She turned, a gun in her hand.

'Captain Lownie, I was told to stop this ship myself if you wouldn't listen to me.'

'Were you?' he said gently.

'Go over to the intercom. And give the order to stop engines from here.'

'If I refuse to move?'

'I'll put a bullet in your leg . . . first.'

He smiled.

'Well. Is that what they taught you at your training school?

The fog-horn went. John kicked over the table in front of him. Her bullet split it. She lifted the gun and took aim again. He was down behind a chair, and, in the bellowing beyond them, she saw the chair lift. She fired. He gave a shout that was loud as the siren ended, making her jerk forward. She fired again as he rushed her, but without aim, and was pinned back against the teak door, both her arms against the wood, out above her head. Pressure on one wrist forced her fingers open. The gun fell. He said, into her face:

'Well, bitch?'

She kicked him. He pushed his weight against her, almost casually, holding her that way, reaching out with one hand to yank down the woven silk cord which held back the curtains at a port-hole. He swung her round, against her struggles, and the cord bit into her wrists. He put a hand over her face and an arm about her waist, dragging her back into the cabin.

He held her in the middle of the floor, waiting for the siren, and when it came threw her down hard. Gerda cracked her head against the splintered table. She saw him go for another cord and pushed herself up, making for the inner cabin. She called out as he caught her again. He pulled her over the sill and got her to the berth. When she screamed he put a pillow over her face, holding it there until all she could think about was breathing again. He let her do that, and while she gasped tied her feet. Gerda couldn't even fight the gag he made from two handkerchiefs with an almost boy-scout deftness. Leaning over, he forced her clamped jaws open.

A blanket was ripped off the berth from under her. He took this to the small bathroom and dropped it on the tiles. Then he carried her over. There was no port-hole in there, just an extractor-fan which whirred while the light was on. He left the light on.

. . . .

SIGNAL H.M.S. AVENGER TO ADMIRALTY STOP TOP SECRET STOP VESSEL PROCEEDING UP CLYDE WITHIN RADAR RANGE STOP ESTIMATED SPEED TEN KNOTS STOP CLEAR INDICATIONS UNDER-WATER CRAFT MOVING SAME SPEED SURFACE VESSEL EITHER JUST TO STERN OR UNDER HULL STOP ESTIMATED SUBMERSION EIGHTY FEET STOP HAVE MADE NO ATTEMPT RADIO IDENTIFICATION STOP INSTRUCTIONS SIGNED ASTON COMMANDER.

Gregory turned his head.

'What instructions are you going to give, Admiral?'

Whitcomb lit a cigarette. His fingers were shaking. That was somehow surprising. Gregory didn't think the admiral's fingers had often trembled.

'We could pick her off,' Whitcomb said.

'And what would that do to the *Maree Tarn*?'

'Blow her to hell, too.'

'That bomb could be primed now. Wouldn't a secondary explosion trigger it?'

'I just don't know! And I don't think anyone could tell us.' He got up and shouted: 'Get me charts of the Clyde above Bute.'

Under the admiral's hand the chart did a lot of talking. Islands bar the entry into the inner Firth of Clyde. There is the massive bulk of Bute, then a narrow channel between a point on it and Little Cumbrae Island, with another channel between Little Cumbrae and the mainland. Beyond Little Cumbrae the channel is much shallower.

'Once past Cumbrae, that sub. can't stay down at eighty feet,' Whitcomb said. 'She'll have to surface behind the *Maree Tarn* or somewhere near her. I'd say astern, to pick up the agent. This could be the rendezvous point they've fixed up. The ship is bound to cut speed here to a point which would let the agent get off safely over the stern.'

'What about the Chinese sub. picking up the *Avenger* on their Radar?'

'No risk of that. We've got them at maximum range. Latest equipment. Far better than anything on an old-class Zirnov submarine. And believe me, the Russians won't have given away their best Radar. No . . . the Chinks think they're getting away with it. They can't know they're tailed.'

'Admiral, if the *Maree Tarn* gets past Cumbrae and is continuing up-river, we can take it that the girl hasn't been able to do anything. So we've got to. Somewhere a good way before Gourock. The *Avenger* must close at speed now.'

'For a kill?'

'What else, man? What else can we do!'

'Nothing,' said Admiral Whitcomb.

Gregory put a finger down on the chart.

'We can't risk letting the *Maree Tarn* beyond here . . . Toward Point. Will your sub. be in range for a torpedo by here?'

'Easily.'

Gregory's eyes took in the names of the towns that would

be in the area of total destruction from an atomic bomb. Little towns, Rothesay, Wemyss Bay, Innellan . . . nothing to what lay up-river. The few instead of the many. God help him!

The ceiling speaker hissed.

'News flash just received. The Prime Minister of China, Liu Fa Tsu, has walked out of the Lake Garda Conference. He is now *en route* by plane to China.'

It was another confirmation for that computer eject pattern in Gregory's brain.

.   .   .   .

On the *Maree Tarn*, night visibility was nil. Even with the foredeck cargo-lights switched on, the peak of the bows and the look-out stationed there were at times hidden from the bridge by swirling fog-drifts. These came like grey, illumined sorties from a massed blackness beyond. At ten knots, the ship trembled gently and each blast of the horn beat against nerves.

Haslett, at the Radar screen, was a frightened man. This was in his voice as he called out:

'Little Cumbrae on the screen, sir!'

John took a deep breath. The muscles in his arms ached.

'Right. Engine-room, three knots!'

The relief at this order was something felt. It was quickly acted on.

Milton was on the bridge, too. The second mate had a curious instinct for the climactic moment. He had missed being about at the discovery of Leslie's murder, and the second murder, but he was missing nothing else now, up here when it wasn't his duty, as though to be an eye-witness to what could easily be an unnecessary marine disaster brought about by a skipper's idiocy.

The second mate wasn't obtrusive, back against a bulkhead in half-shadow, but John felt his presence like an emanation, a man waiting in something near to detached interest, the intelligent observer. It was easy to see him at an inquiry, giving his evidence with a modest economy calculated to show

206

up the correctness of his own performance against the folly of a superior. He had been on the bridge because of the natural anxiety of a deck-officer over his captain's eccentric handling of a situation. Ten knots up an inland waterway at night in maximum fog was enough to alarm any man.

John was quite certain that Milton had never wasted half an hour of his living in any emotional blind alley. His life was the spinning of a cocoon with each new strand making the spinner more secure.

It was an odd moment to be thinking about Milton, or any member of his crew. They had all been assembled by others for his command, and not one a real friend. A kind of paternalism had seemed something valid at moments, but he knew this had been just a by-product of authority. His heart had not really warmed to any of the people who sat with him at table in the saloon, voyage after voyage. Leslie, perhaps. But the radio officer, too, had been a solitary.

John knew that the world which had made him had also put down a bar of strangeness. And each return to the Far East had seen a curious lifting of spirits, always for disillusionment, but recurring, as though any promise for him was in some pattern at the other side of the world on which he had not yet stumbled.

Mabel and the house in Singora.

He was covering what he had to do by these speculations, not wanting to look at what waited. For there was nothing to think about there, it was fixed and certain, inescapable now.

His feet told him of the altered engine tone, and a diminishing vibration. The glowing screen-eye behind picked out familiar landfalls, but for his eye there was only the black fog, the lights below increasing the feeling of a moving ship held in the night's blindness, a captive. The siren was a voice of distress and of terrible loneliness.

John turned.

'Haslett, you're in charge.'

'Yes, sir. But we'll be in the channel in fifteen minutes!'

'Stop engines in seven minutes,' John said. 'Then anchor.'

He turned away to the bridge steps.

CHAPTER FOURTEEN

Captain John Lownie stood on the steel-grilled platform just beyond the main door to the engine-room, on a balcony suspended above moving machinery, with beneath him an oiled, clean inferno that was still hot and smelling, and with its own elaborate mysteries. It was Henderson's kingdom and the captain was an intruder.

He saw Potkin, twenty-five feet below, moving about with an outsize oil-can, his head a little on one side as though even in that din a trained ear could detect a wrong note. He spent his life listening and oiling and wiping away sweat. He didn't look up.

John checked his watch. It was the seven minutes. Haslett would certainly be punctual about stopping the ship. The captain stood there hearing his own order reaching the engine-room and seeing the moment of Potkin's slight surprise. Then the man went to a control panel, pulled levers, and the piston movement showed alteration in seconds. Potkin walked down the steel decking to a closed door. He knocked on that door but didn't open it, as though the place was a sanctuary barred to him. John heard the shout above engine noise.

'Chief? The bridge has ordered full stop.'

The pistons were slowing as another two oilers came aft, one of them dragging at a cigarette and keeping an eye on the old man's door as he did it. They didn't look up, either.

The door opened. Henderson was wearing a jacket, which

seemed formal for an eighty-degree atmosphere, and it some-how made him look bundled up. The noise of machinery began to subside into the cushion of a soft, continuous hissing.

'Full stop?' The chief sounded angry. 'What's happening up there?'

John said:

'The bridge is obeying my order.'

Heads lifted, but that was all. It was like a sudden still-shot, everything frozen, the two oilers almost at attention, Potkin with a rag in one hand. The uniformed skipper up there at the entrance to their steel cave was a shock, a break with estab-lished tradition. They expected his voice but never his presence.

'I want to see you, Chief,' John said, and started down the curving iron stair to a narrow gallery half way up from the engine-room floor. From there it was a steel ladder the rest of the way down.

Even the hissing had gone from the engine-room. The captain's feet made dull thuds on metal treads. He looked down, and, as he did, Henderson turned, suddenly running, down aft, hidden by machinery, Potkin and the oilers staring after him.

There was a water-tight bulkhead door at the end of the engine-room leading to fuel stores. Henderson had only to close it and pull down one of the clamps that was on his side when he was through the opening.

John swung around again and went up the stairs. Henderson was working aft through a labyrinth of the ship's guts. John had to go up two decks, one iron stair to the galleys and crew's quarters, and from there another flight to the ship's lobby.

Ginnis was in the dining-room, setting tables. He stared through glass doors and dropped a spoon. John ran down the long corridor to the door just beyond Malthorp's cabin, which opened out onto the aft shelter-deck. He yanked this door open and pushed against the rail, peering down.

Glow from an oyster light deepened the darkness of the well-deck, but a figure emerged almost directly below John. Henderson had thrown off his jacket and was wearing a light-coloured, vest-type life-preserver which seemed already inflated. This picked him out, a whiteness jerking around the first covered hatch, then wavering down open deck towards the raised poop at the stern.

John took the gun from his pocket. He didn't call out. He fired.

Henderson did a curious spinning step, like a dance movement, then ran on into fog-screened dark. John swung over the deck-rail and jumped down onto a hatch cover. By the time he had straightened up, the Chief was at the poop steps, scrambling up them, just seen. At the top, the whiteness steadied. A bullet stung into deck-boards. John zigzagged. There were two more cracks, then the rattle forward of the *Maree Tarn*'s anchor chain going down. The siren had stopped sounding. There were voices back behind, up on the boat deck. Another bullet snapped at him.

'Four,' he thought. He dropped down into the deep blackness by the rail. A bullet probed for him as he crawled forward. Five. Not more than two left in the Chief's gun.

The voice above him was very near.

'Put a foot on those steps and you'll get lead in your skull!'

John made no sound. The obscenities were in his brain, held there. He went in flat against the poop bulkhead at well-deck level, with a slight overhang above him, two inches of protection. Mist-damp metal was rough against one hand. He put his face against it, for the coolness, his breathing held slow, controlled.

But that was the only control. The rest was hate.

'I know where you are,' Henderson said. It was almost a whisper and nearly directly above. The man must be down on his hands and knees. He only needed to hear a sharp breath or one word. He had steel for his own shield and could reach out over it, and down.

John didn't move. He was back in his day-cabin, listening to the girl. Then he was beyond that, in Shanghai, at a trial where an old man was weeping, his fear and terror a performance. Because it wasn't then they had put their claws on Henderson. They wouldn't use a new recruit for this horror. The Chief had been theirs for long before the trial, tested out, well rehearsed. He could have smuggled opium on this ship, pulled in that way, held, trained, learning to move behind the carefully studied hypocrisy of a part, the bluff Scots engineer with the flaring temper.

The Chinese needed someone in authority, with complete control in the areas of his jurisdiction. A captain or a chief engineer, nothing less, and the engineer was the sounder choice, his home in the bowels where the unspeakable thing must lie.

John's hate was personal from betrayal. Twenty years of shaped, planned living had led him to this moment. He had built only one thing in that time, but something complete, his command, a small ship on the high seas on which there was order, and neatness, and a discipline which made routine reliable and sure. This had been enough for him, more than most men had, but turned into a foulness under his feet while he walked his decks with the silly pride of a boy. The foulness had been breeding beneath, unsuspected. And for this done to him, he would kill.

He had planned to kill in a stillness of feeling, a recess in hate. He had gone from the girl up to his bridge thinking quite coolly of the murderer in his little cubby-hole off the engine-room, a man waiting for the right moment for what he had to do. He'd have had terror for company down there, from things going wrong with planning, that fog waiting.

John had no doubts that Henderson's line of escape lay to a submarine. There had been one in the Indian Ocean and there was one here. How else could the Chinese track a ship to the western world? A submarine could stay hidden until called for. The Chief had only to summon this taxi back into life, leaving death behind him. He must have had radio down there. He had been able to speak to his masters and to hear calls from Admiralty.

On the bridge John had faced a choice of action. He could take his gun and go down at once for Henderson, perhaps coming on no evidence of what he knew. Experts had found nothing in Singapore. He had decided to wait, to make things seem to be going the engineer's way, cutting speed at that point where someone who knew the river was gambling it would have to be cut. John had waited for a later kill, for the evidence of flight, for a man caught wearing a life-preserver and on the way to collect payment.

What were they paying him? What would they have paid a captain? And suddenly John knew the answer. Extended authority. Power. For an old drunk, too, some vast dominion of authority, a taste of strength before the trembling years came.

He put out his hand slowly to the back of the stairs onto the poop. He got a grip. He jerked his body forward and back again. A bullet rang off metal. One left.

There were running feet on the shelter-deck, voices. Under the cover of noise, John pushed along the bulkhead. Then he shouted:

'Don't come back here! Haslett? Hold them! Get cargo lights on.'

Henderson didn't shoot down. He wasn't wasting that last bullet.

Flat against metal John worked his way towards the port steps up onto the poop. He knew that Henderson couldn't risk being forward of the deck-house up there when the lights came on. He must move back.

John swung out, ran for the steps, and reached the top of them without that last bullet coming. He went in against the deck-house, his gun up. There was no sound, no movement. He ran down the short length of covered deck to the open area just behind the stern-rail. The cargo lights came on. They were only a reflected glow here, but enough.

At the stern-rail was a bundled shape, heaving up, clumsy, a foot scrabbling for a push-up hold. John fired twice. The shape sagged at the second bullet, hung on the rail for a moment, then rolled off into the sea like a sack pushed overboard.

John stood at the rail looking down into darkness. He put the gun in his pocket and rubbed an oiliness from his hands into the wood.

'I had to come, sir.' A whisper from Haslett. 'What in hell's name . . . ?'

In hell's name. That was about it.

'Get the lights on in the sick bay! Those stern ports may show us something.'

'I've a torch here.'

It showed them something. The mist was close in behind the *Maree Tarn*, but not a wall of it. The wall was broken by a whale's snout of metal. And on the flat top forward of the merely sketched hint of a conning-tower were three figures in black, rubber frogmen's suits. They had a rope ladder down over the submarine's bulging sides and trailing into the water.

'Keep that torch steady,' John said, taking out his gun.

He fired.

'No!' Haslett shouted. 'How can you? Who are they?'

'I know.'

He fired again. But already the figures were running, back down the flat deck towards the conning-tower. John emptied the gun, two bullets. Over the noise of this he heard a kind of whimpering from Haslett. He threw the empty Luger into the sea.

'The sub's going under,' John said. 'In a hurry. Leaving three crew behind. There'll be Chinese bodies washed up on the Ayrshire coast.'

'Chinese?'

In the light from the torch, John saw the mate's eyes.

'The boy believes I'm mad,' he thought.

.   .   .   .

Gerda sat in a chair in the day-cabin. Beside her was the smashed table. She had put a half-empty glass of brandy on the floor, and was rubbing her wrists without seeming to be aware she was doing it.

John had emptied his glass. He stood by the desk, half turned away, conscious of what a lot had been put between them by his violence and the world's, but with no real feeling from this. He was sick tired, that was all.

Down in the cubby-hole off the engine-room they had found Henderson's radio, but not easily. It had been well hidden. But the *Maree Tarn* was in touch with the world again, Milton in charge of that, giving their position and at once getting the

Admiralty order back to stay anchored and prepare for boarding-party. Soon the ship would be invaded as she was in ports, with strange feet running on her decks and sounds that were not a captain's business.

He went on with his explanation to Gerda because it was owed her.

'If I'd stopped this ship when you wanted me to, it would have been a straight tip to Henderson. He knew I was making for Gourock as hard as I could. Just what he wanted. He also wanted me to slow down for that channel, sure I would. So I did. Making it easy for him to get off. Giving him the feeling that everything was suddenly going right.'

Gerda shook her head.

'I don't see how you could go up on the bridge and just stand there. Knowing he was probably priming the bomb right then.'

'I didn't know that!' John had to control his voice. 'Henderson may have primed that bomb yesterday, as soon as we were in calm water and would stay in it. Look, Miss Lane, it took us twenty minutes to find that radio set. And we've found no trace at all of where the bomb is. It could be anywhere on this ship. We just don't know. Supposing I'd taken my gun and gone down to Henderson's little room? Surprising him. What then? An innocent man. Evidence of nothing. Don't you see? For what I was going to do I had to have a man convicted by his own action. I went after Henderson as an executioner.'

He saw her draw in her breath.

'I'm sorry,' she said.

Gerda reached down for the glass, took a sip, and put it down again. She stared straight at the cabin wall.

'Do you think he was a communist?' she asked.

'No. Though they must have had a hold over him. Tight!'

'Even then I can't see anyone doing this. Why?'

John's voice was hard.

'The price was right.'

She stared.

'There are quite a few people about these days, Miss Lane, who you can buy for anything if the price is high enough.'

She closed her eyes.

'Sorry about the rough stuff,' John said.

Gerda's head bent, her hair falling forward.

'You didn't think of trying to explain the position?'

'I'm not the sharing type. I just wanted you out of the way. Damn quickly. Somehow I didn't have the feeling you'd honour a girl guide's promise to sit quietly in a chair.'

He came a little way towards her.

'Any more questions? If not I suggest that you go and find out how Miss Colleridge is bearing up. The sound of guns brought her out on deck. She asked where you were. I said helping me.'

She was looking at him again and he smiled. This got no response.

'You could also be getting on with your packing,' he said.

'With that bomb under us?'

'It either goes off or it doesn't. If it doesn't, nicely packed bags will save you a last-minute rush.'

Gerda still didn't move from the chair. She was remarkably unbattered-looking for a girl who had worn a gag for some time. No make-up left, but it didn't matter with that tan. The colour of her eyes against the colour of her skin was quite startling. Even now he noticed it.

'Miss Lane, I was trying to be polite. But it's too much of an effort. I'm tired. Will you please go.'

When the door to the deck had shut, John went into his night-cabin, stripped, and stood under the cold needles of a shower. He came out from this quite suddenly, and, still dripping, went across to a chest of drawers, opening the third one down. From under sweaters he pulled a silver-framed colour photograph of a girl with hair that was redder than nature had intended. He adjusted the frame-support and set the picture on the chest.

'Well, Mabel?' he said.

.   .   .   .

It was 2.15 a.m. Gregory Hartshorn read the signal again, slowly. It was dispatched from the Area Naval Command Clyde, time 1.17 a.m.

PRIORITY TOP SECRET STOP BOARDING-PARTY ON MAREE TARN ANCHORED ONE MILE SOUTH LITTLE CUMBRAE ISLAND STOP BOMB DISPOSAL REPORT DISCOVERY OF MEDIUM-POWER PRIMED ATOMIC BOMB IN SPECIAL COMPARTMENT CONSTRUCTED BENEATH CHIEF ENGINEER'S STORE-ROOM AND ENGINE-ROOM OFFICE STOP COMPARTMENT REACHED BY LIFTING PLATE UNDER ENGINEER'S DESK FITTED WITH FALSE RIVETS FOR SCREW-UP STOP ENGINEER'S ROOM ALSO CONTAINED BEHIND FALSE-BACKED CUPBOARD RADIO RECEIVING-SENDING EFFECTIVE RANGE ONE THOUSAND MILES AS WELL AS TWO-WAY RADIO-TELEPHONE LIKELY USE LIMITED AREA CONTACT SUBMARINE STOP CAPTAIN LOWNIE SHOT ENGINEER AS HE WAS ESCAPING TO SUB SEEN AT STERN STOP ENGINEER HENDERSON PRESUMED DEAD STOP MAREE TARN TO REMAIN ANCHORED UNTIL FOG LIFTS THEN ESCORT TO GOUROCK STOP SIGNED HILLWAY.

The computer had been wrong about the captain. Its error was almost a relief.

'You could go back to London,' Whitcomb said. 'That sub. won't get away. When the *Avenger* has dealt with her, we'll let you know.'

Gregory closed his eyes. Tiredness had blurred his thinking, but suddenly he remembered the P.M. asking for some instrument in his hands that could be used by the West to break the dead-lock of containment.

It *was* in their hands. A scrambled call would reach the P.M. at Garda, telling him he must keep the American President and Solvonoff from flying home.

There could still be a little conference at Garda that might turn into the biggest ever held. The Russians would have their face-save over Berlin. This would be anchored waiting for them at Gourock, waiting for their experts to look at and probe, a bomb in its little womb between the two hulls of a British freighter. The evidence was there which could mean the end of all Russian links with China for the whole of Solvonoff's time, and the containment would be narrowed to Liu Fa Tsu's world, a big prison, but still that, with guards watching on every side.

'I'm not going to London, Admiral. I want an Air Force jet now. I'm flying to Garda.'

Gregory got up. He was too tired to stretch stiff muscles. With luck he could sleep in the plane.

The door at the back of the gallery opened and the petty officer came in. This time he handed a signal straight to the Minister of Defence.

VESSEL X DISPATCHED LAT 55 00 LONG 05 30 STOP LARGE OIL PATCH STOP WRECKAGE BEING COLLECTED STOP NO SURVIVORS STOP HUNT FOR BODIES CONTINUES HAMPERED BY DARK AND FOG STOP SIGNED HILLWAY.